WAITING ON FIDEL

OR

How I almost Hitchhiked To Mexico City

WAITING ON FIDEL

OR

How I almost Hitchhiked To Mexico City

A NOVEL

Stephen Edward Paper

Library of Congress Cataloging-In-Publication Data
    Paper, Stephen Edward
Waiting On Fidel or
How I Almost Hitchhiked To Mexico City: A Novel /Stephen Edward
Paper.
CreateSpace Independent Publishing Platform/North Charleston, South
Carolina.
LCCN 2015909202
1. Travel-Fiction. 2. Adventure-Fiction. 3. Mexico-Fiction 4. Fiction 5. Coming of
Age-Fiction.

Book design by Maureen Cutajar
www.gopublished.com

ISBN-13: 978-1514226193
ISBN-10: 1514226197

DEDICATION

For my brothers, Richard and Thomas Paper, my mother Bernice and my father Charles, who all inspired me to love travel and adventure.

ACKNOWLEDGEMENTS

I would like to acknowledge these people for their help in both feedback, support and inspiration: Weston Cookler, Rachel Mostow, Richard Paper, Thomas Paper, Ricki Sawyer, Cary Schwartz, Shahar Stroh, and Dickran Tashjian.

Many thanks to Chaslyn Solomon for the cover art design.

Cover Idea: Stephen Edward Paper

CHAPTER 1

Granola

"Look both ways before you cross the street." –Mom

Marat arrived yesterday. And today, I'm in the goddamned emergency room of a goddamned hospital. Yesterday definitely went off better than today.

This trip was not going according to plan.

Only minutes before I was lying on the hot pavement in a pool of my own blood, an ambulance siren blaring in the distance and a she-devil whining in my ear.

My whole life passed before my eyes in only twenty-three seconds. That worked out to only one second per year. What a let down. I needed to be more interesting in the future.

I heard the voice of an angel repeating over and over again, in a desperate, pleading whimper, "Please don't die. Please don't die." It was like a mantra. Ok, ok, I won't, I thought, if you just shut the hell up. In the meantime, I remembered from the movies or television, or maybe folklore, that you should not move an inch in a situation like this, in case you had damaged your spine, broken your neck, or maybe it was if you were dead. I was in a real state. But I also remembered, probably from the same type of communal wisdom, that if I could wiggle my toes and/or fingers, I was probably not paralyzed. Well, here goes, I thought, although most of my thinking at the time was unprintable and it would most likely have looked something like this in a family newspaper: #%&#-#*##@%, #%&#-##*#@%, and for a much longer duration. You know, if you just bang your knee, or poke yourself in the eye, it only requires an "Ouch, geez, son of a bitch," but this was far more serious. Most of my invective was directed at the angel, whose guilty manner told me everything I needed to know as to the identity of my assassin. No angel: it was a she-devil.

Yes! I thought, as my toes moved. Yes! my brain yelled out to me, as my fingers wiggled. I was not paralyzed! Of course, I still refrained from any other movement, just in case. Better to let the ambulance drivers and doctors figure it out for sure. Then my thoughts calmly returned to: #%&#-###@%, #%&#-###@%, as the she-devil continued to chant, "Please don't die. Please don't die," and started to cry.

The shrill sound of the ambulance siren rent the air in record time. "Could you keep it down," I murmured. "I have a really bad headache."

Weird thoughts began to tumble through my mind: did I really look so mangled she thought I was going to die? *Was I going to die?* Then I'd have to go to a funeral. I hate going to funerals. And now that I think of it, especially my own. How would that help my career?

Then just random: how this would look on the scale of insignificance. If I had to go I didn't want it to be in some mundane, humdrum every day kind of way, like slipping in the shower, falling down the stairs, being shot during hunting season (pretty easy to be mistaken for a deer when the hunters are in heat in Minnesota) or a car accident. Those would never make the front page.

I wanted something unique: like if an eagle clutching a turtle in its talons, spotted your bald head from a 100 yards up, and thinking it was a rock dropped the turtle on it cracking it open along with your head—it happened to Aeschylus; or if you were nude body surfing off the coast of Madras with a six foot tall girl from Mississippi right at shark feeding time and no one bothered to tell you that the German Consul General was eaten there the day before, Jaws 1,2,3 and 4 had not come out yet and the local Jaws came back for seconds; or if you're playing golf with your peculiar swing, you take a cut, top the ball, follow through and club yourself in the head breaking your nose. You keel over onto the ground where a tee impales your brain, and a flesh-eating beetle who just at that time happens to be climbing the tee is plunged inside as well causing a coma, and while the surgeons fix your nose the beetle starts eating all the parts of your brain good at cognition, but you can't alarm anybody because you're in a coma. Then you die in a few months when the beetle finishes every thing on his plate, exits quietly, leaving the doctor to say upon autopsy: "Well, he didn't have much in there, did he?"

"Yes, but didn't his nose turn out beautifully?" the other doctor replies. I think that happened in an early episode of Star Trek.

At least those are pretty unique. Me, I'm stuck with a car accident.

If you're going to be taken out, you want it to at least be interesting. Either that or in your sleep. The former for the notoriety or honorable mention in the Darwin Awards, the latter as easy on the pain, suffering and anguishing bit. Personally, I think a car accident is kind of high on the scale. Happens all the time: over 30,000 a year are killed in the U.S. alone. I could just hear them saying: "He didn't look both ways." I did, but do you think that would stop anyone from saying it? No way. Yeah, I would have looked pretty stupid.

But I guess I have to backtrack a bit. You see, months ago, in October before I left Minnesota for the West Coast, the friend that I was going to travel with suggested we both go see an oracle. We had both been studying the Greeks for our last class before graduating the U of M. and I guess reading Herodotus had affected him much more than I. He was utterly fascinated with how the Spartans, Athenians, Corinthians, Thebans et al always consulted Delphi when they wanted to assault or blockade each other, hoodwink, whack, make an alliance, beat up some Persians, get married, eat some Baklava, launch a thousand ships, make eggs with Feta cheese, take a whiz, build a Parthenon or play the agora. Actually whatever, depending upon their frame of mind or time of month. My friend got it into his head that we should consult someone to see if we'd be safe on our cross-country trip. I considered offering to take him to Delphi to check with the original, but figured he'd only want to consult an oracle before consulting the oracle. Sort of like cleaning up your place before the maid comes.

But he insisted and the more I thought about it the less I liked it. He'd never traveled out of the state before, he was really nervous about such a major trip and I'd never known such an over-the-shoulder salt throwing, black cat side-stepping, ladder avoiding, soothsayer consulting fanatic in all my life. And I'd never seen him step on a crack either. In all fairness, maybe if I hadn't already done a fair bit of traveling—I'd been as far afield as Fargo, Winnipeg and Omaha—I would have been nervous too.

I guess I should've reminded him of Croesus.

So I let him drag me, kicking and screaming of course, to see this old crone that a buddy of his, an albino, had told him about. Like I said, I didn't want to go, but I was too short on money to travel alone. I needed someone to share the expenses and he made it clear he wouldn't go unless we both saw the seer. I had another more profound reason for being loath to visit her, because if someone could tell the future, I was sure that would end any and all possibility of having free will. This was a big thing for me.

I hate it when I start thinking I don't have free will. I had just finished slogging through *War And Peace,* probably the greatest book ever written. There were two epilogues at the end of that book, and both had a huge impact on me. One was about Pierre's happily married family life after all he'd been through. Tolstoy made it so excruciatingly boring that I finally made the decision to leave my girlfriend and snow country and head out west to play tennis full time. The other epilogue was about free will and Tolstoy made the most compelling argument against it and for determination. I cursed him for it, but it was hard for me to go against Tolstoy on anything.

My big fear was if this lady could see the future it confirmed him a thousand fold. How could someone see what was going to happen two, three months or years down the road if it wasn't already set? It meant determination, cut and dried. I *wanted* her to be wrong!

Worse, both of us forgot our billfolds—he probably did it on purpose; you know the type of guy, never brings his own money—and I had to borrow five bucks from the albino (with me it was an honest mistake). Worse yet, I was getting in debt doing something I didn't want to do, and that I didn't believe in anyway. Of course, there was some solace in that, because if I didn't believe in it anyway, it didn't matter what she said. I have a long list of rules: my dad called this one having it both ways.

So, there were the three of us, walking up to this dingy brick building with a glaring neon sign on a narrow side street just off Hennepin Avenue. In big orange letters that flickered on and off, possibly by intention or more likely judging by the state of things, by inattention, the sign read: "Future Told. Ask for Granola," or something like that—I could be a bit inattentive myself.

We entered a parlor with rooms petitioned off by various, dark-colored sheets hanging from a low ceiling. It was dimly lit with red light bulbs and had the appearance of a cheap photographer's dark room. I wondered what would develop. Sorry.

Behind a mahogany table was a shriveled-up, leather-skinned lady wearing a black, floor-length gown covered with various-sized five pointed white stars, and a pointy black witch's hat, which also sported a few stars. A broom leaned against the table near a scrawny arm that peeked out from under the gown and rested on a clear glass orb.

"What's with the getup?" I asked. "Halloween?"

"Don't get me started," she rasped.

"Do you tell the future?" my friend asked, as the albino and I simultaneously used our right palms to slap the front of our foreheads. I guess that was like asking a Frenchman *"parlez vous Francais?"* Naturally, I knew a guy who had done exactly that.

"What do you think I'm sitting here for wearing this *verstunken* outfit?" she said, glancing up at my friend.

She picked her nose, wiped it on the base of the orb, then again under the table, looked up at me to see if I noticed, then opined, "They all say you can't get good help these days, but I say you can't get a good boss. Look what I have to put up with? If I didn't need the work in this economy...But enough about me. This is about you."

Nice for someone to finally realize it, I thought.

"So," I said. "I'd like to know about my upcoming trip."

"Hmph!" she sneered as she looked into the orb that I noticed was suddenly cloudy. I hoped it wasn't from anything on the surface.

"Sit down," she said. "All of you."

We did. By nature somewhat skeptical, I then asked her my Mom's maiden name, my birth date, the last four numbers on my Social Security card and where I was from to make sure she was on the level—she got three out of four.

Then she closed her eyes, hummed a happy tune and started to augur. "Okay. Let's see what we got. Hmm. Not good."

Oh great. Just what you want to hear from a psychic.

My friend's chairs seemed to edge backwards ever so slightly.

"You are going to kill your father and marry your mother. Whatever you do, don't talk to any sphinxes or answer any riddles. You see a sphinx coming, turn and run the other way fast." She peered deeper into the ball. "Hmm. You might have nice looking twins, though." She fiddled with some silvery dials on the back of the globe. "Oops! That's an old one. Sorry. Gotta get that one off the books."

Whew! She must've been at this a long time. Luckily I didn't believe her anyway.

"Okay. Okay. I got it." She took a deep breath. "You will meet an Arab and you won't like him," she said. "And talking about Frenchmen..."

Now, I was worried. Had she read my mind? "Shut up," she said. "I'm trying to work here." She raised her uni-brow in a threatening manner. "You will meet a Frenchman and you will like him."

I would've figured just the opposite.

"You will quit the game you love and will do so willingly," she said. "At least for a spell."

Quit tennis, I thought? Hardly. What a piece of bull. But I kept listening, after all it was a nice choice of words.

"You will be a mentor to one you do not know and will continue to not know."

"You will fly through the air without the use of your own power or an airplane."

By then I was confused.

"Did you know that sixty per cent of Americans between the ages of sixteen and twenty-four don't know what country borders us on the south?"

"Huh?" I stammered. That seemed somewhat random.

"What country is that?" the albino asked.

"See," Granola said.

"I'm twenty-six," the albino said.

Granola looked at him knowingly. "Because later, you will fly all over Mexico in an airplane...but you will not have to pay."

"Huh," I wittily repeated.

"Remember. It is a brave man who farts in Asia."

"I thought you said I was going to Mexico?"

"I did. But a brave man who farts in Mexico doesn't have the same ring to it."

"Well, what about Montezuma's Revenge?"

She curled up her forehead and stared at the crystal ball. "Oh. You'll get that too. By the way," she said as if to show off her powers. "You are a great admirer of Tolstoy."

"Wow!" She was really good.

"I hear it's even better if you read it in the original French."

I take it back.

"You will cut the Gordian knot," she said.

"You will descend from the sky like a god, only to ascend a pyramid that reaches the stars."

Right. Was there a Giza or Turkey in California? Maybe Sacramento? Definitely a lot of Turkeys there. I knew there were some pyramids in southern Mexico. Otherwise it looked like I was going to spend a lot of time in the Middle East.

"On this trip?" I asked.

"Why? Are you taking another one?"

She was a wise ass too.

I was quickly losing confidence. She sure couldn't predict geography.

"And you will go upward in a drug-induced frenzy."

"I don't do drugs," I said.

"You will," she advised.

"No I won't."

"Yes you will," she said tauntingly.

"Nope. I'm in training."

"I'll bet you double the five you paid me that you will in the future," she dared.

Wow. Just like my younger brother.

My friend started to open his mouth. Before he could get a word out, she said, "Yes, your trip will be safe."

He moved his chair back to the table.

Then the albino started to open his mouth. He was quick enough to get out, "Will...?"

"Yes, you'll get your five dollars back."

He looked relieved, then moved his chair back as well.

"Can I have my money back?" I asked. "You didn't help me very much."

"I can help put a curse on you?" she countered.

I could see my two friends were looking askance.

"Nevermind," I said.

"And you will smoke a Cuban with a Cuban."

"I don't smoke."

"You will."

Here we go again.

"There's one last thing," Granola said. "You will meet the girl of your dreams, and you will know her because she cannot correctly pronounce the name Chicago."

Fair enough, I thought. But that brought up another question. After all, I already paid. "Can you tell me what happened with my old girlfriend?"

"Sorry, I don't do the past," she said. "Only the future."

"Well," I asked, changing tack quickly. "Will we get back together?"

"Sorry," she said, glancing at a small sundial directly under a skylight. "Time's up. Unless you have another fiver."

I looked at the albino, who threw up his hands, shook his head and said, "No way."

"Will I ever get married?" my friend hurriedly interjected.

"Better you should ask will I ever get a girlfriend."

"Rats," he said.

The three of us stood up and headed for the door.

"Oh," Granola said. "By the way, say hello to my sisters."

"Huh?" was all I could muster. Good. She didn't get anything right. I knew. I had the best laid plans.

As soon as we were out the door, my friend whispered, "Well, what do you think? Huh? Was she good or what? She really knew her stuff."

"Yeah," the albino said smugly. "Totally. I told you so."

Rolling my eyes, and not wanting to lose my passenger, I summoned my best Minnesota accent and said, "You betcha."

So, back to yesterday and Marat. I picked him up at the bus depot in downtown Phoenix, and within an hour, I had him situated in a fraternity room on campus at Arizona State. Pretty good, I thought. My former girl friend had always accused me of being the greatest manipulator she had ever known—I hope she meant it in a good way—and now, I had just taken a Frenchman, who I had never seen before in my life, and gotten him a free room in a fraternity that did not allow strangers to either stay in or rent rooms. And I had accomplished this minor feat, by befriending another complete stranger, a freshman member of

that same fraternity, inside an hour of picking up the Frenchman.

A feat of legerdemain for sure. I don't know how I did it, but
I was mighty pleased with myself anyway. Then I realized I was
gloating. My college doubles partner always maintained that
nothing good ever came from gloating. I think it has the same
antecedents and derivation as "Famous last words," or when
you're up 4-0 in the first set and you say to yourself, "Well, I got
this one won," and then you lose. Of course, that had happened
to us.

As for the present gloating please see above: "in the goddamned ER."

As a good will gesture, I helped the freshman by outlining an
English paper for him.

Marat just wanted a roof over his head for a few nights before leaving for Colombia. He had lived in Cambodia for ten
months, stayed another two in Laos, and traveled throughout
India, so the dorm room was like a minor paradise to him as it
sported hot showers.

As for me, after Nixon ended the draft there was no longer a
Vietnam in my future. I could live my life as I wanted, and what
I wanted was to leave Minneapolis to travel the world playing
tennis. This was to be my "grand adventure."

On a late October night my friend and I set out down the I-
35W for the west coast in a blue '66 Chevy Malibu, a clunker my
dad salvaged for me. A box of Baklava sat on the front seat between us, the radio was tuned to classic rock, Dunlop Fort
racquets strung with gut were in the back seat, cups of coffee
were in hand and conversation flowed as we drove southwest to
Nebraska. As the signal from Minneapolis died away, my friend
fiddled with the dial till he got a station out of Little Rock Ar-
kansas playing Little Wing by Eric Clapton. Life was good.

Didn't plan it as well as I thought, was traveling more than
training, from Denver to Portland then down the coast to L.A.
Finally got frustrated around Laguna Beach, where I split up
with my friend, and decided I should forget tennis and spend

more time scuba diving. So I headed to Phoenix. Now you might be prone to wonder what I was doing in the desert of Arizona if I now wanted a career as a scuba diver. Well, all I can say is sometimes you get sidetracked.

At the time of the accident I was crashing with friends who lived in Tempe, and was pretty sure they were getting tired of the extra body—mine—in their house. If I brought in Marat, it would be goodbye with a fanfare.

So, everybody got something. Everybody was happy. The freshman got an "A" on his paper, Marat got his shelter, and I got a little breathing space, a few more days before being unceremoniously dumped out on my ass.

Until today.

Tennis is a great metaphor for life. Sometimes, you're in a tennis match and you're in the zone. Everything works. The ball looks like a watermelon coming at you in slow-mo. You have all the time in the world. Your side of the court seems like it's only two feet wide, while their side, you could land a 747 on. Every girl you look at returns your smile or gives you her number, every test comes back aced, any job you apply for is a go. Sort of everything you touch turns to gold. That was yesterday.

Today, nothing worked. The ball looked like a pea traveling at the speed of light and the court sizes were reversed. I woke up with a splitting headache, my mouth felt like something had crawled inside over night and died—a lot of big insects in the desert—and the first person I saw told me I had to move out, ASAP. On top of this the butter was spoiled and the milk was sour so I had to eat my shredded wheat dry. Have you ever tried to eat shredded wheat dry?

You know how you say "I could have beaten him in my sleep?" I then realized I'd dreamt I'd lost to a ninety year old Russian émigré 2 & 3: IN MY SLEEP! And he didn't have a backhand!

I walked out to my car bleary-eyed, tried to start it but it wouldn't turn over. Nobody had cables so I had it towed to the shop. More bad news: it needed a generator and I had to spend the money because I had to have a car especially now that I had no place to stay.

I couldn't find anyone to take me to the tennis courts so all there was to do was wait.

I sat down to read, my second favorite pastime after tennis. Nothing like sitting down with a good book to calm your mind. I'd brought a few books with me: some Nietzsche and Conrad, The Morning of the Magicians, but I decided I needed something light so I picked up a Carlos Castenada, already half way through. I was just at the part where he promised to teach you how to become a Yaqui shaman. I turned the page. ARRGG!! The next five pages were missing. Right at the crucial stage. ARRGG!! Life can be cruel.

Okay. I gave up. I went to sleep. Never should have got up today anyway.

Walking to pick up the car later in the afternoon, I stopped at a crosswalk on University Avenue. A van was making a left, and the driver waved me across. I promise you, I looked both ways, just like my mom taught me, but I was double-crossed. You know how you jog a bit to get out of the way when someone stops and waves you on? Well, I sped up, but just as I stepped out on the other side of the van, a girl in a Volkswagen also sped up and passed him on the right. At least she thought she was going to. Unfortunately, I blocked her way, we collided and I went flying through the air, after first smashing her windshield with my head.

I suddenly found myself sprawled on the pavement. Wet, gooey stuff, that I took to be my own blood, was trickling over my closed eyes, across my cheek and onto the street.

Her car was totaled but that was all the revenge I got. I was whisked off to the hospital, examined, scanned, probed, questioned, x-rayed, scanned some more, stitched up and declared fine, if in a world of pain. "Take ten aspirin and call me in the morning," the doctor said.

My friends picked me up and brought me home. They had somehow found Marat, who was waiting for me as I gingerly limped into the house. I guess I was lucky that only a Volkswagen hit me. Nothing was broken, torn or even sprained, only a few major contusions and bruises. But I was very sore, and in none too good a mood.

It was then, as I laid motionless on their sofa, covered with bags of ice, that something else hit me. I had flown through the air, *just like Granola said!*

Damn, I thought.

Then I realized, I had sort of mentored the freshman.

Then it occurred to me, *MARAT WAS A FRENCHMAN!*

Holy shit! Now I was worried. What was I to make of this? I decided right there and then not to like him.

Back to the present. Still icing, still reeling.

On more reflection, I remembered that I was going to meet the girl of my dreams and get to fly around Mexico for free. Except, Mexico was not in my plans. I still hadn't figured out if I wanted to start tennis again or go back to Laguna Beach to dive.

I should tell you a little about Marat.

Marat was not exactly a *complete* stranger. True, I had never seen him before, but I had heard a lot about him.

My brothers were traveling through Europe around this time. In their sojourn they became friends with Marat.

Marat was a friend of my brothers and that was all the character reference I needed.

Half-Spanish and half-French, he was tall and slender with curly, light brown hair, which he wore short as it was more convenient for travel. Ever practical in matters of hygiene, he liked to say that you never knew when you might get head lice and have to cut it all off anyway.

Marat had flown to Palo Alto a year ago for a reason which for me, an innocent lad from a small town in northern Minnesota, beggars all description unless you just call it French.

Marat was only twenty-three, the same age as me, but he already had two PhDs. I repeat, TWO, count 'em, two PhDs. One of his theses was a study of the evolution of mathematics among the Hindus, starting in 800 B.C.; the other concerned the Pythagorean Theorem. Marat was a model of brevity when it came to the Gallic method of education. In a high-pitched voice that was moderately accented, he explained it to me. "You know, in France, when you are young, they put you through a series of tests. You pass the first one, then you go to the next, then the next, and so on, as long as you pass. The number of students gets progressively smaller with each new series till finally, if you make it through the last test, you are admitted to the *Ecole Polytechnique,* the most elite school in all of France. Once you are admitted, they ask you what you want your PhD. in. You tell them and they say, 'Ok, go study.' In a year, you have your PhD. And they pay you while you study."

However, there was a catch. In order to pay them back after finishing, you had three choices: actually pay them back, get another PhD. or, and this is the part I love, and which is so irredeemably and shamelessly French, become famous.

Marat, however, was not conceited in the least. Maybe that was because he was half-Spanish. I really don't know. I would have been a lot more smug about one PhD. let alone two. For him, it was just his means to a life, no better or worse than anyone else's work or study.

Marat already had his second PhD. from Stanford. He'd got it in less than eight months, so I guess there was something to the system. But it wasn't good enough for Marat. He was going to trump them. Not only did he get his second PhD. but he was going to become famous for his writing, and for good measure, he was going to pay them back as well.

After finishing his second PhD. he traveled a little in Mexico, then went home and into the army as a lieutenant to fulfill his obligatory service. He quickly got tired of the nonsense—it was the French army after all—and promptly told his commanding officer he was a communist.

"Go! We have enough problems without communists in the officers' corps," the commandant said. "Get out of here. You are absolved of your duty."

Now why hadn't I thought of that? While I was in school the

war in Vietnam was still slogging along and I had a very low
draft number. I was certain to go into the army as soon as I
graduated, but I had been anti-war since I was fifteen—had even
put out an anti-war newsletter with a few friends for our senior
class project. It had always been a source of amusement for us,
that for this profound intellectual, political and philosophical un-
dertaking which we were quite smug about, we had received the
grade of "B," while another of our friends had received the covet-
ed "A" for painting the high school stadium football bleachers.

Thus another milestone in my American education; it was
more important that we had a colorful place to park our asses
during football games, than to protest against killing hundreds
of thousands of people in a faraway country that had no way at
all to threaten us.

Yup. I should have told them I was a commie. I had no idea if
the U.S. Army also turned away communists or if they just shot
them but it would have been worth a try. If they had any sense
of humor they would get a kick out of sending a commie to fight
another commie. I certainly would.

So, Marat came here. He finished some business in Palo Alto, and headed for the border, only stopping in Tempe, Arizona
long enough to visit the brother of his friends.

His intention was to hitchhike all the way to Colombia, explor-
ing Mexico on the way. I suspected he could afford a better, more
comfortable mode of travel, but what would that look like in his
journal? No. This way was much more interesting and the journal
of his travels just might provide the fame he was looking for.

"Tomas," Marat asked the following day, pronouncing it in
the European manner. "Are you going to be all right?"

Well," I groaned. I still lay on the grungy blue sofa, elbows,
knees, hips, shins and head covered with ice packs. "I don't
think I'm going to be working out for a while. I can barely
move."

"Why don't you come with me?" he asked.

"Like this?" I sniffed. "I can't even walk. They won't be taking the stitches out for a week."

Marat laughed. "I'll give you a week, then. That's next Friday, December 13th."

"Lucky for me," I said. "You know, I've never even been out of the country." In all honesty, it was really hard to count Canada as out of the country.

"Your brother told me you were getting soft, even with all the tennis and scuba..."

I laughed, and yes, it hurt, but images of Pancho Villa, The Treasure of the Sierra Madre, lost cities and even Hiram Bingham arose in my mind: perhaps this would be my "grand adventure."

It took a few moments for me to realize Granola said I was going to Mexico. Damn. AND QUITTING TENNIS! Holy shit!

CHAPTER 2

On The Road

"The first condition of understanding a foreign country is to smell it." –Rudyard Kipling

So, that's how I found myself standing at a freeway entrance to Interstate 10, with my thumb out, heading south to Tucson. The sky was a bright blue with a few clouds to the east; there was a light breeze, maybe 65 degrees—a perfect day to start out. The stitches were removed thirty minutes before my friends dropped us off on the highway; the bruises and psychological scars remained.

Marat checked his maps, took the lay of the land and stuck his thumb out. "How is hitchhiking here, in the States?" he asked.

A gigantic shiny blue Lincoln pulled up, blaring its horn, as a perfect punctuation to his question. The front window slid down, and the driver, a white haired, leather-skinned cowboy yelled out, "You boys gettin' in or not? I'm eighty years old if'n I'm a day, and I ain't got time to waste. Tucson's callin'! Skaydaddle on in." And it seemed like he threw open the passenger door and the back seat door almost simultaneously.

Marat picked up his bag and jumped into the back seat and I 'skaydaddled' into the front of what was the longest, sleekest automobile I'd ever seen—complete with fins that could have gone on a rocket ship, brown and white cowhide seats, a toma-hawk hanging from the rearview mirror, a gun rack right behind the front seats, and believe it or not, Texas longhorns on the grill.

Soon as the doors closed, he squealed onto the entrance, cutting off a semi in the process. I swear we were doing seventy before hitting the freeway.

"So, you like those longhorns," the old man said, noticing my stare. "Well, old Brutus there served me real good. I got his horns in front, and our asses is restin' on his hide. Just like mine was forty years ago in the rodeo."

I looked at him questioningly.

"Yessiree Bob. I saved his horns and hide till I could afford this dandy automobile. Et the rest of him. Some of the best steak I ever et."

He shook his head with satisfaction.

I turned and looked in the back seat. "Marat," I asked. "You all right?" That caused a minor international incident.

"Marat?" the cowboy asked, with more than a small accent on the rat and a lot of pique in the tone. "What kind a dang furiner name is that?"

I could see the wheels spinning in his head.

"Are you a commie?" he asked.

I started to say, "As a matter of fact..." but just then I looked at Marat and was waved off.

"It's French," Marat said.

"I never met no Frenchman afore," the cowboy said. "Why y'all call yourselves frogs?"

Before Marat could come up with an answer, the old man looked back at the road and caught a glimpse of something.

Look over to your left," he said as he pointed with his right index finger. "See them mountains. Them there's the Superstition Mountains. Home of the Lost Dutchman. Heard of 'em?"

"A little," I said.

"Well, you know, I went up there one day, when I was a youngster, maybe twenty years ago. Started out from Apache Junction. Took a backpack and a mule and enough food and water for a week. Thought I'd have a look see. Durned if I didn't get shot at soon as I passed the foothills."

"Shot at?" I asked. "Why?"

"Them there's the Superstition Mountains, boy! That's why. That poor Dutchman discovered the richest vein o' gold in the country, boasted about it in the city, then he was murdered on his way back. Some say by Injuns, others by lowdown robbers. I say by ghosts of the guardians of the treasure. That's what I say, I do."

"Now there's all them old coots up there, lookin' for the mine. They's all crazy, they is. Shoot anybody they see. Thinks they's hornin' in on 'em, after the gold."

Looking out the window, I could only see the foothills. It was a barren place. No trees, no grass, only dirt and rock, no coots—the only coot I saw was in the car with us. I looked in the back seat. Marat was asleep.

"So. You from these parts?"

"No," I said. "I'm from Minnesota. My friend's from France." I was so nervous about his driving, I forgot an earlier part of the conversation.

"So," he cackled. "I guess you and no frog never saw no rattlesnake. Course, lots o' frogs in Arizona saw then plenty." He laughed at his *bon mot* and reached under his seat and grasped a burlap bag.

We were doing ninety by now, and I wished he would have done it while keeping his eyes on the road. But then, as he sat back up, I heard a high pitched sound, like a blender. Then, it sounded more like a rattle. I'd heard that sound before. Anyway, it seemed familiar.

Laughing gleefully, he stuck the head of a four-foot rattler in my face. Not more than inches away.

"You boys know why them cowboys always hit the snake in the movies?"

He turned around to make sure he had a full audience. "Wake up, boy!" he shouted at Marat.

Marat opened his eyes to the sight of an open-mouthed rattler, fangs extended. He was wide awake in short order.

The old man turned around. "Now where was I? Don't you nevermind the rattler. He gets nasty, I jes club him." Then he let go of the steering wheel with his other hand, made a fist and pretended to punch the rattler. "Where was I? Yessiree Bob. That's right. In the movies, when the cowboys see a snake. They shoot it, right? And they never miss. Know why?"

The snake rattled in a fury, the car shot up to ninety-five, and I thought, if they miss they probably have to do a retake, so they aims real good.

"Cuz the snake's so dang fast, it strikes the bullet. Always gets 'em. Or," he said, a mischievous glint in his eye, "the snake always gets it. Snake's fast, but not too smart." He laughed and put the snake back in what I hoped was a bag sealed by Price Waterhouse and dropped it behind him. I noticed that Marat quietly pulled his feet up off the floor and put them on the seat next to our packs.

We were about halfway to Tucson when the old timer peered off to the west. "See them mountains," he said.

I first glanced at the speedometer, now registering a hundred ten mph. This was going to be a fast trip, if we survived it.

"There's a pass over there. *La Picacho*. My grandpappy fought along side Captain Sherod Hunter, in the battle for *Picacho* Pass. He was with the rebels. Arizona tried to go Confederate cuz those Yankees was real assholes."

"Well," I asked with the utmost courtesy, "what happened?"

"You never heard of Arizona goin' rebel, did y'all? That's cuz they got they asses whupped! That's what happened. If'n they woulda knowed how to fight, meybe we woulda won the war, God dang it."

"Later, he rode with Crook against Geronimo. And you know what?"

"What?" I politely inquired.

The speed was up to 120.

The old man burst out laughing, let go of the steering wheel and clapped his hands in what I took for jubilation.

I started to cover my eyes, so I wouldn't have to see the certain crash, my second in a week after avoiding them for the first twenty years of my existence, and one that would certainly put an end to that existence.

"That ol' Crook never knew my grandpappy was a rebel!" he hooted. "Ol' Crook, the dumb coot. He was fightin' alongside the durn enemy."

Suddenly, his arms straightened as though bracing against the steering wheel. The car flew up an exit and screeched to a halt at an all in one rest stop, gas station, restaurant, truck stop.

"Well, here you boys be," he said.

I could see he was thinking about something. A flash of remembrance had entered his eyes. He cackled. I think he thought he had our number.

"Either o' you boys ever heard of a Gila Monster?" he asked. "Those Gilas, once they bite you, they jes so dang ornery, nothin' make them let go. And they jes keep squeezin' the poison into you."

Before I could answer, he bent over to reach something under my seat, and he pulled up another burlap bag. This one was wriggling. But Marat and I threw open the doors, dove out and made our escape.

"Nothin' to worry about, boys," he yelled from his window. "I jes club 'im if'n he gets nasty. I'm going on to Tombstone, to visit my pappy's grave. Right there on Boot Hill. If'n you want to see a real piece of history..."

We hid in the rest stop, gas station, restaurant, truck stop, till he and his fancy wheels were out of sight, each of us having a shot of whiskey to calm our nerves from the ride. Then we headed back to the highway.

Out went the thumbs, and our eyes kept peeled for Brutus' horns just in case. After an hour had passed, and the only people to even slow down, did so just to wave, make a face, or for some unbeknownst reason, give us the finger, we realized hitchhiking out of Tucson would not be so easy. Two hours were gone, then three. Nobody stopped, not even a Volkswagen.

Something was wrong here. Volkswagens always stopped.

Took a friend and I some thirty different rides to go from Rhinebeck to Woodstock and back again one summer in Upstate New York, and I swear that twenty-eight of those rides were in Volkswagens.

"Bus," Marat said. "We have to find a bus."

We walked back to the rest stop, gas station, restaurant, truck stop, looked in the phone book, found the location of the nearest bus depot and started walking down the dusty shoulder of the road.

It was a long walk from there to the depot. We talked for awhile, then seemed to get lost in our own thoughts. At least I did, so let me digress a bit.

There's a place, just outside Whiskey Creek, my hometown, called Black's Grove. A Captain Black, after retiring from the high seas, built a house a mile-and-a half west of the town. He left the land to the township in his will, if they'd turn it into a park, so they did.

A pretty small nondescript place, for most adults I suppose—just a pleasant, forested park—but for a little kid raised on a diet of war stories, westerns, pirates, Jungle Jim and Tarzan, it had everything magical and adventurous a kid could ask for and more. There were vast forests, hills, a river meandering through it. There were many dirt paths running through the woods, and we imagined Indians traversing the forests hundreds of years earlier. Maybe my brothers and I were the first ones on those trails since the Ojibwa or Sioux. Who knew what discoveries those slender dirt paths might lead to. I saw my first snake in those woods—a non-venomous garter snake, but a snake nonetheless, and my first deer.

Run-down shacks near the entrance definitely had to harbor ghosts. There was a narrow path leading to a fallen tree on which you could balance your way over the creek to an island, so tiny you could run around it in five seconds. Treasure Island, my father called it, and who were we to argue. To us kids, it was an amazing place. My first time there, he pointed out an "X" plainly visible in the soggy ground. It was spring, but the snow had stayed on the ground until only a few weeks earlier, and thin ice was still covering parts of the stream. He told us to dig, and within minutes we found coins. It became the first place we'd run to every time we went to Black's Grove.

Even though it had a circumference of only fifteen yards, and only one tree, and mostly consisted of mud and a few spears of yellow weeds, it was magical. It was only when we got older that we realized we could simply walk across the shallow stream.

One time, my older brother and his friends made mounds of dirt in an area by one of the ghost houses, to make it look like three fresh graves had been dug. They even put crosses made of twigs over each grave. Then one of them came to me and my little brother and told us that my older brother and two of his friends had been killed by the ghosts. We cried. We mourned. But he told us we must never tell our parents or the ghosts would come for us next.

As we grew older, we played Capture the Flag during the winter. We could run across the frozen river or trudge through the snow, tracking footprints in our games. We camped there with the Boy Scouts, and cross-country skied with the adults.

There were often rumors of bears or wolves, though I confess, I never saw one. We did manage to scare the hell out of one particularly annoying young camper, by making the sounds of a bear outside his tent one night. I swear he ran all the way back into town, running through the snow in only his underwear.

I had my first brush with "that far country" when one of the other scouts fell in the icy water and slit his leg open on some rusty barbed wire, just below the surface. Most likely thinking I was in a movie or cliffhanger serial, I sprinted up a riverbank, about thirty feet high, to get the first aid kit at our camp. About three-quarters of the way up, I lost my balance and started falling backwards. It could only have been through instinct that I grabbed the hatchet from my belt, and threw it forward into the grassy dirt as hard as I could. It held and I didn't fall. After easing myself in close to the slope, something made me look down. Right below me, right where the middle of my back threatened to plunge, was a jagged tree stump. Without the hatchet, I would have been impaled.

Why do I digress? Because ever since those days at Black's Grove, I yearned for adventure. Every smell, sound, tree, or blade of grass in Black's Grove spoke of far away, exotic places. It was a combination of mystery and danger, ghosts and pirates, treasure and discovery: the kind we'd see every Saturday at the local theater's matinee. But, being a properly matriculating student, high school, then college and a little diversion known as the draft, all stood in the way of my freedom to explore.

Now, here I was, embarking on my first real adventure, only an hour's journey by bus, to *Nogales*, Mexico. A foreign country. A different language, different people, culture, and sights, sounds, foods and smells. Jungles and mountains, *Mariachis*, *Federales* and *banditos*. What more could I ask for? I was eager, I was nervous and I was hobbling, but I was ready for anything. As a matter of fact, I couldn't wait.

I smiled as we boarded the bus for *Nogales*. This was the first time in years that visions of the wonders of Black's Grove had reentered my mind.

The hour bus ride passed by rapidly.

As soon as the bus stopped on the U.S. side of the border, Marat jumped down and started running. It was dark, about 9 P.M. I limped as fast as I could as he headed for the border.

"I have to see if there's a bus," he yelled back. "We still might be able to catch one. I'll get the tickets. Hurry."

So I limped across my first real foreign border, heading down *Avenida Lopez Mateos*. If I walked any slower I'd be going backwards.

Marat was an adventurer in the real sense of the word. He had a goal, which was Mexico City for starters. Then Colombia. He'd been in Mexico before, but not Colombia. Some of his friends had made their fortunes in that country, and he was determined to equal their effort or even do better.

But he didn't care how he got there. At every new place, he looked at his maps, saw what was interesting, and then took off.

A route depicting his journey could never be a straight line. He was open to the vicissitudes of the road. If the only bus was going south to *Hermosillo*, he'd find plenty to interest him. And he'd be equally happy heading east to *Ciudad Juarez*. I'm certain he had favorites, or must-see places, but many times, he simply let his plans be dictated by the bus schedule or whatever ride he could get. I learned that the only firm rule was no hitchhiking at night. After all, there were *banditos* down here and both of us had heard warnings of robbery and kidnapping, and people getting their throats slit.

The border crossing was simple. I didn't even need a passport. The smells struck me at once. They were the biggest difference. Even this close to the U.S. they were distinctive: diesel gas, open sewers, dung on the streets—the next thing I noticed was the three-legged dogs and the dilapidated buildings.

As I headed toward the bus depot, I stared bug-eyed at everything. How could things be so strange only one hundred yards from the border? Then I saw him. The albino. I yelled, but he was too far in front to hear me. I tried to narrow the distance, but my injuries still pained me too much. I could only hobble in pursuit and soon lost sight of him. What was he doing here anyway? Had he followed me? How'd he find out I was here? All this for five dollars? What was I doing chasing him when I had to catch a bus?

I headed back toward the depot and arrived in front just as Marat exploded out of the doors. "Hurry! I have two tickets, no? The bus is leaving. *Vamos!*"

He grabbed me by the arm and pushed me through the doors, through the station, and to the back where the bus was sitting, engine already running and belching thick plumes of black and gray smoke.

"Where?" I asked, breathlessly.

"*Aqua Prieta*," he said.

That meant east, towards *Juarez*. Then we'd probably cut south to *Chihuahua*—home, at least Marat said it was, of the most beautiful women in northern Mexico. For this reason, and this reason alone, *Chihuahua* was one of the must-see places. Marat had been talking about the women of *Chihuahua* ever since we'd started out.

CHAPTER 3

The Mexican

"There ain't no surer way to find out whether you like people or hate them than to travel with them."
–Mark Twain

Now I was on a bus to *Aqua Prieta*, a place I'd never even heard of ten minutes ago. I had only scanned the maps because I was leaving all to the experienced traveler in my midst.

It was already past ten, the night was extremely dark, and the road extremely bumpy. I had absolutely no idea where we were, but imagined myself to be heading deeper and deeper into Mexico. Marat was busy with his nose in a language book, refreshing his Spanish. Every once in awhile he offered me the book and I'd take it and try to memorize a few words and phrases. But mostly I stared out of the window, trying to glimpse some of this foreign territory through the darkness.

It was strange to see how many vehicles drove with their lights off. All of a sudden we'd come up to a truck or a car, then pass them, and every time I could not see them until we were almost climbing up their rear end. I quickly realized that many of the cars and trucks coming towards us also drove with lights off. How could our driver see them coming as he passed? How was it going to end? Rear-ending someone that he couldn't see, or a head on collision with someone he couldn't see? And our driver was quick to pass. Marat said that some Mexicans had a theory that you see better at night with your lights off. We were meeting most of them.

At least our driver used his lights.

Then I saw my first wreck. A totaled car put up on a stand. Like a shrine. I asked Marat what it meant.

"They do that to remind everyone to drive carefully," he said. Then he chuckled. "I don't think they pay much attention. You see a lot of those down here."

I think it was on this first bus ride, that I realized that hitch-hiking down to Mexico City was something someone young and foolhardy would do, and that there was a great difference between being brave and being foolhardy. Add to that the friends who cautioned, "You *know* there are *banditos* there...And you *are* hitchhiking. Anything could happen." Second thoughts.

I closed my eyes and began to meditate to pass the time and ease my mind. I was relieved that we had gotten to *Nogales* too late to hitchhike.

And at least we were on our way to the great adventure, but then something caught my ear, something lacking. It was the engine noise. The bus seemed to be quieter, and it was slowing down. I looked out the window, trying to see the road ahead. It was pretty dark out.

"Hey look, Marat. There's another one of those wrecks."

Marat leaned over to look. We were going to come to a stop right alongside it.

Before I could say another word, Marat was up. He walked to the front to talk to the driver.

The bus had broken down. Second time this week it had happened to this particular driver on this particular bus. We would have to flag somebody down.

Quick as a shot, Marat grabbed me, made me take my bag and get down from the bus. We each carried only one bag. Mine was a small knapsack.

"I don't like two things about this," Marat said as we crossed a ditch and walked up a slope across from the smoke-belching bus. The smell of diesel permeated the air, but it was unlike any I had smelled before. Other passengers started to get down and mill about on the narrow shoulder and even on the two-lane highway.

"One. The bus could get hit." And as if to punctuate his statement or to ascribe the gifts of a Granola to my friend, immediately we heard the squealing of tires and brakes as an old beater of a car smashed into the rear of the bus. Strangely, the driver got out and laughed till he was bent over (although, maybe it wasn't so strange as he also wobbled as though he'd had a few shots of tequila).

Marat was not one to lose concentration or train of thought. "Two," he said. "There are *banditos* on the roads."

Great, I thought. Just what I wanted to hear.

"It's safer to be apart from the bus," Marat continued.

Now, we heard the screeching of wheels from the other end, as a beat up old pick-up slammed into the front of the bus.

"Line 'em up," I said. "One right after the other."

The pick-up looked somewhat like an accordion, but the driver, much like the first, got out wobbly-like, examined his vehicle and started to laugh. Perhaps both of them were giddy at the fact they were still alive and unscathed.

I looked at my watch, turned to Marat and said, "Well, I guess it's about time for the *banditos*."

Amazingly, no one was hurt. Another driver said he'd tell the folks at *Nogales*. Another bus was sent out, and within an hour-and-a-half we were back on the road. The *banditos* missed their cue.

At about one in the morning, the bus pulled to a stop at a square, unpainted cement building, that passed for a station. Marat got down first and started asking questions.

I could see a donkey wandering down the middle of the unpaved street, and a few scrawny, stray dogs yapping, and of course, one of them only had three legs. A couple of streetlights lit the depot, but everything else seemed closed. Marat was quick in surveying the place.

"There's a *cantina* open," Marat said. "But all the hotels are closed. Why waste the money anyway? We do not stay here long, no? Let's get something to eat."

We carried our packs two short blocks, with me peering down every alley and around every corner—it's so much easier to be paranoid in the dark—and again came the intermingled smells of diesel gas, raw sewage, dung, gasoline, goats, cigarette smoke, cilantro and meat cooking over grills. Walking past another three-legged mutt we finally entered the dilapidated, dimly-lit *cantina*.

Even at this time of night, it was packed. Cigarette smoke clouded the air. The place was loud, I could not make out any English being spoken, and it reeked with the smell of *chorizo*, tacos, enchiladas and oily refried beans. Everyone looked like the villains in The Treasure of The Sierra Madre—my main reference point for Mexico—and Mexican songs blasted from a jukebox. I was grateful for Marat's Spanish speaking abilities.

He spoke to a waitress, who was dwarfish and ugly, and cursed with a pockmarked face. She was one of the five ugliest people I've ever seen on this planet and pregnant, which I suppose proves there's someone for everyone. Letting out an endearing belch, she led us to the only open booth in the establishment.

Thus continued the longest night of my young life.

It was about two in the morning when our food arrived. And it was not much later that a minor hubbub started with the arrival of a newcomer to the restaurant. My back was to the door, one of those saloon-type, double doors, that I thought only existed in westerns, so I gauged interest of the entrance by the look on Marat's face. Actually, I didn't want to turn around and look, and draw more attention to myself. Enough attention had already been drawn by the fact we were *gringos*.

Ok, so I looked. Just in time to see a grimy, black-haired man walk up to the pockmarked waitress, grab her in the crotch and try to snake a kiss. She giggled, then turned abruptly. He slapped her rear as she started back to the kitchen.

I don't know how I knew it, but I knew this tough-looking

caballero, with the slicked-back hair, a faded red shirt open to almost his waist, and grimy black jeans, was going to sit down with us.

Sure enough, within a few minutes he approached our booth and said a few words in Spanish to Marat, none of which I could make out by the way. Marat answered, got up, and sat down on my side of the table, and the Mexican sat down opposite us.

It was cold in the *cantina*, and I was shivering. We had been up twenty hours straight, and it looked like we'd be up till dawn until new transportation was secured. I hoped it would be a bus so I could possibly sleep; no way could I sleep in a car. Marat ordered more coffee for us, and a Corona for our new amigo.

A conversation which was entirely in Spanish ensued, and I understood nothing. This went on for a good two hours, and was occasionally punctuated with grand gestures and loud outbursts such as, *"Ay carumba!"* or, *"Colonel Ratas!"* from the man. He called himself *Franc* (with a soft "a") *Roma*, and most of the talking was done by him, with Marat only interjecting a comment, or maybe a question every so often. Within that one night, *Franc* achieved legendary status with me.

You have to understand, I was exhausted, and still not a hundred per cent from my injuries—hell, my stitches had only been removed that morning. I was cold, and *somewhat* apprehensive. It was night in a land all too foreign and unknown; this *Franc* seemed cruel, foreboding and awfully large to me, and I was certain, *mucho dangerousio*. With his black, pencil thin mustache, all you had to do was put some cheap sunglasses on him and he would have looked every bit like one of those tinhorn dictators from Guatemala, El Salvadoran secret policemen or Mexican *Federales* that you see in the movies, all, no doubt versed in the art of water boarding. And I couldn't understand a word of what was transpiring.

Then bad went to worse. At around four A.M., Marat stood and said he would check out our options for getting out of *Aqua Prieta*. Telling me to wait in the *cantina* for him, he was up and gone before I could object. This left me alone with *Franc*.

The *caballero* stared silently at me for what seemed like a long time. I had no idea what to do, but boy did I wish I had gone with Marat.

Finally, *Roma* started to very slowly nod his head up and down. Then he spoke, still nodding. "I know you," he said in slow, halting English. "You got trouble." Then he leaned forward and stared into my eyes.

"What do you mean?" I asked with as much civility as I could muster. Not having any idea what he meant, I was still nervous enough to to try to be polite. I thought if I ignored him, he would go into one of his outbursts. His pants were too tight fitting to hide a gun, but his open shirt, revealing a dark brown hairless chest, hung loosely enough to hide a knife. Images of *banditos* entered my mind. Filthy, unshaven, lice-ridden, drug-smuggling, gun-running, white-slaving, cattle-poaching, throat-slitting, goat-raping *banditos*. Yes, I thought, his weapon of choice was definitely a knife.

He moved closer, his elbows now on the table, and focused his cruel black eyes even more intensely on mine and then repeated, "I know you. You got trouble."

I squirmed in my chair, but did it as nonchalantly as possible. I didn't want to show any weakness in front of him and cursed the cold for making me shiver. Then I glanced up and down his sleeves for the telltale bulge of a knife and maybe an ace or two in case he tried to lure me into a game of poker. Putting on my toughest Humphrey Bogart face to let him know I was ready for trouble, I stared him right back. "What do you want?" I asked coolly. The "you asshole," that was meant to be on the end of my sentence was kept discreetly silent but implied. Who knows if he was clever enough to figure it out. I looked around. The other people in the *cantina* seemed to be avoiding my gaze as if to say you're on your own, amigo.

"I know you. You got trouble."

Do I retain some friendliness in my voice? Do I tell him to bugger off? I wasn't sure how many of these people were friendly with him or part of his gang. How long could I play along? Would he pull his knife on me in this crowded place?

Where was Marat? The fact that Marat had bought the man a beer, and listened attentively to everything he said, obviously finding some need to appease him, made me think that I had to exhibit calm, and do the same—play along. Marat was experienced in these matters, I was decidedly not.

I caught the eye of the waitress who waddled over, squeezed Roma's shoulder and giggled. Pointing to the empty bottle I held up two fingers. She nodded, giggled when *Franc* swatted her rear again and sauntered off, soon returning with two beers and a revived spirit in her step. I took a sip and sighed in resignation. "What trouble?" I asked, while wondering if those words marked the limit of *Roma's* English vocabulary.

He leaned forward again, looking around the room a bit, till his black, bloodshot eyes settled once more on mine. Then draining half his bottle, he rammed it down on the table, turned his head and spat on the *cantina* floor. "You want drugs?" he asked in a whisper, eyeing the room as if every last one of the patrons was a narc. "You need drugs."

Now, the blood drained from my face, and maybe that was a good thing because I felt like a guy fending off a Vampire, whose only hope was to be politic, and keep him at bay until the sun rose, or Marat made it back with the stakes, garlic, crosses and priest.

After spending time in the Ramsey and Hennepin County jails interviewing people arrested for Federal offences, I had one hard and fast rule: don't mess with your country's criminal justice system. My whole life, I'd tried very hard to not commit murder, fraud, rape, thievery, counterfeit money—or even the seven sins, and I'd mostly succeeded. The biggest temptation was dope. It was the early Seventies. Everybody did marijuana, or at least experimented—some of them even inhaled.

There were recent newspaper reports of a black guy in Texas getting twenty years for a *single joint*. And in my home state, which was known for being a bit more liberal, a passing acquaintance of mine was shot to death in a drug bust. So this led to a corollary: don't do drugs especially if the authorities are nearby. I had already amended it with, don't even think about doing drugs in a foreign country.

After all, why do you think they call it dope?

The U.S. prison system was bad enough. I'd heard about Mexican prisons and my most ardent desire was to buy drugs and spend the rest of my life in one of them. Great accommodations I'm sure: clean sheets, carpeted floors, nice hole in the floor for a toilet, bars you could decorate, lots of vermin for snacks and my Mom would be really proud of me.

Was Granola going to count another coup? No damn way.

As I looked across at this guy, who was possibly going to slit my throat, or just somehow implicate me in a drug deal gone bad, I tried to figure out if I should handle *Roma* by acting or bluffing my way out. Then it came to me: play dumb, hardly a stretch—see "hitchhiking to Mexico City."

So I sipped the beer and smiled at him like some twit.

Marat had told me about buying grass in Mexico. You pay your money and the dealer gives you the grass. But then he can turn you in, get his grass back and a reward from the cops, plus he keeps the money you already paid him. Now you talk about your perpetual motion machine. What could be a better business model? Just sell the same thing over and over again. You could make a living on one lid of grass, not to mention the extra cash from the rewards.

"I know you," *Roma* said, interrupting on cue. "You got trouble." He let this sink in before adding, "Drugs very bad, *malo*. But you want drugs. *Franc Roma* has drugs."

The closest I ever came to being busted for anything was back in college, when my brothers and I lived in an apartment on Seven Corners, and we were getting ready to drive down to Florida for Spring Break. I had taken my last final and had come home exhausted not from the final but the all-nighter that proceeded it, to find two of Minneapolis' finest writing up a report on our refrigerator being stolen.

Unfortunately, we had a habit of leaving the door open when we were home and usually left it open if we went down the hall to visit friends. The day before somebody had made off with the refrigerator.

I swear we hadn't left the door open for very long, and we weren't out of the apartment for that long either. My idea was to find the thief and represent him for a contract for either a defensive or offensive lineman for the Vikings. If he could run with a refrigerator on his back, he could definitely break though the Packer's front four.

My older brother was hosting, the cops were friendly and professional, and even joking with me about passing my test. That is, until a friend of ours, Dino, came in with straight brown hair flowing half-way down his back, a full Jesus-like beard, silver granny glasses, a black briefcase and a dark gray, button-down coat reaching almost to the floor.

We were giving Dino a ride to the airport so he could go home to New Jersey over break.

"I know you," *Franc Roma* said. "You got trouble."

Shut the hell up, I thought. I'm in the midst of a reverie.

The cops' attitude changed pretty fast as they looked Dino over—they were no longer friendly to my brother or myself—and looked like their brains were working overtime as they explored every excuse they could think of in order to bust all of us right then and there. As if they were really desperate to show us all the consequences and ramifications for our brains and well-being, for crime fighters everywhere, for cleaning up the streets, for Bubba in prison, for getting haircuts and supporting the U.S. foreign policy whether it meant killing Vietnamese villagers to protect the freedom of our shores for MacNamara, Nixon and Kissinger, or propping up butcherous dictators in all other parts of the globe, and I don't feel like naming them all at this time with *Franc Roma* breathing down my neck—it's a long slippery slope that starts with a single toke. How they would have loved to get this to sink into our thickheaded, long-haired skulls, especially after we were behind bars. I just knew if they could bring themselves to utter the dread word "marijuana," they would pronounce it with five syllables and the "j" as a "j" like in jump.

I could see a mixture of befuddlement, disappointment and even distress on their faces as they couldn't come up with an excuse for a search. Dino, for his part, seemed completely at ease, unfazed.

The policemen left without their quarry and they left in a hurry. I'm not certain, but they might have gone off to get a search warrant, and on our part, we decided to take Dino to the airport immediately. Call it a hunch.

I can't even began to tell you how many times that winter quarter Dino came over to our apartment and, I guess, trying to lure us into a life of addiction, profligacy and dependency, yelled out, "Wanta smoke some dope?" before even getting to the open door or entering. Why he didn't yell it that day I have no idea.

Later in the car, Dino confided that the briefcase he carried contained seventeen lids of grass, he had already smoked some for the flight and thus forgot his usual introductory greeting.

Back at the *cantina*, I could feel the eyes of *Franc Roma* staring daggers into my face. The shivers were gone, replaced with heat and sweat—the same sweaty feeling I had when Dino came into our apartment and I saw the policemen's reaction.

"I know you," *Franc Roma* said. "You got trouble."

Nope. No big drug purchases tonight. Hell, I didn't even use them, and I knew Marat was too smart to buy them, at least in a foreign country. Even if I wanted drugs, I wouldn't buy them from this scary, nihilistic, flea-bitten, alcoholic, knife-wielding villain to give him a three-fold profit. Was he going to try to plant them on me or in my knapsack, and then claim the reward, I wondered? I watched him even more closely and gradually moved my bag closer to my side. I don't think my mind had ever been that concentrated before, not even at match point. I was totally aware.

This went on, for what seemed like hours. Long hours, all of which were spent having this not so illuminating one-sided conversation with *Senor Roma*. Except for looking away, sort of scanning the room, before he first mentioned drugs, I don't think he took his eyes off me for that entire time.

I ordered another cup of coffee, and one for *Roma*.

What options did I have? Marat told me to wait for him here, and I'd be damned if I was going to go outside in this place at night, and look for him. I had no idea where he went. I had no knowledge of the language, and no idea where I was, except somewhere in the middle of northern Mexico.

"I know you," he said. "You got trouble."

I heard the doors swing open and close. I turned around. I could see the sky outside was finally lightening a bit. A very big man in a gray trench coat walked into the *cantina*. He looked at me, then glared at *Franc Roma*. Walking up to our booth, he spoke a few words to *Roma*. *Franc* bowed his head abjectly, almost apologetically, took a last swig of the coffee, and got up and left. The big man smiled at me, then turned to follow *Roma*. A cloud had lifted.

Marat soon returned. "Tomas," he said. "We have to fly out of here. There is a four-seater leaving in an hour."

"Fly?" I asked. I had only been in Mexico for one night, and already I was in no way eager to fly on a small plane. All I could think was that it was Mexican-owned, Mexican-piloted, and worst of all, Mexican-serviced—all this prejudice owing in no small way to the broken down bus and my all-nighter with one *Senor Roma*.

"The only other way out of here is taking a truck over the mountains, on what is almost a goat path. The first bus out, going east or south doesn't leave for four days."

"God," I said.

"Do you want to stay here for four days? I don't." Then he laughed again. "You say you want adventure..."

"Ok, ok. I'll do it. Let's just get away from here. And get south, where it's warm." I was now shivering again. It was probably in the forties. For a guy from Minnesota, I sure was a wimp about the cold.

We paid and walked out of the *cantina*. The dawn had come, and the buildings started to take shape with the light. I wasn't so apprehensive now—I had a reprieve till boarding the plane—and

took in the smells and sounds of the town with a new appreciation. So this was Mexico. Not bad, I thought. I looked up and
down the dirt street. Something was strange to the north. I
peered through the hazy light. What was it, I wondered? I shouldered my pack and started walking up the road, leaving Marat
standing in the street, studying his map.

"Oh my God!" I exclaimed. "It can't be. It just can't." I closed
my eyes and rubbed them, intent upon erasing any illusions or
phantasms. But when I opened them, there, a mere hundred
yards down the road, was a wire fence, and a sign. *In English!* It
read: Douglas, Arizona. Welcome to the United States.

I walked across the border, then back into Mexico. I had
spent the whole night awake, kowtowing to *Franc Roma*, when
I could have got a good night's sleep a hundred yards away.

Some adventure. I was exhausted. I did the only thing possible. I doubled over, laughing so hard, that Marat heard me from
all the way back in front of the *cantina*, and ran over to see if I
was all right.

"We have to go. The plane leaves at seven. Come on," he said.

At the airport, the runway was a mixture of dirt and grass.
We had to show papers—I only had a Minnesota driver's license
but that was ok with them—we had to pay and then still had an
hour's wait for the plane, and who should wander by, but my
nemesis, *Franc Roma*.

Now, in the bright sunlight of the morning, he looked pretty
skinny and dissipated. Hardly someone to worry about. He
seemed, small, pathetic and obsequious, rather than dangerous.
He was hung over and no longer talkative. He lit a cigarette and
looked off into the distance. Who knows what those eyes saw?

The plane, a six-seater, red and dilapidated, with a rough,
clunky sounding engine, arrived in due time, but the pilot took
another three hours before he was ready to leave, due in no
small part to his wanting to fix the twenty or so things wrong
with the plane that the maintenance crew missed. We said our
good-byes, which in this case meant waving to the reduced
Franc Roma, boarded and were off to *Casa Grandes*.

CHAPTER 4

In Flagrante Delicto

*"Good judgment comes from experience, and a lot of
that comes from bad judgment."* –Will Rogers

Aqua Prieta grew smaller and insignificant, as our plane ascended into a clear blue sky. I still couldn't get out of my mind, how small and different *Franc Roma* looked in the bright light of day.

We flew across rolling, barren hills, with just small patches of green grassland and the occasional mesquite and cactus. There were no animals, such as cattle, or villages that we could make out from the plane, even though we were only five hundred feet up in the air. I did try to spot the goat path, but I only saw countless arroyos and chaparral.

I turned to Marat. "What was going on back there? With *Franc Roma*?"

At first, Marat looked at me questioningly, but then a big smile spread across his face, and his head tilted back in laughter. "Oh. That's right. You don't speak Spanish." He laughed some more. "I guess you didn't understand any of it last night, did you?"

"No," I said, barely hiding the leftover anger at his leaving me alone with *Roma* for over two hours. "What was he saying? All I remember is him yelling '*Ay carumba*' and '*Colonel Ratas.*'"

"I was just playing along with him," Marat said, "to keep myself amused. There was nothing else to do, and he's probably the town drunk. Why? Were you worried about him?"

Now, I stared daggers at him.

Marat laughed again. "Calm down. He was harmless. What you Americans call full of shit. All that talk—he was trying to get money from us," Marat said. "He needed money to help feed *Colonel Ratas'* men in the mountains. He said they were revolutionaries, fighting the government. When he slapped his forehead and cried out *'Ay carumba,'* he was saying he just remembered that the men were depending on him, to bring food, and he had got drunk and forgot."

"But he yelled *'Ay carumba!'* more than once," I said in a thinly veiled, and very annoyed manner.

"He kept remembering," Marat said. "Then," Marat added, "he wanted money for getting us drugs. Then for the society of the poor, then for an orphanage, then for the Sisters of the Holy Trinity. One thing after another, though he kept coming back to Colonel *Ratas* and the starving men in the mountains."

"I simply told him that we didn't have any money and wouldn't have any until we went to a bank in the morning."

"Oh," I said, taking this all in. "Then why the hell did he pester me all night?"

"I guess he didn't believe me any more than I believed him," Marat patiently answered.

"That's all he talked about for all that time?" I asked out loud, but more to myself. I was incredulous. *Franc* had talked almost non-stop. So much for how well I can ascertain a person's character.

"That's all. You know," Marat went on, "*ratas* means rat in Spanish. Colonel Rat."

I went on to tell him about the drugs and the "I know you" bit. "I was terrified back there."

"I guess that will be your first lesson in traveling. We're in his country, so I would not just toss him aside or ridicule him. But I would not believe him, or give him money either. I've come upon many like him in my travels. You have to sound them out, no? Could he really be dangerous? Sometimes, you don't find out until it's too late."

"Then what do you do?" I asked.

"Run like hell!" Marat said. Then we both started laughing.

"Where did he get that stupid name?" I wondered aloud. "He must've made it up. Probably *is* the town drunk. Does Mexico have soap operas like ours?"

"Yes," Marat chuckled. "He could've taken the name from one of them, or from a porno star."

The plane started to hit air pockets, dropping suddenly, along with my stomach.

The turbulence lasted for the rest of the flight, and thankfully, the clunky engine kept turning the prop.

We landed none too soon on another weedy, dirt runway in *Casa Grandes* and were greeted with cold, blustery winds, which seemed to lift most of the topsoil into the air and into my face, stinging it. And I'd thought I'd come south to get warm.

The pilot pointed us in the direction of the road to *Chihuahua*. We grabbed our packs and started walking, hunched over in the strong wind. So, I thought, this would be our first real hitchhiking in Mexico.

We stood on the roadside for an hour. No cars passed by. It was freezing, even for a guy from Minnesota, and I only had a light jacket. Marat loaned me a sweater. He had two from Peru, both alpacas and multicolored, though one was mostly maroon and the other orange; they were large and came all the way down to the knees.

Finally a car. An old Chevy-the driver pronounced it with a hard "ch." But the ride only lasted for a few miles, then we were back to looking for nonexistent cars. A truck picked us up for another ten miles, then another car for five. We still had not slept or washed for two days, and hadn't eaten since the *cantina*.

A bus came by, and I was tempted to walk back to find a stand, but Marat would not have any of that. He was not going to spend any money he didn't have to.

Two more hours. We were out in the middle of nowhere. The sky was growing darker. A bus came by and to my surprise, Marat flagged it down. I'd never experienced that in the States. The second and third class buses in Mexico will almost always stop to pick up passengers, no matter where they are. With the first class buses, you have to be a little lucky. They're a bit more pretentious. I sat down comfortably, read a few pages of *Morning of the Magicians,* and fell asleep.

The next thing I knew, we were in a big city, *Chihuahua,* the city of *Pancho Villa.*

"Where is the center of the city?" Marat asked the first person he saw. This was to be his first question in every city we stayed. For one thing, the center of the city was bound to be where much of the action was. For another, in Mexico, it always seemed to be close to the red light district, usually a "must-see" for Marat.

"We'll find a place to stay," Marat said to me. "Then we'll look around the city. Remember," he said, laughing and shifting his eyebrows like Groucho Marx, "the most beautiful women in all of northern Mexico," as if this was the most interesting fact in all of existence.

"Right," I said, busily massaging my right leg, which had stiffened up during the bus ride. The injuries to my head were not a problem (though some might argue), but my legs were still awfully tender.

We headed down *Calle de Carranza.* The street was well lit, and bustling with life, although I did not see any of what I would call pretty women. When we turned down a side street, it was ill lit and empty. I was about to find out that Marat had a knack for finding the cheapest accommodations, and usually in the dirtiest sections of a city. He had asked a lot of questions in the bus depot and I had no way of knowing the questions or the answers. When I asked him, he'd just say, "Come, we're going to find lodging," or "come, we'll get something to eat." I was on a learning curve and he was the professor. He was the leader, I, the follower. Everything was new and exciting. Every choice had its good points and bad points, and I determined not to argue with him, unless I thought I was in danger. Here, in this place, knowing neither how to read, write, or converse, I would have to rely on my intuition, and hope it worked a whole lot better than it had with *Franc.*

There had been a few, what I'd call, nice hotels, on the *Calle de Carranza*, but everything on the side street was dirty and run down, and smelling of sewage. Marat was eager to engage in the nightlife and didn't want to waste time or money getting a nice hotel, so, like I said, anything cheap would do.

The *Hotel Real Madrid* was a hundred yards down the side street. One lonely light bulb lit the entrance, over which was the sign, half of which hung down at an angle, ready to break off at the first sign of trouble. Marat pulled open the thick metal door, and went up two steps to the lobby, which was only a short hall in front of an imitation wood desk. Behind the desk, stood a tall, unshaven gray-haired man, in a grubby, moth-eaten, dark purple terrycloth robe. After Marat spoke with him, he picked a key out of a box behind the desk and led us outside down a corridor, which had not been cleaned in an epoch. Cobwebs and filth abounded, legions of cockroaches and rats scurried for cover as our concierge led the way with a flashlight. Open cement troughs were filled with water and refuse, giving off a stench I would not soon forget. I covered my nose as I breathed in and out. Approaching a peeling, blue-colored door, our host unlocked it and ushered us into a dimly lit, shabby room. After accepting twenty pesos, he gave Marat the key and left.

Marat closed the door and started laughing. "I'm not sure I want to pull down the sheets," he said. He looked around, and, after close examination, put his pack in a closet. I put mine down on one of the beds, first, placing a newspaper underneath. I didn't even want to touch the bed, and looking around the small room, I realized my options were very few. I did not want to sleep standing up.

"Let's find a place to eat, and then we'll look around the city," Marat said. "I've wanted to visit *Chihuahua* for some time."

And it was then that I made my first big mistake.

"You go," I said. "I'm beat. Just bring me back a banana or something. An orange. I'll be ok."

"Most beautiful women south of the border," Marat said, a twinkle in his eye as though that would tempt me.

I realized that when I'm that exhausted, nothing tempts me. Besides, I had not liked the look of the city. Don't know why, just another intuition.

"You'll have them all to yourself," I said.

It was seven in the evening by the time we were settled, then Marat took off to explore. I eventually was too sore to stand, so I moved the newspapers to where the pillow was, and sat down on them, with my back against the metal headboard of the bed and began to read, soon dozing off. The metal was solid, no vermin to worry about there.

I guess a couple of hours passed.

I awoke with a start as the door to our room opened. It turned out our room was the only thing that was open.

"I wandered the streets for a while, and found them empty," Marat told me. "Everybody disappeared. No restaurants were open, no night clubs or *cantinas*. No music." Marat seemed pretty disappointed. "No people about. No hot women. Perhaps it's a holiday."

Maybe we were in the wrong quarter, and there were more interesting sections of the city, but I did not feel like being stuck in *Chihuahua*. I started casually playing up all the bad particulars of the place, hinting that better times awaited us farther south. After all, I was a master manipulator.

Surprisingly, Marat ran with the idea, and almost immediately—I'm not sure what persuaded him, for he was set on spending time in *Chihuahua*—said we should go to the depot and check for outgoing buses, just so we were aware of the possibilities. Also, I sensed something new in his manner, maybe a little more urgency, but barely.

There was hope. I picked up my boots, but before putting them on, I turned them upside down and shook them, just in case.

It took about fifteen minutes to reach the station, Marat out in front and me hobbling after him. We didn't see one living person the whole way there, not even a three-legged dog.

"So this is where all the people are," I said as we entered the station. It was packed and there were lines at every ticket booth. Looked to me like everyone was trying to escape. Marat checked the schedule. "*Merde!*" he exclaimed. "There is one bus only going south. And it leaves in forty minutes. Nothing else leaves for five days. There's some sort of strike. Look. Almost everything is canceled. What do you think?"

"Well," I said guilefully. "You know, we haven't really seen the city, or the women." Somehow, I knew this was the right tack to take with him. "And I think our place is really interesting, and I really like it."

Marat looked at me. He was deep in thought. A look of decision appeared in his eyes. That must have decided it for him. "You stand in line," he said. "Say '*Dos boletos a Torreon, por favor.*'"

Yes! I thought to myself. Goin' south.

"Go ahead. Repeat it."

I repeated it.

"Good. Now stand in line. I'll go get our stuff."

Marat took off like a sprinter, and I stood in line, nervous about communicating in a foreign tongue. "*Dos boletos a Torreon, por favor,*" I said in a low voice. I kept repeating it over and over in my head. The line moved relatively quickly, and I could feel my pulse racing. For once in my life, I wanted a line to move more slowly. Beads of sweat formed on my forehead and ran down the middle of my back, but I didn't stop to analyze why I was so apprehensive, or try to talk myself into being calm. I just kept repeating, "*Dos boletos a Torreon, por favor,*" and hoped it didn't come out something like, "Your mother is a goat and pygmies from *Torreon* turn their noses up at her."

I looked at my watch. Five minutes already gone. It was going to be close. I got to the front of the line and ordered the tickets, and paid. The clerk handed me two tickets. They said *Torreon.* What was the big deal? I could've done it in my sleep.

But a lot of time had passed. I looked at my watch. Thirty minutes to midnight and departure. Where was Marat?

Time passed, now quickly. I didn't want to leave the station, but he should have been back. I also didn't want to get on the bus alone, plus Marat had all our baggage. He should've been back. So we miss the bus, I thought, who cares. But then we'd have to stay in this place for five more days, so I cared.

Against my better judgement, I started walking, trying to remember exactly the way we'd gone when we left the station earlier. I had always been pretty good at directions, but it was dark and I'd never been in *Chihuahua* before. If he was coming back and I missed him—I didn't want to think about it. Unfortunately, besides trying to remember the way, I could think of little else.

The *Calle de Carranza*. Ok, so far so good. Brother, that was only the first street. One side street looked a bit familiar. I took a deep breath and turned the corner. It looked much narrower than I remembered. Were all those second stories hanging out over the street, which was more like an alley? Were all these buildings that shabby and faded? God! I wasn't at all certain. Had it taken this long to get there? But I kept walking.

Finally, after limping through the dark streets and alleys for what seemed like a long time, there it was, the broken down sign, *Real Madrid*, the hotel probably named after the soccer team. I rushed down the path to our room. Turning a corner, I saw Marat, bent down on his knees, fiddling with the keyhole to the door. He had been in such a hurry, he broke the key off in the lock. And he had spent the last ten minutes trying to somehow, force it or jiggle it out.

For all his smarts, he had missed the obvious and easiest solution. I decided to take over.

"Go to the office and get a screwdriver," I said. "We'll take the door off the hinges." I really, really did not want to stay more than the next twenty minutes in this city. Besides, I didn't think our ticket plan allowed for a refund.

"Good idea," Marat said, and rushed down the wet path.

I shook my head. How could he have broken the key? Things like this only happen when you don't have any time. I looked at my watch.

Rushing back, Marat fumbled with the screwdriver until I could bear it no longer. There's a myth about the French. Whether it's true or not, I can't say for sure. But I've heard more than once, that they're not supposed to have "good hands," and that ball boys and girls at the French Open used to carry nets to catch the balls because they were so inept with their hands. I took the screwdriver from him and quickly unscrewed the hinges.

Funny, Marat didn't seem so superhuman to me now.

The concierge wandered up and wondered, I suppose, what the hell we were doing as I took the door off. Marat took care of the explanations and even got our deposit back, then we entered the room and got our belongings.

Marat thanked him and we rushed back to the station. The bus was leaving in ten minutes.

I was much relieved, but the feeling was not to be continued. Marat took one step up to the bus, turned, slapped his forehead with his hand and yelled, "*Sacre bleau!* My notebook!" His face was ashen. "Do not let the bus leave!" he cried, and he took off in a flash.

What was I to do now? Stand in front of the bus? The only word I could think of was halt with an "o" attached to the end. The bus was leaving in less than ten minutes, and the hotel had to be at least a half-mile away. I imagined myself standing in the aisle behind the driver yelling, "Halto, halto, halto!" What if it leaves? I asked myself: what would Cortez do? Nah, that would be bloodier and then we'd have to drive.

The engine was running. I saw the driver check his watch. I looked out the window and saw a slender figure in an alpaca sweater, approaching at great speed. It was Marat. Relief again.

I might have made fun of Marat's ability with his hands, but I'll never make fun of his foot speed. I swear he set a world record time. By my estimate he had gone and come in less than four minutes. And that counts retrieving his writing—the work that covered over two years of his life of travels and that he hoped would one day secure his fame.

Marat sat down heavily in a seat next to mine. He breathed deeply a few times, then started laughing merrily as the bus started out of the city.

"You know," he said. "I didn't waste time going for a key. I figured the room would still be open, but the door, it was already back in place so I knocked on it. A voice from inside said, '*Uno momentito.*' But I didn't have time to wait. I tried the doorknob, just as it opened. A woman, pretty sleazy-looking, and wrapped only with a sheet peered out. There was a man in bed. I had not even suspected. I knew we were in the red light district, but I didn't know we were in an actual brothel. We were in a hotel of prostitutes." He laughed again. "I knew there was something about that place. I guess I still have *some* of my instincts."

"Well, they didn't have to change the sheets," I said.

I thought it was curious the way he accented the word "some," but I was too tired and too sore to pursue it. Besides, I had got my way. We were headed to warmer climes and I didn't have to do any heavy manipulating. I was quite satisfied, except that we'd been in a brothel and I didn't even get to see a woman of the night.

On to *Torreon*.

CHAPTER 5

The Quest

"Adventure is someone a thousand miles away having a rough time." –Marat

The ride to *Torreon* was another all-nighter. I drifted in and out of sleep, never quite knowing whether I was actually sleeping, dreaming or awake in a semi-stupor, the only constant was Marat going over his vocabulary and the racket from the bus engine.

When I was awake, which happened now and again, I focused on a tennis ball. Now, of course, I was damn near crippled and had not brought a racquet or tennis balls on the trip, but I had read somewhere that Billie Jean King would stare at a tennis ball for five to ten minutes before a match to help her concentration and to become as "one with the ball." Bored when I was awake, but too tired to read, I closed my eyes and visualized a bright yellow Penn tennis ball, number and all, and tried to keep it in my mind's eye as long as possible. This effort at concentration would wake me up, then I would read, which would put me back into a fitful sleep and so on through the night.

Sometimes, the motion of the bus was so shaky, that I'd dream I was the ball in a giant pinball game, ricocheting back and forth from bumper to bumper—I was queasy, but I did score a lot of points.

As the light of daybreak began to filter into the bus, I woke up and was surprisingly refreshed.

Marat was asleep in the seat in front of me, as were most of the twenty to twenty five other men, women, children, chickens, goats and one burro who took up a whole row of seats. Excuse me, the burro was awake. My mistake.

To the east, all I could see were barren foothills and most of the land looked like desert and scrub brush, but it wasn't long until we were passing through the outskirts of a city: run down, faded shacks, fences, the smell of cattle and dung, a gas station. Soon, I began to see fruit stands and *torta* stands. A burro by the side of the road brayed, and my companion (not Marat, the bus traveling burro) answered him in what I considered a plaintive call for freedom, sex, comradery or against motion sickness. I wasn't sure which.

Marat was awake by the time we reached the *Torreon* station, and once more he surprised me. He went right up to the ticket office and asked what time the next bus heading south was due to leave. No luck. There was nothing for hours, so he walked across the street to a *Pemex* station and started talking to anybody with a car.

Why wouldn't he want to explore *Torreon*, I wondered?

I watched him as I gorged myself with bananas and oranges from a fruit stand by the bus depot. I had been warned only to eat fruit that could be peeled and cooked food. No lettuce, tomatoes, no raw vegetables or even an apple. Water was out of the question. Marat said only soda or beer, and we always wiped the mouth of a bottle before drinking.

"Tomas," Marat yelled as he motioned for me to come over. He had secured a ride to the east and we were soon on our way.

There was only one problem. In his haste, he had misunderstood the driver, and after an hour ride that covered about eighty kilometers (I'm trying to fit in) he was turning down a narrow country road where it would be impossible for us to get another ride. We were obviously better off hitching from a highway—much more traffic. By my count we had traveled some seven hundred miles since *Nogales* and this was only the first ride we hitched that took us more than ten miles since Tempe. Not too successful.

I thought I was in a Marx Brother's bit.

Chico, along with Harpo and Zeppo, all disguised in long fake beards and playing Russian aviators who flew across the Atlantic were being feted in New York City. In a thick Italian accent, Chico says: "Da first-a time we fly a across-a da ocean, we get half-a way across, den we ran out-a gas, so we go back. Da next-a time, we take-a plenty a gas and-a we get-a plenty close, only twenty yards to land...and we run-a out-a gas, so we go back. Da next-a time we take-a so much-a gas, but we forget-a da airplane, so we sat-a down in da middle a da Atlantic and-a we talk it over and take-a dis large boat. And-a dat is how we fly across-a da ocean."

And-a dat's how we hitch-a-hike down to Mexico City—we take-a da bus and we take-a-da plane.

Now as we began to walk and thumb anything that moved, I had a lot of time on my hands and I began to wonder about Marat's recent haste. It wasn't like him at all. I guess I didn't really know him too well, only for a little more than a week, but it was curious. He didn't even want to wait for the next bus out of *Torreon*.

Everything seemed to be going well. Just as I hoped, we were heading further south, and the sooner we got south, the better. We hadn't even stopped for more than a few minutes in *Torreon*, and I was beginning to think that old girlfriend was right—I was an expert manipulator, without even knowing what I was doing. But that didn't last for long. I started wondering, you know, what's with Marat? He didn't even say anything about stopping in *Torreon*. I began to think, Marat doesn't find anything here? Nothing of note he wants to see in *Torreon*? There were some interesting things here. Like links with *Pancho Villa*—he fought battles for the city three times. There were famous mines and a ghost-mining town. Those were the sort of things both of us liked to see. I was kind of surprised. I started to think, he's been wanting to move faster and faster.

Why *Torreon*? Because it was the first bus out, he said. The only bus out of *Chihuahua*. But why did we have to move so quickly. I had my own reasons. I'm from Minnesota. I'm starved for warm, hot climates. I didn't want to stick around the north. Hell! People here were wearing stocking caps. It's winter up here.

Now I'm a pretty trusting guy, a pretty optimistic guy, but it occurred to me that there could be a reason he wanted to move a little faster. The only way to find out was to ask him, but I figured I should be subtle about it, after all, it was probably nothing and I didn't feel like making a fool of myself over it.

I decided to start my interrogation slowly.

"So," I asked very slyly, "What did you say your second Ph.D. was on?"

"Pythagorean Theorem," he answered.

"Pythagorean Theorem?" I said, and then added, to show off my sense of humor, "I woulda thought they figured that out a long time ago, like in Greece."

"Well," he said, somewhat taken aback. "I worked on a new proof..." It was then I realized Marat was a literalist.

When I was younger, I used to really be annoyed by literalists—they just take everything too seriously. Everything is taken at face value or is painted in black and white to them. But now, I kind of enjoy them—they're really easy to mess with.

"Why?" I asked with the utmost innocence. "We already know it's true."

Marat looked at me with a combination of utter hopelessness and Gallic disdain.

Then I grinned. The grin my older brother said was award-winning, that he said always got me out of trouble.

"I know. I know," I said. "Just fucking with you."

But I think he was still pissed off at me—like I didn't take his education with enough seriousness. But now I had him on the defensive. Next, I started a new topic, one with great interest for me, but from experience, one guaranteed to make the listener fervently desire to talk of anything else.

"So," I asked innocently, "Do you believe in free will?"

Marat looked at me with a puzzled expression. I guess the question did seem like it came out of the blue.

He held up his right hand, the forefinger extended as if to have time to gather his thoughts.

"There is free will," he finally intoned, "but, I believe, only in one instance."

"What?" I asked eagerly.

"If a person has a choice A and a choice B, where A is the right thing to do, but is disadvantageous and might even cause harm to the person making the choice, and where choice B is wrong, but is beneficial to the person, yet still the person chooses A. That is the only instance of free will."

Nothing like mathematicians. See, now even I was getting bored. I was now one question away. "What about virtue? Do you think a virtuous life can be lived in this day and age?"

Now he looked like I had stabbed him or caught him out, further arousing my suspicion. I thought it was time.

"So," I asked before he could answer the virtue bit. "Anything interesting happen in *Chihuahua*? When I stayed back in our illustrious hotel, I mean?"

He hemmed and hawed for a little bit, gave me innocuous answers telling nothing. But then it came out. Maybe I was a better interrogator than manipulator, because I now found out I had not manipulated anything. While he was gone in *Chihuahua*, he had his way with the wife of somebody, and he wasn't quite sure just who he had cuckolded.

"I didn't think you needed to know," Marat said, just a tad disingenuously.

"Well, you're right," I said, relieved. I had been suspicious for nothing. "I don't care who you sleep with. It's none of my business."

But now he became more apologetic. "I promise you, she made the move to me," he said. "I walked around the city, no? Not much was open. Then I saw the lights of this little kiosk—a travel agency of sorts, in front of a house. I saw the travel posters and thought I could get information, no? Next thing I know, she led me upstairs to her apartment and took off her clothes. She was trying to seduce me. And I let her. It was so stupid. And I know better."

"Like I said, I don't care," I said. So the more apt description was that she had her way with him. "You can do what you want. I'm not your keeper."

Marat was a good-looking guy. His short, golden brown hair, with a shock hanging down the right side of his forehead was appealing to women. He had a moderately aquiline nose, sloped just enough to give him a certain hint of dignity and a slightly patrician look, without it diverging into snobbishness, and bright blue eyes full of elan.

"Well, you should care," he said, laying a haymaker on me. "Because she was the police chief's wife, or maybe that of a *Federale*, but that doesn't matter."

"Why?" I calmly asked.

"Because...I, ah...Whoever it was...I think he might be after us," Marat replied. He was less calm.

"How do you know it was the police chief?" I asked none too pleasantly.

"He came home, right when we were in the act," Marat said excitedly. "She told me to hide under the bed, but I jumped out the window. I didn't want to take a chance."

"So what's the problem?" I asked solicitously.

"I am sure he saw me," Marat said.

"How could he?" I asked, now concerned. "How would you know?"

"Well...I heard the two gunshots go off," Marat said, "and zing off the pavement in front of me."

"Oh," I said.

"And the 'You little white bastard *gringo puto*. I will hunt you down and stuff your *cajones* in the mouth of my giant guard dog,' that he yelled after me."

"Are you translating?" I asked.

"Yes," he said.

I did some quick figuring and came up with, "Oh shit!"

Now I didn't know whether to jump in front of the next car going east, or hide from it. Did the threat cover my *cojones* as well?

"Man," I said. Now I knew I was distraught. I'd never use "man" as an address or exclamation unless I was. "He'll never follow us this far south. We've come over five hundred kilometers (I started to say three hundred miles but changed it in mid-sentence cuz it sounded further) from *Chihuahua*. He's got a job, you know, beating up people or torturing them. He's too busy if he's a police chief or F*ederale.*" Then, the thought occurred to me that he might have some vacation time coming.

"I'm too light-complexioned," Marat said. "I look too much like a *gringo*. Too bad I'm not tan like you. I stand out too much."

I'm not sure if I took the opposite tack because I wanted to soothe his nerves or if I just realized how unlikely it was for this hombre to pursue us, but I did.

"Stop worrying," I said. "He'll never come this far."

"Tomas," Marat said. "This is a Latin country. I've heard of men acquitted of murder, because they caught their wife with another man. Hell, my father would kill somebody for this kind of thing."

"That's why I wanted to get out of there fast. I didn't even know she was married..."

For a split second, I imagined Marat fiddling with the key stuck in the door at our luxury brothel suite, as a big policeman with a pistol and a bigger dog (probably with four legs) tapped him on the shoulder from behind.

A car slowed down. It was full of people, but apparently they wanted more company, so we got a ride all the way to *Saltillo,* as we gradually made our way upward into the foothills of the *Sierra Madre Oriental.*

"Anything interest you here, Marat?" I snidely asked, when our ride stopped and we got out.

Saltillo had once been the capitol of Texas before we rested it (Texas) away, and a major battle was fought at *Buenavista* a bit south of here, when Zachary Taylor defeated *General Antonio Lopez de Santa Anna,* the villain of the Alamo (to us *Norte Americanos* anyway) giving him one more comeuppance after *San Jacinto.* But that wasn't my point.

I guess I could have split up with him, although it was not as though he got us into trouble on purpose. This sort of thing could happen to anyone, especially if he was a guy. Most guys would kill to get "lucky" like that. He didn't know she was married—I believed him on that count.

Though I hated to admit it, quite frankly I was more afraid of traveling here alone without the language, than being chased by somebody who was six hundred kilometers away. I suppose I could've just gone back to the States, but what kind of adventurer is that? What would I tell my grandchildren? I decided to stick it out with Marat. I would just make sure I kept more of an eye on him.

Everybody has their moments, stupid things are done sometimes inadvertently, but I've noticed that really, really brilliant people do really, really stupid things. Maybe these aren't any dumber than stupid things done by stupid people, they're just less expected and can have much worse ramifications. Perhaps there's another axiom: the more intelligent you are, the less common sense you have. Or, really intelligent people and really stupid people have a lot in common. Certainly it doesn't apply to everybody, but here's a real simple example: once upon a time you have these brilliant guys and they make the atomic bomb. Did they think it wouldn't be used? Or that they could stop it from being used? Had they ever heard of the military? Now we're in a world where whole cities can be destroyed in seconds and isn't it nice to reason that no sane leader of a country would ever use the bomb because of mutually assured destruction. Was Truman sane? The Japanese might not think so.

But I guess the scientists did give us the ability to save lives by destroying lives.

I have to admit I'm a little ambivalent on that one. For one, Europe's had almost thirty years of peace because of the deterrence factor. An example of the law of unintended consequences? Maybe that's the trouble with being a middle child—I always see both sides of the argument. And maybe I'm ambivalent for purely selfish reasons. Was it a truly necessary to drop A Bombs on Hiroshima and Nagasaki? My father wasn't disturbed by the making of those bombs or the dropping of them. He thought it saved his life and many of his friends. If we invaded Japan, he would've been one of the first on the beaches. He was an army engineer and had already been one of the first to hit the beaches in MacArthur's island hopping campaign and he'd seen a life's worth of carnage. They were projecting over a million casualties if they had to attack mainland Japan. My dad didn't want to be one of them. He already had his share of purple hearts.

That's one reason for my selfish ambivalence—Maybe I'm here because my dad didn't die on some beach in Japan.

Of course, if you want to talk about intelligence and common sense, I was still here with Marat with the possibility of a rabid, murderous torturer on his trail, so I guess that means I'm either really, really intelligent with no common sense, or just plain stupid.

After giving me a dirty look, Marat defiantly stuck his thumb out as he walked backward down the road.

We ended up walking through the whole city, and it was pretty large and spread out, but it was still barely noon and sunny and soon our spirits were high.

Three more rides got us further south along the road to *San Luis Potosi*, but the last one dropped us off in the proverbial middle of nowhere, as the driver was going off on a narrow mountain road that probably could be qualified as another goat path.

These rides had not gotten us more than a hundred miles south of *Saltillo*, but the more I thought about it, the more I believed what I'd said earlier, that we need not worry, and they were still longer rides than I'd gotten from any Volkswagen.

There was no way that enraged husband would follow us all the way down here. We were out of his range. Besides, this was a huge country. He might have tried to track us from the *Chihuahua* bus station, but that was the last bus we'd taken. There wasn't a million-in-one likelihood he would've chanced upon the drivers that had got us this far. No, I was pretty sure we were safe. Does that sound like "famous last words?"

The last driver, so Marat told me, was certain we'd get another ride soon. There was a lot of traffic through the mountains on this road, he'd said. We'd be in *San Luis Potosi* before we knew it.

So we walked. And we walked. And we walked.

The mountains of the *Sierra Madre Oriental* run about two hundred miles wide and extend southward through eastern Mexico running parallel with the Gulf, and we were now fully in them. It was cooler up here, even during the day and the air was very crisp and clean. I've always loved the mountains.

It seemed like we were spending the whole day walking and Marat had his face buried so far in the current Newsweek, that I took it to mean that he was tired of my banter and still sensitive about my wisecrack in *Saltillo*.

A few semis passed us, breaking up the quiet of the road and belching black diesel smoke that befouled our noses, lungs and clothes as they rumbled by. Also smaller trucks and pick-ups, but nobody stopped no matter how vigorously we waved our thumbs.

For some reason, my mind wandered back to Vietnam. I've long had a reputation of starting a story or discussion and letting one tangent after another lead me off the path. But sooner or later, I'd come back to the original item, and so, in true form, I went back to a discussion we'd had the first week we'd met. Maybe it would break the tension.

"Who gives these old men the right to send so many others to their doom anyway?" I asked.

Marat looked up at me and laughed. "That is a long story interruption. Even for you."

What'd I tell you?

Marat had his own ideas about the war. Certainly a French commie would have an interesting point of view—if he really was a commie. He had left it an open question as to whether or not he had just lied to get out of the army.

The French had been there before us. We'd only gotten into it to aid them a little before *Dien Bien Phu* in '54. So if we were to say, "Well they started it," and the North Vietnamese answered, "No, you did!" and we said, "Did not. You did," we would both be wrong (but this would definitely be a better way of disputing it, than with real weapons). The French started it, and we only took over for them. And that's in modern times. In earlier days, it was usually the Chinese and Vietnamese that were habitually killing each other.

"So many of us go through life knowing little and caring less," Marat said. "Unless it concerns our little scope of interests and appetites, always pertaining to ourselves. One striking feature being that it all goes by so fast—what is the latest football score, the latest tennis result? Who did something for me? How many women did I make love to? How much money did I make? What kind of pretentious car do I drive?" He wryly laughed. "We do not bother about the war unless it affects us directly."

"When I was a student, we bothered," I protested.

"Perhaps you did, but most only did when they brought forth the lottery. Many students in your country care only about exploiting their new freedom. They are finally on their own, away from their parents. There is sex, drugs and rock and roll to put it simply. Your leaders on the other hand, care about three things: getting and maintaining their power, stopping communism or any system that is antithetical to their own, and acquiring as much wealth in any form—and all are related.

"Tolstoy's *How much Land Does A Man Need* should be required reading for everyone, especially the ones that need to acquire everything they see or encounter."

So, he liked Tolstoy. It was in this conversation that I knew we would become friends. Goddamn it! Friends with a Frenchman. Another coup for Granola.

"And what is worse than some old man deciding you have to go to war and kill other people with their narrow interests?" he added.

"It has taken the loss of some fifty thousand men, and only some of your leaders begin to see the error of their ways. Most would still press on, forever seeing the light at the end of the tunnel."

"Every one of those lives was precious. Every one had their own intimate thoughts, goals, dreams. They had parents and brothers and sisters who loved them, had girlfriends or boyfriends they wanted to build a life with. And they had the same thoughts of sports scores, nice cars, love and a future. And what of the millions on the other side that were lost? Did they not also have people loving them? We French were no better. How did we get so barbaric? What makes us so?"

"You, with your knowledge limited to newspapers, tv, periodicals and perhaps discussions," Marat said, "could have made better decisions than those 'best and brightest' did. Or at least your decisions could not have caused any more destruction than theirs."

"Another required work for your government officials should have been Bernard Fall's *Street Without Joy*. Had your presidents read this, they would not have gone to war in Vietnam."

"I read it," I humbly said.

"Then I rest my case," Marat said laughing.

"Naw," I said. "Those men would have just thought they could do better than the French with their hands tied behind their backs."

Marat thought for a bit.

"If the old men want to fight a war, let them fight it themselves. After all, they've already lived, loved, eaten, danced, played, traveled, acquired, perhaps read a great work though I doubt it. Now it is our turn. Why should they not let us do the same? They should not have the right to send us off to die before we have our chance to experience everything about life."

He went back to his magazine.

"Yeah," I agreed. "If you're seventy or eighty, go fight your war. Maybe even sixty. Younger than that, you should get to live your life."

I wasn't saying that if a guy was seventy or eighty, he didn't want to have that one last steak or one last pepperoni pizza, make love to a stone fox (that's the way some of us talked back then), or listen to Beethoven's 9th one last time, but you've had your turn. Give someone else a chance. Besides, you might survive. Who knows? You may end up being constipated a lot out there on bivouac but you could still survive. Better yet. If they had to do the fighting maybe there would be no war.

As my thoughts got carried away, Marat was once more engrossed.

"This is curious," Marat said excitedly, handing me the Newsweek. "Look. They killed *Lucio Cabanas*. The *Federales*."

"Who's that?" I asked.

"*Lucio Cabanas*? He is a famous rebel leader. Operating in *Guererro* State. Southern Mexico. The *Federales* report they kill him every six months or so." Then, with a completely straight face, Marat said, "Looks like they got him again."

I'll never forget that. It was not to be my last encounter with *Senor Cabanas*.

As for the war, I decided that it was against my better interests to shoot at some stranger or to have them shoot at me. And that meant getting out of the draft.

As luck would have it, an attorney friend of mine said he would trade tennis lessons for advice on avoiding the military.

Of course, there were other ways to get out. You could go to Canada, you could go to jail, you could cut off a toe, preferably one you were not overly fond of or used too much.

One of my friends dipped a cigarette in ink before going in for his physical. His chest looked black under the X-ray. Another friend gorged himself with licorice—I can't remember if it was the red or black, but whichever it was, it raised his blood pressure over the limit. Both got out. I, unfortunately, was not so creative. I passed my physical.

What I really remember about that day, and I think it took almost a whole day, was the math test to see if you were smart enough to join the army. A sample question: if Johnny has one dollar and goes to the store to buy a candy bar for twenty-five cents, a coke for thirty cents, and a piece of gum for five cents, how much money does he have left? That was one of the harder ones. I am not making this up. It was rumored, that if you failed this part of the test, they would make you take it over until you passed. It was a three hour test. There were some determined souls who managed to fail it over and over again, but they were better men than I.

One big guy with red blotches all over his arms and legs (I never found out if those were the results of a licorice-like ploy) failed the hearing test a few times. A supervisor took him into a different booth and, unsurprisingly, he passed with flying colors.

I later asked him a question, but he said he couldn't hear me.

One of my best friends got the golden award, one to kill for. He got number 365 in the lottery.

For the lottery, everybody's birth date was randomly assigned a number. If your birth date, say, April 1st, was number one, and they were calling up draftees, and you were of the right age, you had to go. Well, no one thought they'd go through all the numbers. Everyone knew he was safe, except for my friend.

Another friend received number 197 and gave up his deferment, because in the rules to the new game, if you gave up your deferment and your number wasn't called for a year you were off the hook. My number was low and was called. That's why I had to take the physical. One quarter, I dropped below the number of credits needed to keep my deferment, and before you knew it I was turning my head and coughing.

My friend with the golden number panicked. As soon as he graduated, he joined the National Guard. That year, the numbers stopped at 196.

My attorney's plan of attack: file for 4-F. It would take them about a month to turn it down, then another three months for the draft board to turn down our appeal. Next, file for hardship. Another month for them to turn it down, and another three to turn down the appeal. And finally, file for conscientious objector. He thought we could drag it out at least a year, and by 1972, the war was winding down. Turned out, I didn't have to do any of it. Nixon ended the draft about two days before I graduated. But I still liked the commie idea. It had class.

Then I returned my thoughts to the present, and that meant one step after another. All we could do was to keep on keeping on, one hill after another as we slowly climbed to some two thousand meters. One long stretch of road uphill, then another not quite as long stretch downhill with a couple of switchbacks thrown in for good measure. Some sections of the road were so narrow I was happy to be on foot. As far as I was concerned this offered a lot more control than being on a bus or other vehicle over these narrow roads. I remember quite often reading newspaper articles (usually in a back section) about buses going over cliffs, off of bridges or tumbling over and over as they crashed downhill in some far away third world country. Everyone was always killed and there was always a single German or Frenchman among the victims.

A few buses passed, but as usual, Marat didn't want to ride a bus unless we were desperate, which meant that we wouldn't flag one down until it was getting dark and the *banditos* were due out. Marat would just trust to his luck, which seemed a little strange to me, considering he felt he was on the run. Maybe by now he'd relaxed about his pursuer and dalliance.

As the sun began to ebb behind the hills and outcroppings to the west, it became much cooler, after all we were up over 6000 feet, and I was not looking forward to the weather if we didn't get a ride.

Now Marat said, "We'll take the first bus that comes by, regardless. We don't want to be out here at night."

I'll drink to that.

Unfortunately, no buses came and I was out of water.

As the light began to further diminish, I could see Marat thinking about what to do. The brilliant wheels were turning.

"We don't want to walk on the road at night, Tomas," he said. "It would be stupid of us to do so. And not only because of the drivers—those without lights and those with lights. You never know when one will be drunk or just plain reckless. *Banditos* are definitely a danger. I don't want to needlessly worry you..."

Well you are.

"But you need to know the concerns," he continued. "If no bus comes before it gets dark, we need to find a place that will shield us from the cold, but also gives a clear sight down the road without us being seen."

"Do you have anything that's white?" he asked.

"Only underwear," I answered after thinking for a second. I had taken darker clothes to keep warmer. I pulled one unit of underpants out of my pack.

"Nothing larger?" he asked.

"That's it," I said. Too easy to make a joke at my expense here, so I will refrain.

"Look for a stick," he said.

Following his lead, I began to look for a long stick as we continued walking. We also kept our eyes open for the requisite shelter.

Waving my underpants at poor, unassuming drivers, I thought—the horror! The horror! At least they were clean.

The underpants would be tied to the end of the stick to be waved in case a bus came by in the dark. But we'd only wave if the vehicle looked big, we wouldn't trust to anything smaller than a bus. Too dangerous to try to flag down cars or pick-ups in the dark.

We found our stick and soon after we found a hideout on the west side of the road, between two large boulders that rested on either side of the bottom of a v-shaped opening between two small but steep bluffs. We were almost in the middle of a long straight away, as the road declined toward us. Marat hoped we could see the silhouette of any vehicle as it topped the crest to the north and its beams were shining upward in the darkness.

As I looked west between the rocks and into the arroyo gently receding below, I could see beautiful hues of purple, brown and blue. There were few trees in this spot, but cacti and a lot of scrub brush.

Now we pulled our few remaining snacks from our knapsacks and hunkered down.

"Lots of traffic on this road," I murmured under my breath.

Marat laughed. "Very astute, our last driver," he said.

"So this is adventure," I said.

Marat laughed again. "Adventure is someone a thousand miles away, having a rough time." Then we both laughed.

"I think Camus said that," he added. "I would not want to steal his line without giving credit, no?"

"Magnanimous of you," I offered. "But it sounds like something you'd say anyway."

As the sun went down, it got colder, and quickly. And I couldn't understand why I was having so much trouble with the cold. There was a two week period in my home town of Whiskey Creek where it never got above minus seventy-two degrees and for two days, the temperature went down to minus ninety-two. Now, of course, that was with the wind chill factor, but as far as I'm concerned, minus ninety-two is minus ninety-two.

I, unfortunately, was sick during this time, or I would never have gone out, but I had to go to the local pharmacy to get medicine.

When my younger brother took me there, we encountered a poor, misguided person who had neglected to start her car at least once every hour during her day at work. The car was completely dead. We all have tank heaters in Minnesota to plug our cars in, to keep the transmission fluid and oil warm—you usually plug it in overnight (especially if you park outside), but you never think of it during the day.

My younger brother, the good guy that he is, was determined to come to her rescue and try to start the car, and he wasn't hitting on her or anything like that. He was just trying to help.

We were all bundled up pretty tightly, only our eyes were uncovered, but my brother had to take his gloves off to jiggle with the battery and anything else.

The lady watched for awhile and then retired to the warmth of the store. I lent whatever assistance I could—mostly encouragement, for I know nothing about cars except to turn the ignition key or roll down a window.

I don't know how quickly you would die if you just sat out there, but I swear he worked on that car for over ten minutes, before going inside to get warm. Then he went back out for another ten minutes and then came in to get warm and so on. I had to take my glasses off because they were so cold, they were burning into my brow, giving me one of those brain freezes you get when you drink something that's way too cold and you drink it way too fast. I gave up pretty quickly and went inside to give the lady moral encouragement from there, while my brother still worked.

He never did get it started, though he told me he had it worried, but if I could stand outside in that weather for ten minutes when I was sick, I certainly shouldn't have any trouble with the piddling cold down here. Nonetheless, it was obviously bothering me. It must have been the accident, I thought. It must have shaken out all that native Minnesotan hardiness from me. To be perfectly honest, I used to get depressed in June that winter was just around the corner, so who knows?

Occasionally from our vantage point, we could see a thin pinprick of light coming from the north, and as we watched, the pinprick would grow, finally becoming two distinct lights, then whoosh, it would pass us by.

It wasn't even all that occasionally, just a few trucks, one car and surprisingly—buses comprise a major part of the transportation system in Mexico—no buses.

Once more, Marat turned over one of his sweaters, and if I'd been mad at him before, by midnight, I was ready to canonize him, genuflect and pray to the idol that was Marat, for the Blessing of the Sweater.

It had a nice ring to it. Maybe this could evolve into a myth— the Blessing of the Sweater. Perhaps a whole religion would spring forth from it.

Obviously, the cold was making me hallucinate.

But thinking of myths got me started. I didn't have anything else to do except look down the highway, so I decided that I needed a myth, a quest, at least a loftier goal then trying to get south to get warm, or running from an irate husband. Something like heaving a ring into a volcano in Mordor, though *Popocatepetl* was more along my way. Could I use the Holy Grail? I wasn't certain if I had to look in Glastonbury or Jerusalem, however I did consider that a worthy start. Perhaps we could go off the main roads and stumble on a lost *Aztec* or *Toltec* ruin, like Hiram Bingham stumbling on *Machu Picchu* in Peru.

"Marat," I asked. "Was *El Dorado* in Mexico or Peru?"

He looked at me as if I'd just asked the most random question possible.

"*Pizarro* looked for it in Peru," he answered. "I don't know about Mexico."

"Did he ever find it?" I asked. This was becoming important to me.

"I don't think so," he said.

"Good," I said. Now I had my quest. I'd search for *El Dorado*. And it had its benefits if the Spanish were right. Lots of gold. It did not matter to me whether or not it was in Mexico, or if I had a ghost of a chance of finding it. It was the principle.

By one in the morning, we'd given up and we both started to search our meager surroundings for a semi-comfortable place to try to get a little sleep.

Now I imagined a Gila monster sucking on my toe as I helplessly slept. Just squeezing that poison in there, and me without a club "if'n he was to get real nasty." I wished I'd brought a tennis racquet along. Then at least I'd have a weapon.

And so I drifted in and out of sleep, this time, dreaming I was on a whaling ship in the arctic, and the great white whale I was pursuing strangely had Marat's facial features.

Maybe I wasn't as forgiving as I thought.

CHAPTER 6

The Arab

"Dying is a very dull dreary affair. And my advice to you is to have nothing whatever to do with it."
–Somerset Maugham

The sound of a "pop," like a firecracker, woke me up. I looked at my watch. It was about two in the morning. I'd slept less than an hour and I felt almost hung over.

I looked down the road and I couldn't see anything. Then I looked south—nothing in that direction either.

There was another "crack," coming from behind me, from the west.

It didn't take me long to pick out another pinprick of light. It looked to be pretty far off down and across the arroyo, and it was moving.

I didn't know there were any roads there, of course, I didn't really know where I was, so how would I know if there were roads down there?

It was a starlit night and quite dark. All I could see were the lights of this vehicle. Now that I really listened, I heard it grind its gears and gun its engines over the night sounds of insects and the occasional coyote.

The lights went up a little bit, and then would slip back down, as though it was trying to climb something like a sand dune, but couldn't get the traction to keep going.

I didn't think there were any sand dunes about. Then again, like I said, I really didn't know. It did this for awhile and the lights would disappear for awhile, and I wasn't certain, but it did sound like it was coming closer.

There were a few more cracks, like a cap going off, a firecracker, a whip, a backfire...or a gun.

Crawling over to where Marat was still sleeping, I said, "Wake up. Get a load of this."

Marat's eyes opened slowly, but then another "snap" went off and he was up in a second.

"I was dreaming about someone whipping a horse, like in *Crime and Punishment*," he said as he peered into the darkness— the lights were now out of sight.

It took me a few seconds to get the allusion.

"Do you think it's backfiring?" I asked urgently. This was something I needed to know. "Or do you think it's gunfire?" I hadn't heard a gun go off since I was in boy scouts and those were only .22s.

"Sounds like what I heard in the army," Marat answered. "Let's get closer. I think we should investigate."

I don't think he could see me looking at him as though he was crazy. He was too absorbed by whatever conflict was going on below us. And that's when I made my second big mistake.

"Ok," I said.

Still a wee bit apprehensive, I added, "You mean you want to cross over this scrub brush and cacti and God knows what else is down there between us and them? In the dark?"

On Marat's other trip to Mexico, he had traversed a hundred miles of jungle in the *Yucatan*, swimming across a few *pirana* infested rivers—at least I imagined they were *pirana* infested— and stumbled on hidden *Mayan* ruins.

"Yup," he said tersely. I think his English was improving.

Now having grave second thoughts, I said, "And we don't even know who they are. They could be *banditos*."

Marat was single-minded in his desire to know things, and

by now, *Popocatepetl* couldn't have dislodged this new curiosity. He was far beyond deciding if we should go or not. He was already on the "how."

"There must be a road from this highway leading down, even a goat path," he said. "We haven't passed anything like that for miles or hours, so I would guess it's probably ahead of us. We'll just walk till we find it."

"If we don't find it, we'll be further along, and if we do, we'll take a look."

Sure enough, he was right. We hadn't walked a hundred yards before we found two dirt paths, like a jeep track, leading down into the canyon. So we headed down.

The road descended at a steep angle. The canyon seemed even darker than up above by the main road and we were pretty much walking blind.

I hadn't heard any popping for awhile, or the engine of whatever was down here. I confess I was relieved and once or twice, I hoped they'd left the area all together.

Besides, we had no way of knowing if we were on the right track. When I had peered into the arroyo at dusk, I had seen so many hills and valleys below, that we could in all actuality wind up as close as a quarter-of-a-mile away and still be separated by a whole mound of earth. Something to wish for.

Now the path started a series of switchbacks—I'm not too partial to heights and was happy I couldn't look down. Well, I could, but I couldn't see anything anyway. Then it went up, then down again.

As the track then started up once more, I could hear the engines again, and this time it sounded like there was more than one.

Our eyes were as accustomed to the light as they could be by now, and I saw some movement about a hundred yards away at the top of the incline, and in the direction the road was now leading. Whoever it was, was on the same road we were.

Before I knew what had happened, I felt like I was on a football field being tackled by a vicious Carl Eller, as Marat grabbed me and threw me behind a large outcropping of bushes.

"Don't move," he whispered.

"But..."

"And don't talk. We don't know what this is."

I'd never been one for melodrama, but somehow, here, it seemed to fit.

"We'll see what this is soon enough," he whispered. Then there was silence except for the thumping of my heart.

In seconds, seven shadowy figures could be seen above the crest and heading our way, down the parallel dirt tracks.

By the time these shapes descended along the trail enough to blend in with the darkness, we could see two searching beams of light above the crest of the ridge, trailing off into the night sky.

The vehicles were right behind them, and in seconds, the first appeared over the ridge and barreled down toward us.

For an instant, my eyes were blinded, so I looked away. As they readjusted, I could see four larger figures, which I took to be men, and three smaller ones, that I couldn't tell whether they were women or children. Strangely, they all seemed to be hunchbacks. Then I heard screaming—definitely from a woman.

From what I could see, the first vehicle had the silhouette of a jeep. As it bore down on the fleeing peasants or *banditos* or whatever they were, the second, similar vehicle crested the ridge. This time, I turned my head immediately, to avoid the beams of light.

Now, there were more "pops." It was gunfire and they were shooting at these people.

I don't think my heart had ever beat so rapidly. I was now sweating profusely in the cold night air and would have taken off the sweater if I wasn't afraid of making the slightest move.

By now we could see them clearly, lit up in the streams of light. They weren't hunchbacks, they were carrying backpacks which I imagined contained every last meager possession they owned. As I turned my head ever so slightly, aware of a new sound, I saw another pair of lights coming down the same path Marat and I had taken. It must have come from the main road.

Are they *banditos* about to be caught, I wondered?

What was I thinking? There was no doubt they would be caught. They were surrounded. The jeeps were still too far off for me to be able to tell how many soldiers or policemen were involved, but there were three of the jeeps and these people had no chance. Then again, we couldn't see any insignias on the jeeps. Maybe the *banditos* were in the jeeps and the fugitives were just peasants. I hadn't considered that.

Now, there was light all over our hiding place. I was certain we stood out as plain as day and we'd be seen.

Marat was calm and seemingly unmoved, as though he'd seen sights like this countless times in Laos or Burma. Except for his eyes, which absorbed everything.

I now noticed that he kept his eyelids almost closed as though he was squinting, and I thought, God! This guy's smart. At certain times of year, when you drive on the highway at night in Minnesota, you always have to keep an eye out for deer, and one of the ways you spot them, is if their eyes get caught in the headlights—you spot a lot of animals that way. Hopefully, you'd see the deer before they'd run into your car—one time when I was driving north with my dad, I didn't and the deer was killed on impact.

Marat later told me that in the Amazon, you shine a light on the surface of the water to spot caimans.

I began to squint.

Just then, I felt a nudge in my side.

"Don't breath so loud," Marat whispered.

And I realized I was making enough noise between my breathing and my heart that they wouldn't have to see my eyes. Once they turned off their engines, they'd have us.

One, two, three, I began to count. I breathed in to a count of ten and I breathed out to a count of ten—an old scuba diving trick taught me by a college roommate. It also calmed me down and slowed my heart.

The fugitives ran past us, but they only got to where the road dipped and started up again, before the third jeep was right in front of them. Now they scattered, trying to climb out of the trap, but here the sides of the hills on both sides of the track were too steep and slippery and they kept sliding down no matter which side they attempted.

All seven of them now quickly put up their hands, and the other jeeps soon pulled up to their rear.

Now a uniformed man jumped out of the rear vehicle—the first one we had seen—ran up and began screaming at the peasants in Spanish.

He was an officer—whether he was *Federale* or policeman, I couldn't tell at this point—but he was tall and fairly thin, and his face, I couldn't believe his face. It looked like pictures I'd seen of Hafez Assad, the president of Syria. What was Assad doing here, I wondered in my disconcerted state? I thought he was busy killing people in Hama. What's he doing killing people here, expanding his business? That whimsical thought left me almost as quickly as it had appeared—although he would look good in a kaffiyeh.

The Arab!

Other men quickly got out of the jeeps and pointed rifles at the seven, who in the light really looked to me to be peasants. Of course *banditos* could look like peasants. They certainly did in *Viva Zapapta,* another one of my Mexican movie references—strange, what thoughts go through your head at a time like this. So, I still had no idea who they were, but Marat was listening intently.

As the officer screamed at them, all seven slowly moved to the edge of the path and got to their knees, each of them pulling off their backpacks and placing the bags in front of them as if it was part of the rules. The soldiers raised their rifles—or maybe the peasants didn't want to be encumbered on their way to the afterlife.

Oh God, I thought as they pulled back the bolts on their old bolt-action rifles.

I was astonished. Just then, Marat grabbed my arm to still me. I guess he thought I might do something stupid, idealist that he took me for, but I was too shocked to move.

I don't know to this day whether I would have been stupid enough to jump up at that time. As if it would make any difference to them if they killed us as well. The peasants would already be dead anyway.

They'd just say the *banditos* killed us, and they would probably claim they put an end to our executioners after finding our bodies, and then they'd bring our bodies home to our parents and get a reward.

They'd probably end up looking like heroes for all their trouble—either that, or they'd plant drugs on us.

I could see Marat looking intently at me. He was still grasping my arm. He very slightly shook his head, "No," as if he was still worried what I was going to do.

Assad now pulled out a cigar, bit off the tip and searched his pockets, apparently looking for a match. He pulled his hand across his throat in a signal to a man I took to be his sergeant and walked back to his jeep.

I looked back at the impending slaughter.

Then, one of the larger men turned around, half stood and plaintively pointed at his crotch like he had to pee or something, as if it would really matter if he had a full bladder on his way to judgment—like it might really be a long trip—so the sergeant, in a gesture of magnanimity, waved for him to get up. The man hurried behind the sergeant, walking hunched over, his hands pulling down his pants as he moved.

I quickly looked back to see if the bastards would shoot before he returned and from my vantage point I saw something weird. While the soldiers attention briefly wandered to the first man, the other peasants or *banditos* or whatever their classification was, were all quietly digging into their packs, still out in front of them.

No sooner had the large peasant gotten behind the sergeant, who closed his eyes as he yawned, when the peasant tapped him on the shoulder. The sergeant turned, mouth still open in mid-yawn, just as the peasant let fly with his pee, soaking him from head to toe, not to mention giving him a drink.

The guy not only had a full bladder but pretty good aim. It was bright yellow so he might have been dehydrated. I kinda had to pee myself and considered joining the rout, but Marat must have sensed it and held me down.

As if on cue, the kneeling peasants extracted papayas from their bags and hurled them at the soldiers, catching a couple in the groin and some in the head.

Now there's a couple of weapons I wouda never thought of. I hoped the papayas weren't ripe.

The seven peasants, as if by plan, then jumped into one of the empty jeeps, squealed the wheels in an abrupt turn and raced up the track toward the highway.

Assad ran back and angrily fired his pistol off after them, emptying his clip.

"Nincompoop!" or something similar he yelled at the sergeant in Spanish.

Frightened of their commander, the soldiers of the firing squad sheepishly piled back into the vehicles.

Assad furiously grabbed an automatic weapon from one of the vehicles and, stomping up and down the arroyo, raked the surrounding bushes with salvos. Then he threw the clip away, loaded another and scorched everything he'd missed the first time. As he put in yet a third clip, there was fire in his eyes. The sergeant charged over to join him, proceeded to trip on a rock, did a somersault, tuck and roll with his finger still on the trigger, which sent another fusillade in all directions, sending his men jumping out of both jeeps for cover, knocking Assad over and spraying bullets within inches of my head and Marat's. I gave him an 9.4 for his style and degree of difficulty, but I confess I made it little higher than I normally would because I figured the Commie ducking beside me would purposely give him a lower score out of principle.

The sergeant jumped up quickly from his tumble. "I'm good!" he said.

"Meshugina!" Assad yelled as he got up. "Get in the jeeps!"

Then the sergeant brushed himself off—although a lot of dirt and stuff stuck to him on account of the wetness—and ran back up the trail and jumped into the second jeep. Assad then threw his arms up in the air and screamed, "Aarrgg!! I just can't get good help!" But then he quieted down and started looking around.

Maybe Assad sensed someone's presence.

I squinted even more and didn't move. I breathed as softly as I could.

At one point I swear he was looking right at our hiding place, right into my almost closed eyes. But after what seemed like a long time, he walked back down to his jeep and gave a command to his men, who revved up the engines of the two jeeps.

Assad's jeep, the one on the upward slope, moved backward and forward, turning a small degree with each movement, and finally turned around and started up to the main road. The other jeep followed him.

So now we waited, a million thoughts and questions going through our minds, at least mine. And we waited.

We let those jeeps disappear into the darkness till we could no longer see them or hear their engines.

"We should report this to the authorities," I whispered.

"They are the authorities," Marat said.

This was good to know. "Are you certain?" I asked. This was just what I wanted to hear right now. "How could you know?"

"There is an insurrection down here," Marat said. He seemed to be weighing his words carefully. "I told you about *Cabanas* earlier."

Marat went to one of the backpacks littering the ground and retrieved two papayas. Tossing one to me, he started walking up the dirt track.

As we reached the main road, I looked north and south.

"What now?" I asked.

"We don't stay here," Marat said. "We take our chances walking on the road, even if we walk all night. We'll hear or see anybody long before they see us, and we can hide on the shoulder if someone comes." He looked at me. "Put on something darker," he said.

I found a navy blue t-shirt in my bag and changed it with the sweat-soaked shirt I was wearing. I already had on jeans so that was dark enough. He put on a black shirt and then we both stuffed the sweaters back in our bags.

We didn't need to keep warm at this moment—we were flushed with heat and adrenaline. Neither did we need more sleep—I've never been so awake.

It was three in the morning. By the time the light started coming out, we had put maybe twenty kilometers between ourselves and the spraying.

And we were both on edge and exhausted. There had only been a couple trucks that passed us during the walk, and we scrambled into the ditch as soon as we heard them. No buses, cars, pickups or jeeps. The scariest part had been crossing bridges. We made certain there was complete silence from the road before we'd run across. No place to hide on a bridge, unless you wanted to dangle underneath, which I didn't. You'd have to have a flair for the obvious to come to the conclusion that we were both shaken, even Marat.

He barely said a word the whole time, only encouraging me to go faster. I was still limping. I thought the accident had given me shin splints. At least something had given me shin splints and I'd never had them before, so I figured they were one more gift from the "Angel" in Tempe.

They were quite painful.

As it got brighter, I could see Marat looking stonily ahead. I swear he walked like that, silently staring off into the distance for another hour, in which we dodged five cars, two pickups and two semis.

"We have another problem," he finally said, and after a night full of silence, it seemed to come out of nowhere.

"Great," I said, eagerly awaiting his good news.

"That husband that shot at me," he said. "The one in *Chihuahua*...he wasn't a police chief. He's a *Federale* officer."

"Why worry about it now? Don't we have enough to worry about?" I said. Another thing I didn't want to hear about just then.

"Suit yourself," Marat said.

But as we walked, I couldn't get the thought out of my head and my curiosity got to me. "How'd you figure it out?" I finally asked him.

"Well..." Marat said haltingly. "That's him. The big fellow leading the *Federales*. The one you called Assad."

"Oh shit," I said.

CHAPTER 7

San Luis Potosi

"The optimist proclaims that we live in the best of all possible worlds; the pessimist fears this is true." – James Branch Cabel

We walked another four hours, and traffic gradually grew heavier. Now, every time I heard the sound of a car, I wanted to duck into the nearest ditch. No more hitching for me, not until we were entirely out of this region, and in this, Marat and I were in complete accord.

Unfortunately, not a single bus came down the road, and even to Marat, this seemed odd. Now my mind came up with every paranoid reason possible as to why—and they all somehow involved Assad and us.

But around nine, we heard the rumbling and knocking of an engine behind us, and sure enough, the top of a bus soon appeared over the last ridge behind us and we flagged it down.

It took us to a village that was only another twenty or so Ks down the highway, so we'd hardly gained anything.

The bus driver's route took him back toward *Saltillo* after this stop, which amounted to one of the ubiquitous Pemex stations and a *cantina*-general store. The *cantina* was the bus stop.

Every last one of the passengers got out except us. Marat grabbed my shoulder, holding me in my seat. He pointed toward the *cantina*. There were two mud-splattered jeeps parked in front. On one, you could just make out the mud-covered *Federale* markings.

We had no idea if these were the same ones that had been at the scene last night, and obviously, we had no desire to find out. The *cantina* was some thirty yards from where the bus let everybody off. Paying the bus driver, we got down and started walking. Luckily, the bus was parked a bit south of the *cantina's* windows, and we were able to keep it between us and the line of sight from the *cantina*—doing this as long as possible. By the time we reached a point where we were once more in the line of sight, we were quite far down the road. Now I tried to ignore the pain and walked as fast as I could.

Just then, a farmer pulled up along side us and slowed down, waving for us to get in his old '64 Chevy beater. He didn't have to ask twice.

A lot of Spanish speaking went on during the next hour and like usual I understood nothing. I was still quite tense and could not care less that I was left out of the conversation. Finally Marat grinned and said, "You know, he picked us up because he thought you were Mexican. He thought I was a *gringo* and wondered why we were traveling together. That is why he picked us up." Marat then laughed. I could tell it was a nervous sort of laugh. He must have repeated it to the driver, because they both started laughing. I didn't. I couldn't find my way to laughing yet.

How would I have felt if Assad succeeded in the execution? Of course the peasants could have really been *banditos* and Assad was ridding the country of nefarious criminals who would have slit our throats just for the fun of it. But if that was the case Assad was all thumbs and that was definitely better for us,

As the ride wore on, memories of the previous night began to fade somewhat. There were incredible vistas everywhere I looked. The sun shone down from a cloudless blue sky on mountains and valleys which went on and on for miles.

No doubt it sounds like a cliché, but how could something like last night have happened in such beautiful country? Had we collectively hallucinated it? Had Marat slipped peyote into both of our snacks? I fervently wished that was the case. I was so mentally and physically exhausted during this ride, that for a long time I could not tell fact from illusion, but after an hour I began to relax and enjoy the panoramic view as we winded through the *Sierra Madre Oriental.*

Sometimes, the road was so narrow, the shoulder was non-existent and if you edged over two feet, you might be taking a one way trip downward into one of those beautiful canyons. *Enrique,* the driver, seemed to think he was in the Indy 500, and I sincerely hoped he wasn't into passing other vehicles, especially slow moving trucks going up hill. Even staying in your own lane seemed precarious when we met a truck or bus coming from the opposite direction. Sometimes I swore we were going to scrape paint or side view mirrors off the larger vehicles as they passed by.

The ride lasted about eighty Ks till we pulled over at another village *cantina,* right off the side of the road. It was the end of the line for the farmer, but he invited us to have breakfast, so we went in and sat down with him at one of only four tables. We were starved and never did a bean and egg burrito taste so good to me.

Enrique wolfed down his burritos as quickly as we did, and then ordered *café blanco* for all of us. As we sipped at the steaming *café,* he looked me, the real *gringo,* in the eye and said in halting English, "*Senor,* you should not travel here this way. Like I find you. It is very dangerous in these hills."

I stared back at him.

"You don't say."

Now the tension of the night reached its apex and Marat and I looked at each other and started laughing hysterically. Our farmer friend, with an uncomprehending look on his face, gaped at us as though we were village idiots and no doubt, that's what we sounded like—personally, I preferred something like misunderstood lunatics.

When we finished our *café, Enrique* insisted on paying for us. After our outburst he probably reckoned we needed all the money we had.

As we walked out behind him, I quietly asked Marat, "Should we be traveling in daylight?"

"Do not worry about it, Tomas," Marat answered. "They're a hundred kilometers behind us now. It is a million-to-one chance he was following us or he saw us. First, if he saw us, he could have done something about it then, and with less danger of discovery for himself. Secondly, he's some sort of federal officer. He must have responsibilities countrywide, or at least for the north and central. So it's no surprise that he was south of *Saltillo*.

Still not at ease, I now hoped that Marat had a good understanding of Mexican jurisdiction.

"Perhaps his duties bring him to this area, while he lives in *Chihuahua*. Who knows?" Marat said rhetorically. "I don't think it's worth worrying about."

"Well," I said. "I'm still ducking if I hear something coming. I'd rather just get on a bus."

"Then you'll be happy, because *Enrique* says buses come by here on the hour."

I had my doubts, but just then we heard the sound of a car from the north. *Enrique* started running to the road and waving his hands wildly above his head at an approaching Chevy pickup, faded blue with any number of rust-colored spots and good-sized dents. It looked like it would break down with a good kick. The driver screeched to a halt and *Enrique* went up to the smoke-filled cab, and leaned inside to talk.

Then he came over to us and spoke to Marat in Spanish.

Marat soon smiled. "See," he said to me. "I can always trust to my luck. Whenever I need something, it happens. It's been that way my whole life."

Marat's luck!—see earlier chapters plus gloating rule.

As far as I was now concerned, this game of chance wouldn't conclude till I was back across the border. It's when I hear statements like Marat's, that it's time to look over my shoulder as if I wasn't already doing it. And I hadn't even seen the albino in some time.

"*Enrique's* gotten us a ride all the way to *San Louis Potosi*."

So we climbed into the box of the dilapidated pickup—there were two children, a goat and a big dog sitting in the cab. I sat against the back of the cab and Marat sat leaning on the side of the box at a perpendicular angle. We were on our way.

"Yes, Tomas," Marat said, putting his hands behind his head and sinking back into them. "This is the best of all possible worlds."

"Huh!" I said. I knew I'd heard that somewhere before, but in any event, I was too tired to argue with him and just happy to be able to keep an eye on the road behind.

Once more I was relieved, and Marat, he was downright effervescent. I thought he had been a lot more scared than he'd let on. He was a tough minded man—anyone that would cross rivers and jungle at night had to be and he certainly proved his mettle to me when we were hiding in the arroyo—but still, it seemed like a weight had been lifted from his shoulders as well and he became talkative.

We had become much closer since the past night, and a bond, if it hadn't been there before, was certainly forming.

"This ride is so different," I said, my back resting against the cab. "Looking backward from where we've come, instead of almost always looking forward to where we are going."

"A novel metaphor for travel," he opined. "And perhaps life."

Somehow it seemed very extraordinary, looking at the rolling hills and barren valleys receding from us in this way. The rocks, grass, weeds, wild flowers all took on strange hues, and some whole sections of land were darker as clouds came between them and the rays of the sun. What a magnificent country this was.

Marat started to tell me more about his friends from Colombia—how they made their fortune.

"Drugs?" I ventured.

"No," he laughed. "You are always suspicious of me, Tomas," he said, but in an amused way. "Perhaps deservedly so, after *Chihuahua*. No. They made their money in textiles, importing to France."

Enrique had driven like a madman, whereas this new fellow took his time—I don't think he could get his pickup over forty miles-an-hour, even going down hill, and there were still plenty of switchbacks and uphill grades. I wasn't as concerned about an accident this time. Even if we had one, the impact would be slow and there was much less of a chance of going over the side at this speed. I casually wondered if *Federales* responded to highway accidents. Maybe Assad was the guy that propped those wrecks up on the side of the road.

Marat said he was always doing things that other people thought were either risky or foolhardy. Going in, they never seemed like that to him, probably because he was either fascinated or caught up in the moment. He felt it was important to push yourself, to push your fears. The challenge was in trying—and in surviving I might add.

I liked to imagine I did the same sort of things, but somehow, during the actual escapade, I'm not so sure I was so happy to be there. But they were great to talk about after they were done with. Especially if you were still around to do the talking.

Marat made me look like a stay-at-home type.

We had been in the state of *San Luis Potosi* for quite some time by now. *San Luis Potosi* was also the name of the capitol. An old silver mining town founded in 1592, the Spaniards named it after *Potosi*, Bolivia, possibly hoping that if they gave this city the same name, it would prove to have the same wealth in silver deposits.

As Marat and I gabbed away, the time passed quickly. The ride was bumpy, but neither of us minded. It was breathtaking to see how high up we were and to look down to see roads we were just on, that were now a hundred meters below us. The road winded around hills, then dipped into valleys, then climbed again. The mountains began to loom larger as we started descending. Although our driver went slowly, it wasn't long before we started passing farms, haciendas, *Pemex* stations, a quaint little cemetery with painted tombs with wreaths of flowers, icons and jewelry laid upon them, then small market stalls, as we reached the outskirts of *San Luis Potosi* around three in the afternoon.

Before long, we got down near the *Alameda* and started to walk and soon enough Marat found another one of his favorite cheap, dilapidated run-down hotels, south of the *Plaza de Armas.*

Now, all the worries of traveling departed. We were a long way from *Chihuahua*, a long way from the death squads. Here in the middle of the city even if those men had followed us or saw us I didn't think they'd dare to do anything. And now, with the help of distance, I was certain Marat was right—if they'd seen us, they would've done something right there. I definitely felt safer being in a city and I was able to put it to rest.

Now, I wanted to see everything. I was exhilarated. I felt free, I felt safe for the first time in a long time.

It was only Tuesday! We'd only been on the road for three days! It seemed like a lifetime had passed. Of course, I was only twenty-three so having a lifetime pass wasn't a very big deal for me.

Why to travel: every day seems like a lifetime. You may not get out of this life alive, but you can certainly slow down time. Dig a ditch, clean a latrine, wash dishes—this will always take longer than doing something you like. You won't actually live longer, but it'll sure feel like it. Traveling with Marat seemed to involve long interminable stretches of boredom, intermixed with brief sheer moments of terror. If you traveled with him and died at the age of thirty, you'd still probably feel like you lived to be a hundred and thirty.

Why to travel in a third world country: the length of time, especially when dealing with foreign bureaucracies or modes of transportation, is magnified to the nth degree-as are the moments of terror. So, make that two hundred and thirty.

Just then, I recalled Marat telling me the guy shot at him right in the streets of *Chihuahua*. So, maybe we weren't so safe here after all. Damn. Now I was beginning to sound as neurotic as Woody Allen.

The room had two beds and hot water. These were the first beds I'd seen since *Chihuahua,* and they were quite clean in comparison. I took my first shower in days, then shaved while Marat cleaned up.

The washing and shaving seemed to wipe all the past away and I really did feel like a new man.

We left the hotel and headed out into the streets. It was still light out; dusk was maybe an hour away.

Marat had a thing for the slums. He felt that the majority of the people of this world lived more or less like this, rather than like the middle class or even working class Americans or Europeans, and that's who he wanted to write about.

As we walked back toward the *Alameda*, he pointed out various places from his travel book.

"Look," he said as we approached the *Templo del Carmen* and I saw the many sculpted angels. "This is spectacular and I love looking at things like this. But this is my objection. Man must have art, and religion will always inspire him, but one has to wonder how much this cost even in the 1700s? How many native people died building it? How many people could have been fed, clothed and housed for the cost?"

"All peoples are appetitive to some degree," he said, in the Aristotelian sense. "But, we westerners, and you North Americans in particular, grab so much that we not only leave little for the rest of the world, but we destroy much of our own surroundings and theirs to satiate our greed."

"You will never in your life see such a disparity between rich and poor as you will see in almost any third world country. And the rich here, are to the poor, as your country is to the rest of the world."

"Is that why I keep hearing that foreign countries hate us so much?" I asked. "I thought they used to love us."

"Well...they are somewhat jealous for one thing. But, I think it's the promise, the hope...that the idea of the United States once gave to everyone. Then they see how your government treats other countries. This is the hypocrisy of, 'Do as we say not as we do,' and how your people, represented by your tourists and your foreign officers seem to condescend to them."

"So it's all right for the Europeans to do things like that, but not the Americans," I said defensively.

"That's it, exactly," Marat said. "Everyone knows the history of certain European countries...and they expect such actions from them, my country included. Don't blame me. Your country is held to a higher standard."

"Take you," he continued. He was back to the class struggle. "Neither you nor your family are particularly wealthy by your country's standards, but here, you are rich. Myself as well. We can come here as tourists and move with the lower classes that serve us at a hotel, or by hitchhiking or taking buses or walking where we will walk this afternoon. But as a tourist and a Caucasian and even more so as a tennis player you can dress in some, say, Ellesse or Fila, and go to a tennis club and mix with the upper class."

"Their good tennis players can do the same."

"That is my point. For a native of this country, or most of the countries I've visited in the last few years, one would have to be very upper class to do that because with very few exceptions, only the upper classes would have an opportunity of reaching that stature in tennis. None of the poor would ever dream of attaining it."

"Most of the people here have no such mobility, and there are oceans of difference between the upper and lower classes here and what you experience at home. From what I've seen in your country, even the working class lives better than the middle class in most European countries."

Maybe he *was* a Commie.

"I busted my butt for those skills," I said.

"All people should get a chance. That's all I say."

"And then there is the issue of color," he went on. "We also have mobility here because we are white, and even with your tan, we will never be mistaken for a *mestizo* or Indian."

"I already was," I joked. He took offense.

"Come now," he said. "Not once you opened your mouth."

"Okay, okay," I said.

"And that makes it even more difficult."

"Why?"

"Because in this country," he answered, "and many third world countries, the majority of the poor are darker and the majority of the rich are lighter, perhaps of European descent or a mixture. Over the years they have had better food and more of it, better shelter, sanitation, education and opportunity. It is very difficult for the poor to rise out of their situation."

As I've said, Marat wanted to be a writer, and I think, that whether he was a communist or not—I still hadn't decided on that one, or whether it made any difference to me—he did want to see from the perspective of the common man. And for him, the common man was unfortunately poor and destitute. Perhaps he thought that by writing about them, he could do his small share in alleviating their suffering by bringing at least some awareness to it.

As for me, I figured the "higher-ups" were already quite aware, and were either too busy, too greedy, too cynical or too uncaring to bother with it. Marat would probably describe their attitude as "screw you, I've got mine."

I took off my shoes to walk on the cool grass of the *Alameda*. After crossing the park, I noticed the buildings and streets on the other side seemed to be becoming more and more run-down.

"So you think economics determines politics?" I asked Marat.

"Still trying to ambush me, aren't you?" he asked, laughing. "Where did that come from?" This he said in a sarcastic tone. Maybe he wasn't as literalist as I thought.

"For most people," he said, becoming serious once more as we walked down dusty streets, littered with garbage and open sewers that stank, "if they have food, a warm shelter and security, perhaps health for their children, they will be content. Most importantly, there has to be hope."

My eyes grew large as I looked up and down the streets. I was truly amazed at what I saw. I had never before seen such poverty.

Children in dirty clothes ran around playing, boys in torn long pants, little girls in soiled but colorful dresses. One small

girl—she couldn't have been more than four—looked at us and
gave us the prettiest, most vibrant smile. Some played soccer,
others looked like they were engaged in an intense game of tag.
A mother stood by with a baby nestled against her breast. All
quickly cleared the street as a diesel-spewing truck lumbered
into sight, blaring its horn and raising dust, disappearing as
quickly as it had come, and then the children quickly filled the
street once more, though almost invisible in the thick black
clouds of diesel air. The smell of *chorizo* and beans blended
with that of the gas, sewer and wood-burning fires, making an
acrid but sweet odor.

Lively music erupted from different run-down *cantinas* on
either side of the street as dusk approached, and another woman smiled at us from a doorway as her body swayed with the
music.

The hotels here seemed worse than the one we briefly stayed
at in *Chihuahua*—even more decrepit and tawdry. None of the
buildings, whether they were places of business or residences,
had seen any work or paint in years.

Still, and this is what amazed me, though you could see they
had next to nothing, the people seemed so happy, so full of life.

Kids would come up to us and touch Marat's skin, perhaps
wanting to see if white skin felt like their own. I guess they
didn't see too many like us down here.

Some would speak to me in Spanish, rather than Marat, then
laugh when he answered and they saw I was the bigger *gringo
blanco*, not him.

Marat directed me into what was a slightly cleaner restaurant, but only just, and we sat down and he ordered for us.

I remember hearing the words *"mucho caliente,"* but what
did I know then? I was just the bigger *gringo*. This was Marat's
first prank.

When the food came I noticed Marat staring expectantly as I
took my first bite. Immediately my mouth erupted in flames. I
began to sweat. Steam certainly came out of my ears and my
nose began to run like a faucet; tears streamed down my cheeks

as my throat and mouth expanded like an alarmed blowfish. I was loathe to drink the water so I had ordered a beer and the fizz just served to exacerbate the heat, and Marat was sitting across from me, bent over in laughter. I don't think I've ever seen anybody laugh so hard.

In between convulsions, he said, "I told you to learn more Spanish." He now started another two minutes of unbroken laughter. He was having trouble catching his breath and I hoped it was a heart attack. I'll be damned if I give you CPR, I thought.

"I even gave you my book to look at," he said, and then he shook merrily once more.

Not generally a violent man, still, as it dawned on me that Marat was the cause of my agony, I reached over the table to strangle him, but he was bent back so far in his laughter, my hands couldn't reach. However, I noticed little beads of sweat from my arms dripping onto his tacos and into his drink. And so I lingered in my attempt. He needed more salt in his diet anyway.

As I sat back, I now gave up on immediate thoughts of revenge and started doing some hard thinking about coolants. I grabbed the daypack that he carried, took his Spanish book out and found the word for banana.

"*Platano!*" I yelled at the restaurant owner or manager or whatever he was. "*Platano! Platano! Platano!*"

Rushing over as if he feared not one, but possibly two *gringos* might expire in his bistro, he hurled a banana onto my plate, retired off to the side and raised his hands in supplication.

I cut off the head of it with a knife, pealed it down and mashed it between my teeth, sucked on it and rolled it into every corner of my blistered mouth. It took five more minutes of this to finally lessen the pain. I swear Marat was still laughing, though now it had ebbed to the occasional chuckle, between paroxysms—and worse, he seemed to be enjoying his food.

Then, a very humble looking middle-aged-man came to our table. He was partly stooped over, with straight black hair that went down over his ears to the bottom of his neck, and wore a white, long-sleeved shirt and dark pants. Cautiously tapping me on the shoulder, he spoke Spanish to me just like all the others, and looked surprised when Marat stopped convulsing long enough to answer him.

Next thing, the man sat down, but this was nothing like *Franc Roma*. He was clean-cut and although dressed quite modestly, had, to my mind, a certain nobility about him.

"This is *Pablo*," Marat said after the preliminary introductions. "He is a teacher."

Ah ha, I thought. That explains it. Of course he's a teacher. That's why he has that look about him.

I've always had a great respect for teachers, although I'm certain that might surprise some of the ones I had back through the years, especially in high school. I've always had fond memories of those years.

This is obviously a simplification, but there was a business and professional community and an education community in Whiskey Creek—I knew people in the former group through my father, and the latter through my schooling. There were bankers, people in hardware and clothing businesses, supermarkets, auto parts and gas stations; doctors and pharmacists, bakers and stockbrokers and insurance salesmen. People in every type of occupation you could name. And then there were the teachers: English, history, math, music, biology, physics and sports. I swear it was like some rip in the time fabric, a concatenation of events that led to all these talented people just descending on, or happening to settle in this small town in northern Minnesota at the same time. Whether a finer group of people ever existed in the same place at the same time I can't say, but they inspired our young minds—I know they inspired me and most of my friends. It was a close community, and along with our parents, they molded us well. I've always believed I was lucky, growing up in Whiskey Creek.

Marat ordered *café* for the three of us, and with a twinkle in his eye, he looked at me, then the manager, and then pointed at me and said, *"Uno café mucho caliente, por favor,"* then started laughing all over again.

Must've been a mathematician's thing like when Descartes put Ben Gay in Pascal's jock strap or when Archimedes soaked the toilet paper in water right before Euclid had to go. Yup. Marat was like one of those guys.

The best I could do was roll my eyes.

Pablo and Marat conversed and I was now so versed in Spanish I could pick out words like, '*banyos,*' '*habla,*' and '*casa,*' but not much more. I did, however, know the word '*poco*' by now, and Marat had made sure I could say '*habla despacio,*' which he felt were the most important two words to know in any language besides '*no comprende.*' I should probably ad '*no chilis*' to the list.

So I just sat back and treasured the fact my mouth had returned to normal, even sipping the *café*, and felt glad to be alive. One more day, I found myself thinking, and I was surprised I put it in terms like that because I'd never done that before the car accident.

As we left the restaurant, Marat said, "*Pablo* wants to meet with us again. I've arranged for us to meet at a *cantina* a little closer to our hotel, but you should go by yourself. It will be good for you, and I have other things."

My eyebrows inadvertently lifted at this—I could just imagine him getting us into more trouble.

As if he read my mind or body language, Marat laughed and said, "Don't worry. There are some murals here I want to see. I won't even look at a woman. I promise you."

Right, I speculated.

"This will be good for you," Marat said. "You will work on your Spanish, and he wants to work on his English. He was not that interested in speaking more Spanish to me."

So it was set.

∗   ∗   ∗

I have to admit I felt a little weird that evening. Not for the meeting with *Pablo*, just for walking through the city and especially the slums by myself. It was pretty much my first time wandering through a Mexican city alone, if you don't count *Chihuahua,* where I was so consumed with the urgency of the matter that I never thought about danger lurking in every alley. I guess I should add the fact that I was routinely imagining Assad's face popping up out of everywhere and any place ever since we saw him in the arroyo. And now I was going into the slums alone with the knowledge that there were certainly places even in Minneapolis that I wouldn't want to go into alone at night.

Back in L. A., a policeman told me there were parks he wouldn't go into at night, even with his partner, and they were armed. So I don't think I was paranoid. That's another thing about growing up in Whiskey Creek: you never had to worry about being robbed or mugged. We left our house doors open, our cars unlocked. In the coldest days of winter you might leave your car running when you went inside to have a cup of coffee or visit with friends.

There wasn't a murder there in all the years of my existence.

I had only two fights the whole time I was growing up, both before I was thirteen, and one of those guys became a friend. It was an idyllic existence.

So now, as I walked through these streets, I was aware of every movement, every sound.

Maybe I've seen too many movies.

That's one thing I was learning to love about travel: it just seems you're so much more aware. Living in the States is easy, probably too easy. Even if we didn't have the highest standard of living in the world, there's no place where life was so easy and comfortable, no matter what your income or status. I now vowed that whenever things were going exceedingly well, whenever things were becoming too easy or were already at that point, I had to challenge myself, and to me, at this instant, that meant leaving the country.

Though I was relatively poor—I had worked three jobs for about five months to save some seven thousand dollars in order to travel out west, and then to join my brothers in India in the fall. I had slaved at a cottage cheese factory from four in the morning till noon; a half-hour later I was on a tennis court teaching, then I'd play tennis for four hours, run, jump rope, and maybe two times a week, I'd go to the county jails and interview anybody who needed a public defender. It was a busy summer. I'd usually go out with my girlfriend at night, get in around midnight, get up around a quarter to four, grab a doughnut, and race to the factory where I'd assemble the machinery so they could mix the cream into the cottage cheese.

About once every two weeks, I'd come home at noon and fall asleep till a quarter to four the next morning. I have to admit I loved that factory job. When I was done for the day, I was done for the day. It was totally mindless, no thinking involved.

I was still wealthier by far then any of the people I saw here. I knew it, they knew it, so I figured I was definitely a mark. And everybody had warned me how dangerous it was in Mexico—and I could not, so far, contradict that opinion—but I kept walking to the assignation.

And there was something else. I don't know what it is about the driving in Mexico—I guess the wrecks along the sides of the highways should've given me some kind of hint. I was already a little paranoid about crossing the street since the accident, but here in a big city like *San Luis Potosi* it was strange. You could look up and down a street and see no traffic, not a single vehicle. You start out into the street and you could be a quarter of the way across and nothing would be coming, but as soon as you reached the halfway mark, where it was the same distance for you to run back or go across, every bus, car, taxi, bicyclist and horse-drawn cart in the world would bear down on you, from both directions, and most of them would swerve toward you rather than away as if it was a carefully laid trap and they were gunning for you. You had to sprint for your life, dodging in and out and around or jumping over the traffic, and every driver seemed to think he was in the Baja 1000. It was quite unnerving and it did not matter a whit if you were walking in a crosswalk and had a green light.

Driving is definitely different down here. I saw a guy run a red light and crash into another car. They got out of their cars and instead of yelling at each other, they started laughing. Marat's uncle told him it's all right to run a red light here, but if you cause an accident, it's your fault.

Soon I started to hear lively music coming from one of the haciendas, then another and another, and it brought me out of my reverie.

By that time, I was pretty far into the dingier side of town and I spotted *Pablo* in the distance, out in front of the restaurant he and Marat had picked, and I hurried up to greet him.

What followed was three fast, simplistic hours of conversation, his half in English and my half in Spanish, and I'm being quite generous on my part about the Spanish.

Pablo taught history at one of the local, poorer schools and his English was better than my Spanish but not by much. Many times he would write out a word on the paper place mat or a napkin because his written skills were much better than his speaking skills when it came to English, and if he wrote down words in Spanish, I could sometimes see the similarity to English words and at least get an inkling of what he was trying to say, and so we had our conversation.

We spoke simple words, wrote down more complex words and ideas, and gestured when nothing else would suffice. We covered history, politics, revolution, sickness, philosophy, classics, class systems, sanitation, humor, movies and more.

Something I'd been told about travelling by my older brother, and I was now picking up on myself, is how fast two people can become friends—and I'm not talking about myself and Marat. We were travelling together and it was obvious we'd either end up hating each other or forming a great bond, and the latter, so far, had come true. What I'm getting at, is you form bonds with people that you just met, spend a few hours with—perhaps you'll never see them again—and there's a brotherhood that is just formed, and it's not simply the brotherhood of the road, because *Pablo* obviously wasn't travelling like we were, but there was a closeness that developed instantly. Maybe it's the intensity of travelling like this: you become friends faster, you hate someone sooner, you fall in love with a woman in a single evening—well I suppose I could do that anytime. But everything is magnified.

Pablo was compassionate, warm-hearted and good, and contrary to popular opinion, he was not offering me his sister. He cared for his people and wanted to do something to better their lives and so became a teacher.

As we were about to part, he knowing he would be stuck in his life—I could see that there was just the smallest bit of envy for Marat and my freedom—but for the most part, preferring it, because he was an idealist and he was happy helping kids learn. Still, as he bid me luck on our next step on the way to Mexico City, this look of hope entered his eyes, and he said, "You go to the mountains. You go and join *Lucio Cabanas.*"

"I thought the *Federales* killed him," I said.

"Sure they kill him," he replied matter-of-factly. "They kill him a lot. But he comes back a lot."

He tore off a piece of the place mat and wrote on it:

LUCIO CABANAS
MONTANA DE GUERRERO
SIERRA MADRE DEL SUR
AL ESTATE DE GUERRERO

I probably should have asked for a house number.

There was such an inordinate disparity between the rich and the poor in Mexico that it was inevitable that guerilla groups would arise. Now, this soft-spoken man showed emotion. He told me that *Lucio Cabanas Barrientos* was a former rural schoolteacher, much like himself. But *Cabanas* was braver. He wanted to overthrow a brutal, indifferent central government and replace it with fairness and reforms: expropriating factories and facilities for the workers' benefit; enacting broad financial, judicial, educational and social welfare reforms that focused on workers, peasants, Indians and women.

Were ambushes of military and police units, kidnappings, bank robberies and other armed actions of his group justified? He didn't know, but was the constant squashing of the poor by the government any more justified?

I knew Marat would like this *Cabanas.*

Then, he proceeded for the next twenty or so minutes to try to convince me why I should do this and what the poor in Mexico were up against with *Echeverria* and the P.R.I., during most of which, I thought, why me?

Well, got to go.

I looked at the address, then got up. I felt badly when he would not let me pay the bill-it was so small it meant nothing to me—but he would have been insulted had I insisted.

We shook hands, then hugged. And I was sure there was a tear in his eye as I turned to leave.

Maybe Marat was right: the people in these third world countries look to the U.S. as a beacon of hope. I even got the feeling from *Pablo* that he felt we could do anything, even bring justice to his countrymen. From what I could see they don't hate us *Norte Americanos*, they just despair when we don't deliver.

As I walked back to the hotel, once more I was taken by how these people seemingly had so little, in comparison with what we have in the States, or even compared to what people had in the district of our hotel, and that was a poor area as well. Still, they were so dynamic, so happy, and so enamored with the same crap and worse that all of us have to put up with. There was a lesson there somewhere.

It didn't take near as much time to get back and the room key was gone, so I knew Marat had already returned. As I entered the room, I saw he was reading.

"So you didn't get into any trouble tonight," I stated, but I guess it was more of a question.

"No," Marat said. "Just looked at churches and old architecture. All the museums were closed. Then he asked, smirking, "Did you eat any hot food?"

I grimaced then told him of our conversation, including the invitation to the mountains.

"Well," he asked. "Is that what you want to do?"

"I don't want to fight. This isn't even my country. But I can understand. You don't have to look far...but I would be interested in going up into the mountains, and finding these people...maybe telling their story."

"Good," Marat said. "If you go up there, you will not be able to ever return."

"Why?"

"It is most likely, the *Federales* will become aware of a *gringo's* sojourn," he said. "And when you come down, they will find you, and ask you information, perhaps in not so polite a fashion."

"And you will tell them," he added after a pause in which he stared into my eyes so intensely I had to look away.

"I will?"

"You'll tell them," he said. "I guarantee it."

"There are, perhaps, laws in this country against torture," he continued. "But I doubt they ever stopped anybody. How long do you think you could hold out against torture?"

"You mean like listening to the Archies?"

"If you really intend to go up into the mountains, this becomes a serious question deserving of a not so flippant answer."

It didn't take too much thought to know he was right.

"I'd last maybe a second or two," I responded. "Soon as I saw a blade or a fingernail extractor, I'd spill my guts." I knew this journey into the mountains was just another of what my father would have labeled "pipe dreams."

"Good," Marat said. "One should not enter another's business, unless he has something to offer. To be just a voyeur would help neither you nor them. What you might learn would not offset the misery you might bring in your wake."

"There are and have always been disputes between the haves and have-nots. It is simply more exaggerated in a country such as this. In the end it just comes down to who has the power and can they keep it. If *Cabanas* wins, he will just exchange their oppression with his own, and then, he will stay busy oppressing the previous oppressors. A different group will then be impoverished, so what does it matter?"

"I thought you were a idealist?"

"Perhaps, sometimes I am," he answered, "But I am always a realist."

Still, I quietly entertained the idea for some time. What a romantic notion: fighting to free an oppressed people. I tossed it around, explored every angle and wondered if I could actually do it—it would have been easier if I wasn't still limping. I once had a friend who was one of New York's finest. Also a black belt in Karate, he told me that the first option in any confrontation was to run away, and I think that's what finally sealed the question for me. It had been less than two weeks since my accident and if Marat and I were in a tough situation, I couldn't run if I had to. If we had been spotted in the canyon, I would have been a goner. Besides, if I wanted to fight injustice, there were plenty of causes in my own country, and as for Marat, let's don't even get started about France.

CHAPTER 8

Guadalajara

If God lived on earth, people would break his windows. –Jewish proverb

The next day I felt incredible. I had the first full night's sleep since we'd left Phoenix.

Going outside, I spread my arms and breathed in deeply, then coughed for two minutes as the diesel-permeated air entered my lungs.

We caught a ride early from a young man, mid-twenties, jet black hair slicked back with thick cream, sporting a pencil-thin mustache, and heading southwest to *Guadalajara.*

Soon the land started to change as we headed up into the *Sierra Madre Occidental* through barren foothills. As we went higher, I could see that these mountains were far more rugged and with steeper canyon walls than the mountains we had traversed earlier, and soon we were passing through forests of Douglas Fir, oak and pine. Switchbacks multiplied and some of the drop-offs could literally make you think you were hyperventilating—and figuratively too.

At times, it seemed we were heading straight up and at others, downward in a plunge. Every time we hit a straightaway, the smooth-skinned lad would gun the accelerator to the floor. We made good time.

It wasn't long before we were descending, also in leaps and bounds. I'm not certain his Ford had brakes—in any event, he didn't find need to use them. In one piece, he let us off on the other side of *Lagos de Moreno*. I held out some money for him and he shook his head 'no' and grinned. By now this seemed typical of the hospitality of our rides.

For the most part, we were through the *Sierra Madre Occidental.*

Now we walked and our newfound luck with the thumb didn't hold. Six miles passed slowly, but at least the road was fairly level, even sometimes at a slight decline.

You're killing me, I said silently to my legs. My right side, from under my arm to my knee, was still a darkish purple from the accident, and now, I was so out of shape, every step brought a new ache. This time it was both shins.

But the air was clean, and our hearts were light. We were far away from the arroyo, and though I felt a twinge of guilt every time I thought about it, for not doing anything to stop the *Federales*, by now I realized I would have only succeeded in getting us all killed.

And so, we continued down Mexico Interstate 80.

Life was good. We were relatively healthy. After all, I could have been dead under the car that hit me a scant two weeks ago, or dead from a bullet only a couple of nights ago. Now, I looked forward to losing myself in the adventure. What could happen to us now that could in any way come close to the danger in the arroyo? Nothing. Now was the time for looking forward, not backward, and my anticipation of all this country could offer was great.

By the time we hailed down a bus, I was barely crawling and Marat was cursing audibly. Mustn't upset the pocket book or timetable, I thought. What timetable, I wondered? But at least he agreed to flag down the bus.

Now the highway gradually descended as we came down from the mountains and traveled through the rolling hills and sweeping valleys in the southern half of the *Altiplano Central*. I could see large tracts of cultivated farmland and cattle feeding off the grassland.

It was late afternoon when we began to see the first signs of a city, heralded of course, by a *Pemex* Station.

The bus stopped at an outlying, single-story half-painted stucco depot. While I stretched, Marat went up to a man and asked him directions to the center of the city and which bus to take. He listened intently, thanked him, and as soon as he walked off, Marat went up to someone else and asked the same thing. Marat would usually ask three or four people whenever he needed directions, and if two of the answers meshed, he figured they were telling him the truth.

"When I was in Laos," Marat said as we found seats on a bus headed into the center of *Guadalajara,* "on my first trip overseas, I asked somebody directions and I felt confident, or at least had no concerns because he spoke French. I had spent most of my time in small villages far out in the countryside where most people I met spoke only their native dialect. When I found someone who could speak French I naively trusted them." He now laughed. "How is that for trusting someone simply on account of speaking the same language? I ended up in some jungle. I don't know if they were having a laugh at my expense, or if they just didn't know their way around and were trying to be nice and have an answer. They might have felt they'd lose face if they did not tell me something, regardless if it was correct or not. Or they just might hate foreigners or Frenchmen. Now, I am a little more cautious."

Marat could be a bit loquacious in his explanations.

As we got down near the *Plaza de Armas,* I happened to glance up, and lo and behold, there was the *Roma Hotel.*

"We have to stay there," I said to Marat. I imagined sauntering up to the desk where they would say they had no rooms, and replying, "I know *Franc,*" and them giving me the best suite in the house.

"I think it's a little rich for us," Marat said, laughing.

"You see," Marat now mused, "the sons of the rich have time

on their hands. Never having to worry about where the next meal comes from, or having a roof over their heads, they go in one of four directions. They either live a life of dissolution, wasting their resources with as much alacrity as is possible, or they become more acquisitive, even Calvinistic in their zeal—these are the possibilities of the Right. Those of the Left, either follow that same descent into dissipation, or turn to helping the downtrodden, with the extremists among them, attempting to overturn the whole of society."

As we continued down *Avenida Juarez*, crossing *La Calle Maestranza*, Marat solemnly gestured upward at the giant *ROMA* sign on the top floor. "So it must have been with *Franc*."

"Churchill said, 'If you are not a Communist by the time you are twenty, you have no heart. But if you are still a Communist when you are forty, you are an idiot.'"

"So it must have been with *Franc*," I said with impeccable timing.

Then we crossed *Calzada Independencia Sur*, a major thoroughfare, and believe me, I looked both ways. As I've said, drivers in the cities were somewhat reckless. In addition, I don't think they like pedestrians all that much.

Marat found a hotel to his liking on *Avenida Javier Mina*—not too big, not too small, dirt cheap and rundown, but comfortable. For me, this was the nicest, plushest hotel I'd been in since leaving the States, which by now seemed to be a few years ago. Of course, these things are relative, and if my mom saw it, she would have rather seen her middle son in bondage than ensconced within its dingy rooms.

Oh well, what to do. I would refrain from sending a picture post card.

Now, I had four days on the road behind me. I was a seasoned traveler and this place looked like a Hilton to me. I tossed my pack on the bed nearest to the window, lay down, and shut my eyes.

Marat went into the bathroom and I could soon hear the sound of the shower.

Coming out scrubbed and smelling like soap, his hair combed back and wearing his best clothes (in addition to the maroon alpaca sweater), he shook my bed.

"Come on, Tomas," he said. "Let's go. Let's explore the city. Get ready." He shook the bed again as I had not budged. "This is Mexico's second city. It's incredible. It has museums. It has art, murals. It has history, nightlife and beautiful women. It has music, food, life. Let's not waste time, let's go."

But I was exhausted. The long period of walking had really done in my legs. I would have been upset if I was not so worn out. Normally I would be exhilarated. I was used to having boundless energy, but since the accident, I was physically unable to keep up with him. And it wasn't just my body that was fatigued, it was also my mind from everything that had gone on. There had been so much stimuli to absorb, so many new experiences, smells, tastes, sounds, stresses, close calls. Perhaps I was overwhelmed. Mentally, there was a certain fuzziness, as though I just couldn't think or concentrate—like I had had too much sugar. I think if I had a sports page in front of me, I'd probably have to read a score eight or nine times before I could comprehend it. 'Let's see: Vikings over Packers, 24 to 10. What does that mean?' That's how debilitated my brain was. I'm not sure what else I needed, except that I knew I needed rest.

"Marat," I said in a supplicating manner, "I have to just sit still for awhile. You go. I don't even care if you get into trouble. Do your worst. See if the mayor's wife is available. I just can't move from this spot."

"You're certain?" he asked. "This is what you came for. The other country. This is the exotic, the foreign, the real Mexico. You will love this I promise you. Where is the mental toughness of the athlete?"

But I was in bad shape. "Just let me die with my boots on," I said. I don't think he'd seen enough westerns to appreciate my wit. "You go. Have a great time. I have to lay down or sit or something."

I half expected him to glare at me for my weakness, but he didn't. Instead, he handed me one of his books and then turned and left.

I closed my eyes and dozed off into one of those dreams that are so deep and real that when you wake up, you aren't sure whether it was a dream or reality. Then I felt the weight of the book, still resting on my chest.

Bertrand Russell's *Principles of Mathematics.* I started laughing. Shows how much he knew about the state of my brain. Right. I couldn't figure out Ashe beats Newcombe in five, and he wanted me to read this. Yet, I turned to the opening page and I started reading. I went over the first section of the first chapter for an hour. That's one hour for about four pages, and I was so determined to do it, that I focused and concentrated and reread and tried to figure out each proof and equation, over and over. I studied with such fixation, that when I heard the door open and Marat walked in, I was wide awake. I'd concentrated so hard, I was completely alert. I don't know that I understood that section, but somehow it just woke me up. It was like drinking ten cups of coffee without getting the jitters. Like concentration drills or meditation. I highly recommend the book.

I was sitting up on the bed, when Marat returned. He had a little paper bag and came over and sat on the bed.

Reaching in the bag, he took out some kind of salve.

"Let's see if this helps," he said. "Pull down your pants."

Hmm, I thought. I didn't think he was that sort of guy, but warily, I pulled them down—I still had on bvds.

He squeezed some of the ointment into his hands and started massaging my calves and shins. Then, he handed me the tube.

"I'm not doing this by myself," he said.

So I rubbed the stuff, which had a faint smell of wintergreen, into my quads for a good twenty minutes.

Marat then stood up, went over and washed his hands and said, "Let's go."

Within minutes, we were headed east on *Avenida Javier Mina.* It was dark out, though the streetlights were on. As we walked, I began to hear music coming from a distance.

Marat had a smile on his face as he led me down the street to a plaza. As we turned from the street, the music grew louder and I saw what must have been over a hundred guitar and trumpet and fiddle cases, and God knows what else, spread out on the ground near the wall of what looked to be a church.

Inside the plaza, which was crowded with people sitting at tables, there were a dozen or more *Mariachi* bands all playing at once. Some of the bands were on a stage and others moved from table to table, serenading the patrons.

"This is called *Plaza de los Mariachis*," Marat said loudly over the din.

The place was crowded to standing room, and Marat and I were forced to be on our feet for over a half-hour, when a table near us opened and we swooped down on it like ravenous vultures.

After half a *cervesa* (following Marat's lead, I carefully rubbed the top of the bottle to clean it, after the cap was off—Marat even insisted on the waiter taking the cap off in front of us), we ordered tacos, and I had the biggest smile on my face.

Marat laughed. "I knew you would love this, Tomas," he said.

"This is what I came for," I agreed. Forget El Dorado, I thought. This was the music and the food and the culture of Mexico. Everything tasted better and felt better in this environment. I was in love with every minute of it, and perhaps for the first time in my life, felt a part of the grand pageant that made up our existence, rather than just viewing it from a distance as though I was clinically watching and not taking part.

"I met a woman, *Louisa*, when I was out," Marat said.

"Oh oh," I said with a laugh.

"No, no, no," Marat said. "This is a nice Mexican girl. She's about our age, and she wanted to practice her English. She thought I was a *gringo*." Now he laughed. It was becoming our private joke. "This seems to happen to me."

"Well," I said. "Why don't you lie out in the sun for awhile?"

"And turn red like the lobster."

Prepared for the worst, I asked, "What transpired?"

Marat shook his head, knowing what I meant. "Listen," he said. "These Mexican women...they do not have sex until they are married. If you meet a woman down here, don't even think about it. It will not happen." He finished his beer.

"Why?" I asked.

"They are very religious," he answered. "And their legs are very strong, no?" Then he laughed again.

"When I was here before," he continued, "I tried. Friends told me this is a very Catholic country. You might kiss them, and maybe feel their breasts but no more."

"She wants to meet with us tomorrow," Marat said. "So we're going to meet at a pizza place." He hesitated enough to mischievously raise his eyebrows—he did this a lot when speaking of women. "She said she would bring some girlfriends."

There's always a woman, I thought. I must've got that from some private detective movie. The voice over probably started with, "It's always about a woman," but then, it always is.

Around eleven, the *mariachis* began putting away their instruments and packing up their equipment. People lingered for awhile, but Marat had other places to go, so we paid our bill, walked back out to *Avenida Javier Mina*, then headed west to what he said was a first-rate night club.

Some ten minutes later, as we approached the entrance to the club, a man, who reminded me of *Franc Roma*, but not quite as debonair, and in a soiled white t-shirt and dirty torn jeans, came up to us wanting to make friends. Obviously drunk—he stumbled and slurred his words—I knew immediately this man was not an upstanding citizen. He kept putting his hand to his back pocket and I would not have been surprised in the least if he pulled out a knife. There were only a few people around and they all seemed to want to keep their distance from this hombre. Marat always reminded me that this was their country and you don't want to get too aggressive unless your safety depends on it. At this point, I could feel a trickle of sweat run down the middle of my back. I had one eye on Marat to follow his lead and the other on the drunk, just in case. I didn't know what he wanted with us, but I was certain it could not be good. Grabbing my arm, he tried to lead me away, as he slurred his unintelligible

Spanish—of course, all Spanish was still pretty unintelligible to me. Gently, with regard for the proprieties of his country, I removed his hand. Then, Marat would pull me the other way. This happened not a few times, till I felt I was back in the pinball machine. Next, he walked around me and grabbed Marat's arm, and Marat ever so politely removed it.

Marat saw that I was about to punch the guy—nonviolent man that I am—and he got between us and shook his head.

"No, Tomas," he said in a whisper, once more reminding me. "You do not want to do that. You're in a foreign country. You do not want to get entangled with the legal system in a foreign country. You might become lost forever in one of their jails."

Damn. What was I thinking? I already knew that rule.

The man stood in front of the club entrance and kept speaking to Marat in Spanish and Marat kept speaking back in a calm tone, I guess, trying to pacify him.

Then, another Mexican man approached us, got between us and the first man, yelled at him in Spanish and pushed him backward against the brick wall of the club.

"Follow me," he said to us in heavily accented English, as he started to walk quickly away from the club.

I looked at Marat. I was suspicious about everything these days, but Marat started down the street after him, and I limped after them as fast as I could.

Glancing back, I saw the drunk was trying to follow, but he couldn't keep up with us and was soon out of sight. Who knows, maybe he just got turned around and didn't know where he was anyway, but I was glad to see the last of him. He might have been too far gone to harm us, but another thing I'd learned on this trip was to go with my instincts, and I knew he was trouble.

Our new friend *Jorge* informed us he lived in Denver and had worked in Chicago—he pronounced the "Ch" like the "Ch" in Charley. Now I was concerned. If he couldn't pronounce Chicago correctly, maybe others also couldn't. Maybe nobody in this country could pronounce Chicago correctly, so how was I to know when the girl of my dreams turned up? Granola wasn't as smart as she thought.

Jorge was home visiting his family. Not a citizen of the United States, he just snuck back across the border every time he wanted to go back to work in Denver.

Going into Mexico was not a problem. Getting back was the problem, but he seemed to have it all worked out.

"That hombre was *malo*," *Jorge* said, when Marat told him how we traveled. "I hear of other hitchhikers getting their throats slit." Then he moved his hand across his throat in a cutting gesture.

Jorge took us to a different nightclub. Once he'd gotten us a table and ordered us *cervesas*, he went off to the dance floor with a woman I took to be his friend.

When the beers arrived, the waitress informed us they were already taken care of. Marat took a sip then got up and went over to one of the most beautiful women I'd ever seen. She was small and seemed a bit young, but had long dark hair and bronze skin and a delightful smile; definitely movie star features. He talked to her for a bit and then they moved to the dance floor.

So I sat, nursing my third beer of the night and I was getting pretty buzzed, with a big, shit eating grin on my face. I was happy.

And there was Marat. It was the first time I had seen him dance. He was in his long maroon alpaca that came down to his knees, and I guess I wouldn't really call it dancing. He held her closely and bounced up and down to the music, occasionally turning in a circle, the young *senorita* following his lead and bouncing with him as best she could. Strangely, to my mind at least, every time he would turn so that the girl was facing me, she would give me the biggest smile and so I'd return it, after all, I was happy, though I felt sorry for Marat. Why? Because he was dancing with this beautiful woman and had no chance to take her home unless he married her, and even if he wanted to, that would take some time. As far as I knew, there were no Las Vegas chapels anywhere near, plus, he'd have to deal with in-laws.

Earlier, Marat told me how he ended up with the two alpaca sweaters and the intricacies of his bargaining methods. He was in Peru and had gone to a market place in a small Andean village outside of *Cuzco*. While looking around, he saw a man who had a stand where he sold the sweaters.

"How much?" he asked the villager.

"Eight hundred soles," the man replied.

"No," Marat said peremptorily. "Four hundred."

"No," the man said emphatically.

So Marat turned around and left.

The next day, Marat went back to the same kiosk, same time, same guy, same sweater, and asked the same question, "How much?"

"Four hundred," the man said.

"No," Marat said assertively. "Two hundred."

"No," the man said determinedly.

So Marat turned around and left.

The next day, Marat went back again.

"How much?" Marat asked.

"Two hundred," the man said.

"No," Marat said insistently. "One hundred."

"No," the man said resolutely.

Marat was out of there, but, he returned the next day, and pointed up to the same sweater.

"How much?" Marat politely inquired.

"Ok. One hundred soles." This day he looked different, Marat said, almost resigned.

"No," Marat said with little mercy. "I want it for free."

The guy, positively irritated, looked at Marat as if he was crazy, and yelled, "No!"

Marat shrugged his shoulders and left.

The next day, same time and place, Marat went back.

"How much for the sweater?" Marat asked.

"All right," the man answered, completely exasperated. "You can have it for free."

Marat said, "I want two."

I made him swear on a bible after that one.

Now, Marat left the dance floor and came back to our table, seemingly angry.

"Marat?" I asked. "What's wrong?"

He looked at me and said huffily, "She won't do it with me for free."

Free, I wondered, now in a state of utter bewilderment?

"Do what?"

"Sleep with me."

I blurted out, "I thought you said you couldn't sleep with the women here unless you were married?"

Marat looked at me as though I was stupid which by now wasn't far off the mark.

"Well you can't," he said. "But this is the red light district."

"Red light district?" I repeated in total wonder, trying to get my bearings.

"These women," Marat said, "they're all prostitutes. And you see all these guys. They all have girlfriends, but they can't sleep with them so they come here. Then they wait on their girlfriends till they get married."

Prostitutes, I thought. I guess I'd forgotten about *Chihuahua*. Sometimes, you get something in your head, and it just stays there, no matter how wrong, stupid, inane, moronic—it's like the wires were crossed when you heard it, even if you misheard it. I had listened intently to Marat's description of Mexican women and got it into my head that every last one of them was a virgin. I wasn't thinking straight. I hoped it was just the beer.

Prostitutes? "Well, why wouldn't she do it with you for free? Why *would* she do it with you for free?" Maybe he needed to come back six days in a row.

"I always ask them to do it for free," Marat answered matter-of-factly. "I'm not going to pay money to sleep with a prostitute."

"Paying money for them," I countered. "Isn't that the idea?"

"Yeah," Marat said. "But if you pay, you're just sleeping with a prostitute. If they go with you for free, then you're sleeping with just a regular woman."

I shook my head at his logic and finished my beer.

All this new information swirled around in my liquored-up head for a bit—who knows how long—I'd only seen a prostitute once before and I'm not even sure she *was* a prostitute. When we used to go up to the state basketball tournament in the early spring, and wander around Minneapolis, I remember walking down Hennepin Avenue and there were a couple of gaudy places of disrepute, where the smell of cigarette smoke and stale beer overwhelmed my senses, even from the street. The windows were usually brightly painted over, if there were windows, and at one of those places there was a greasy, mustachioed old man with a big belly hanging over his belt and flaky, slicked back hair, beckoning us young boys to enter (after ascertaining we were over twenty-one years, of course. We were actually about sixteen).

We passed by the place a few times, always trying to get a peak inside, and once I saw a "painted" woman in a really tight, low cut dress come out and talk to the tout.

Boy, I really was innocent, wasn't I?

Anyway, this girl, that Marat had danced with, looked so sweet and natural, I couldn't believe she was really a prostitute. After minutes of mulling all this over, checking all the permutations and ramifications, the qualifications and ins and outs, and recalling how much she'd smiled at me, I asked Marat if he minded if I danced with her.

"Do your worst," Marat said, his tone telling me how pleased he was with my request.

So I wandered over to the beautiful *Leticia* and asked her to dance. It is one of the more intoxicating experiences of life to dance with a woman you're attracted to, especially when it's slow and you can feel her body next to yours and breathe in her perfume and scent, although all I could smell at this moment was smoke and stale beer.

As the first song ended, she looked up at me with big brown eyes and said, "Rich American?" She pronounced it "reech."

Well not really, I thought, so I smiled and said, "American, *si*, reech, no."

"*Si*," she said and then giggled, and we danced for another thirty or so minutes, only broken up by songs ending, and the mantra-like, "Rich American?" question. Maybe she wanted a green card?

Then we went back to the table hand in hand and she sat down with Marat while I went off to the Hombre room.

When I got back, she was in an animated conversation with Marat and *Jorge*. When *Leticia* saw me retuning she sat back, smiling at me like a teenage girl with a huge crush.

"You know," Marat said. "She didn't like me at first, and now she thinks I'm all right." Then he grinned. "And she likes you more."

It's probably the "reech" American thing, I speculated.

"She's only fifteen," Marat said. "She supports her family like this. She has had a hard life. I heard her whole story." He stared at his bottle of beer. The only part of him that moved was his mouth. "She started this at thirteen and has been working nightly. Many of these women would say such a thing to get sympathy, but I believe this girl." Now, he looked up at me.

"She says she wants to come with you tonight," he said.

Leticia still sat smiling at me. I'm certain she didn't understand a word Marat was saying.

"For free," Marat said, and he did so without malice or jealousy. "With *Jorge's* help, I've arranged for her to come to our hotel. She'll come around two in the morning. I've given her the room number and she knows the hotel."

He still stared at his beer bottle, but now rubbed his hand up and down the stem of the bottle. Maybe he *was* jealous.

"And, ah, when she comes, I'll go out."

Once more, I was bewildered. I hadn't been to bed with anyone since I left Minnesota, and that was almost three months ago. Hell, I hadn't even thought about sleeping with anybody—I was, to tell the truth, still a little hung up on the woman I had left. In fact, while first driving out west with my superstitious friend, the lamentations had come fast and hard.

She was a blond Nordic type, but then, a good percentage of the women and men in Minnesota are. To my eyes, she looked a bit like Britt Ecklund, and was quite intelligent, but I suppose I was prejudiced. In any event, she looked pretty good to me.

Had my older brother been there to advise me or warn me, he would've said, "She's baited the hook, now she's trying to reel you in. Watch out for the lure and the net." I would have countered with, "Though I might be easy to reel in, I'm very hard to land." Not that I take pride in this, there was just too much of the world that I wanted to see, and I wanted to see it from all levels and that precluded much travel in comfort, and I imagined that that would exclude most of the women I knew at present.

Once more, I had gotten away, but as my brother would have said, "Then, the lamentations would start."

Finally in despair, the guy I was driving with threatened, "If you ever talk about that lost love again, I'll take one of your tennis racquets and put slice, topspin and an American Twist on your head, and then I'm going to hit it 400 times in a row over the net."

I thought this was a bit over the top. He could have just threatened a poke in the eye with a sharp stick. I would've gotten the picture.

Now, concerning *Leticia*, it wasn't because I forgot how, or that she was a streetwalker or anything like that. This was just different, and I didn't know what to do.

So we stayed and we drank and we listened to the music and we danced and I thought a lot, Marat sometimes switching places with me and dancing with *Leticia*, bouncing up and down like a yo-yo, his alpaca sweater riding up to mid thigh.

We left around two in the morning and wandered around the streets till we saw something we recognized and we were able to find our way to *Avenida Javier Mina*. There was one street where we had to jump from the pavement up to the curb. Running along the curb was the water, waste, debris and stench of an open sewer. Marat nimbly jumped over it, but for me, it was tough on account of my stiff, sore legs. I'm not usually overly concerned about where I step, but for some reason, this just revolted me.

The smell was sickening and I had to summon the strength of will to take a running leap. There was no way I was going to step in that crap.

This in itself, was hardly worth mentioning, but as I touched down on the curb and got my balance, Marat nodded for me to look to my left and down. There was a man on the sidewalk going the other direction and only a few yards away from us. But this man was pulling himself along the ground, using only his arms. Trailing behind his torso, were the sleeves of his jeans, empty from the thigh down. Never glancing up at us, he pulled himself down the curb and across that slime filled water, his jeans soaked and becoming dark, dragging on the street after him.

Marat and I walked solemnly back to the hotel. At some point, our arms were supporting each other and we cried.

Does a man lose his innocence when he first sees a problem he cannot solve? That, even if he can ameliorate it to some extent, his aid only amounts to a bandage?

It was the first time I remembered crying since I was a little kid.

There is a feeling one gets from being able to commune with his fellow man—to feel the joys and sorrows that befall us all. To feel a oneness with all of humanity, something we seldom feel in our sheltered and busy existence in the States. We felt that, at least I did, on that night.

At the hotel, Marat asked the night clerk where there was an open pharmacy nearby.

I went up to the room while Marat purchased condoms.

Handing them to me back in the room, Marat said, "One must be cautious."

But it didn't matter. I had already decided this wasn't for me. If *Leticia* showed up, I would just give her money and send her on her way. She was only fifteen. She was supporting her family. Somehow it just did not seem noble to me. Using another being for my pleasure, then paying for it or not paying for it didn't matter. It was just something I could not do that night. It had nothing to do with repugnance or aversion to a woman who sold herself. She was making a living in the way she could, to have food and shelter, struggling to exist like everyone else. If I could help her, that would be one thing. If I could help her without using her, I knew that would be better for me.

As we sat on our respective beds, Marat writing in his journal, me expectant for God knows what, Marat suddenly threw down his pen and notebook, disgusted with himself.

"You know," he said in an irritated voice, "your brother...he is a great writer, while I am a journeyman."

"Patrick?" I asked, somewhat surprised.

"Yes."

"Why?" I asked. My older brother was talented in many areas, but he loved to draw and paint. I'd seen many of his sketches, but little of his writing, though he always used to correct my papers for me in school, I never knew he was that interested in writing—in fact, I don't think I ever read anything he wrote, whether a school paper or something just for pleasure.

"Because he has something to say and he has to get it out," Marat answered. "Or it will gnaw on him, haunt him, torture him until he does. And that is what makes a great writer."

"I have something to say," he continued, "but I don't know that I have any urgency within myself that needs to say it."

I always thought my younger brother was a really good writer. I'd read many of his creative works and been in some productions he filmed—they were clever, amusing and even intelligent. Now I was astounded. How could I not know this about my other brother? Of all the people in the world, even including the women that had heretofore been in my life, I was closest to my two brothers. There are unknowns and secrets even between people this close—another ideal shattered.

Many times on this trip, from when I'd left Minnesota, if I was lonely or sad, I would think of their faces, of our many times together, and I would smile. Sometimes, I'd even dream about them and wake up laughing.

A year ago last spring, Patrick had written my younger brother and I from Crete. He had a villa overlooking King Minos' palace and he wanted us to come join him, but we both wanted to finish our degrees. A year later, I had gotten more into tennis and headed west. My younger brother joined Patrick in Rome, and the last I heard, they had been moving east through Turkey to the border with Iran. Patrick's last letter said that he had gotten the bug to move east, to see India and they were going overland.

Now we were on opposite sides of the globe and I missed them.

"But your brother puzzles me sometimes," Marat said, looking at me intently as if I could explain away his confusion, and I, no longer certain I could answer a question about either of my brothers with certainty.

"Why?" I asked, resignedly.

"He wants to go to the east," Marat said.

"Yes," I said, wanting to at least appear to be in the know. "He's on his way."

"He wants to enter the monastery."

"I didn't know," I said. Another secret, now made even worse as I realized these were unknowns for me but not for Marat. "What is so puzzling?"

"One only enters the monastery to come back out, no?" Marat answered.

I had to think about that one, but it certainly sounded profound at the moment.

Four in the morning came and went, but no *Leticia*. Marat speculated that she came to the hotel but they wouldn't let her come up, and this was very likely.

CHAPTER 9

First Time In The Mountains

"Because it's there" –George Leigh Mallory

The next morning saw us up early, taking a quick bite and heading off to the buses, where Marat asked his series of four people before we boarded.

This was to be a day of museums and murals, cathedrals and early Spanish architecture. Marat was insatiable when it came to viewing everything ever made, painted, composed, proposed or written—it was easy to see how he had fallen in with Patrick. I doubt that I've ever met anyone else with such unending appetites for learning and seeing as my two brothers and my father. They'd devour museums whole, leaving my legs and patience aching long before my car accident. They wanted to know and see and learn and experience everything.

So, the present day was to be filled with *Orozco, Rivera* and *Siqueiros,* all artists commissioned after the revolution to paint grand murals on public buildings. I think Marat was enthused over the scenes of Mexican history and culture, because they were mostly leftist. The murals were definitely grand, depicting the revolution, tyranny, the peasants, the workers, the heroes and villains of Mexican history, both pre-Spanish and after, and were all over the city—*Orozco* was most visible in *Guadalajara* in the *Palacio de Gobierno* and the *Institute Cultural de Cabanas*—no relation to *Lucio*. I followed Marat throughout the city in search of them. When we had exhausted every possible viewing, we started on the churches. They were all over the city and we went all over looking at them as well. If I added up all the stained glass windows I'd seen in my entire life, before or since, I couldn't equal what I saw in that one day in *Guadalajara*.

By the time the evening arrived and we were scrubbed and dressed in our Sunday best—which for me was jeans and a collared shirt and for Marat was the now legendary alpaca—I was once more exhausted. But, as we were going to meet *Louisa* and her friends, I massaged my legs and sucked it up.

We had barely sat down at the meeting place when in walked *Louisa* with her sister, the sister's boyfriend and another woman who was a dead ringer for Sophia Loren. I'd always been attracted to body types that were halfway between slender and voluptuous—maybe "slender with curves" is a better way to put it. I quickly calculated, capricious as I was, that if *Esmeralda* lost five pounds, she would be my perfect body type. And I guess I wasn't far off from her body type because there was an instant chemistry as soon as our eyes met.

"We're going to *Tapatia*," *Louisa* proclaimed, while I wondered how long I could wait before testing *Esmeralda's* pronunciation.

Soon, all six of us were crammed into an old Volkswagen and on the road.

Tapatia was one of the higher-class discotheques in *Guadalajara*.

As we drove along, running red lights and narrowly missing pedestrians and other cars, trucks and buses, *Louisa* turned on the radio to an English speaking station and all four of our hosts, three of whom spoke no English, began singing along in unison to *Red Rubber Ball*. They knew all the words to the pop songs by heart. How could they sing along with these songs almost without an accent, when only *Louisa* could speak to us? Never figured that one out. To communicate with *Esmeralda* and the others, I added an 'i' or 'o' to every word I knew with Latin roots and pantomimed like I did with *Pablo*. I mostly got derisive laughs in return.

"Do you know Chicago?" I asked *Esmeralda*.

"*Que?*" she responded. Try as I did, I couldn't get anything else out of her.

After a night spent dancing with *Esmeralda*, I knew what Marat was talking about. These poor guys dancing with these incredible women and otherwise not being able to touch them. I was ready to go back to *Leticia*.

Around midnight, we exchanged addresses, made protestations of undying love as they dropped us off on *Avenida Javier Mina* and parted sorrowfully. We waved after them with tears in our eyes and as soon as they were out of sight, headed back to our favorite bar. But, no *Leticia*, no *Jorge*, so we had a *cervesa* and called it a night.

The next day was once more "cathedral day." We went to every church we'd missed on the previous outing, and viewed every piece of religious art in existence in *Guadalajara*. It was an all day project and Marat's energy once more amazed me. As far as I was concerned, you seen one mural, you've seen 'em all. You see one church with stained glass, icons and gold gilded paintings, you've seen 'em all. I'd already had enough for a lifetime and couldn't wait for Mexico City where Marat assured me there was even more to see.

That night saw us back at the plaza of the *mariachi's* and we closed 'em down. Gradually, we made our way around the streets in stops and starts, but with an inevitable drift towards *Jorge's* club. As we jumped across the curb of the swill-filled sewer, there was another man pulling himself across it—maybe the same man we saw earlier—but going in the opposite direction.

I'll never forget those empty flat pants' legs, soaked with the sludge. Marat bent down and handed him a few pesos and I did the same. But the gesture didn't even qualify as a bandage for those wounds. What happened to him? Born that way? Caught in an accident, an act of war or repression? Was it bad luck or did he bring it on himself? As we walked, I tried to imagine myself in his straits.

Thankfully it wasn't long before we entered the haven of the bar. I was certain I'd drink much more than usual, but before the first *cervesa* arrived, *Leticia* appeared with a broad smile upon her face, grabbed my hand and pulled me up and onto the dance floor. Her English had not improved much since our last meeting. About all she was good for was, "Reech American," but that was fine with me.

Jorge came up and told me that she indeed had come to our hotel the night before but wasn't let in by the astute hotel management. *Leticia*, her eyes wide with merriment—which I hoped signified happiness, listened patiently to this exchange, and when she determined *Jorge* had finished, said, "I come you tonight, free," then smiled even more brightly, if that was possible—and thus proving she could speak better English than my Spanish.

Holding this delightful girl in my arms, smelling her smoke-tinged perfume and feeling her big brown eyes staring wondrously upon my face, I realized I just couldn't do this. Call it not my style, I don't know, it just didn't seem right. I turned to *Jorge*.

"Will you tell her this for me," I asked. "I cannot tonight. Tell her we're leaving early, but I want her to have something, as a gift. Something for her to remember me," I said lamely—during the course of my lifetime, I've culled many cliches.

As *Jorge* told her, the smile completely disappeared from her face. She looked like a sad little girl as tears began to form in her eyes, and I felt like a complete asshole. I quickly placed two hundred peso notes in her hand, but the tears did not abate, nor the smile return. She just stood there staring sadly at me.

Leticia finally turned and walked away, still crying, her shoulders slumping and her gait ponderous.

Jorge shrugged his shoulders, looked at me and said, "Women," and walked off.

As I sat and pondered my *cervesa*, I could see *Leticia* glancing over at me now and again. It wasn't hate in her eyes, it was more like betrayal. I don't have that much charm or charisma. Maybe she thought I was her ride out of this place.

I spent the rest of the night sitting sullenly, nursing my one *cervesa*, and realizing that just possibly, the most important thing one has in this world, is hope, and I'd taken that away from her, even if briefly.

I couldn't even get any enjoyment out of watching Marat's unique dancing style, which I had now decided looked like some primitive mating ritual.

I just hoped the money would help her somehow.

Early the next morning, in keeping with our method of hitchhiking, we boarded a bus to the outskirts of town where we were really going to make a serious attempt at hitching.

Strangely, for once a driver stopped right away. An American, with his wife and a couple of kids in a station wagon, so we turned them down. We don't hitchhike with just anyone.

We had scrupulously avoided both Americans and Frenchmen on our trip. "If you're going to be in a foreign country," Marat asked, "doesn't it ruin the purpose to hang out with people from your own country? You might as well just stay at home."

This was a rule Marat lived by and it made perfect sense to me.

And from this, came his axiom: if you want to avoid Americans, just keep away from the most touristy, popular places. If you want avoid the French, don't go to the most out-of-the-way, esoteric places.

"No thank you, sir," Marat told the American in his most polite tone. "We're not hitchhiking. We're just taking a walk."

"But you had your thumbs out," the man said in a thick, accusatory Texas accent.

"We try sometime," Marat said, flashing his most charming smile. I noticed his English got worse on such occasions. He found it easier to fake being stupid, than to explain everything to commoners. "But no one picks up. Now walk, everyone picks up." Then Marat laughed and it was so infectious, that the man, his wife and kids all laughed as well. They waved and drove off.

"Nice save," I said to Marat as I waved after them with a silly grin on my face. I figured I might as well play stupid as well.

As soon as they were out of sight, our thumbs were out again. They were only gone ten minutes when another station wagon pulled up and screeched to a halt. Once more there was a man, a woman and two children, this time Mexican. As usual, they looked at me as they spoke, motioned for us to get in, and off we went.

We now passed through rolling hills, green with trees and grasses. The air was warmer and thick with humidity.

They dropped us on the road to *Ajijic*, just after passing through *Chapala*, a resort city on *Lago de Chapala*.

As we surveyed the lake and the mountains to the north, I could feel Marat staring at me, carefully, almost challengingly.

Standing straight with his arms akimbo and his hands on his hips, he opined, "I think it's about time you got your legs back in shape, Tomas."

"Today," he said, then gesturing at the foothills behind us, "we're going to climb."

He crossed the road and started walking near the narrow dirt shoulder, looking for a path. I followed.

"There is always a trailhead," he said over his shoulder. "Indians and villagers have been walking around these hills for millennia. Man has been here so long that we shall never be the first to explore a piece of land."

"That grates on me," I said.

"I know," he said, turning around and grinning. "That is why I said it. So, we'll just find a used one."

So we walked, searching the hillside for possible trails.

Even back in Black's Grove, my brothers and friends and I always tried to fix it in our imaginations that we were the first to walk down the trails, which begged the question who made the trails. Sometimes I think the world is too small and too old for a seeker of adventure—there are no places left untouched, at least on the land.

Here we were, in a land far removed from Whiskey Creek, in a place I'd never heard of, yet still, after about a half-hour, we found the inevitable trail up.

It was a hard climb from the onset, but my legs were getting stronger. Before the accident, I was playing four go-for-broke hours of tennis a day, running three to five miles, plus sprints and jumping rope. By now, it had been almost two weeks of what was for me, being almost sedentary. I knew I had to start pushing myself or I'd never get back in shape.

There were a lot of switchbacks. There were steep sections which seemed to go straight up, and even tougher were the descents. There were places we had to haul ourselves up on hands and knees, and I noticed a lot of holes in the ground, and had no idea if they belonged to rodents or snakes.

Marat noticed the holes as well, and soon we were singing Rolling Stones' songs over and over, thinking that the cacophonous sounds of our voices would terrify or scare the serpents or large animals away. And if not, it might eventually annoy them into giving us a lot of room.

When we stopped to take a breather, we could see small pools of water way below us, next to haciendas. This was a rich area. I wondered what *Pablo* would have thought about that. Personally, I don't think I'd ever been in a place where the disparity between the rich and the poor was so overwhelmingly great. Maybe he knew. Marat certainly did. I learned later on that many of these rich people were actually ex-pats from the States, moving here because they couldn't afford to retire at home. Could the same disparity be coming to my own country?

These mountains were covered with trees, mostly types of pine, and when we reached what I thought was the top, I was amazed. While catching my breath, I was looking out at miles and miles of unfettered hills and forests. And in the distance, I could see valleys and rolling hills and mountains looming up even higher.

"Marat," I said, "I have an idea for this *Lucio Cabanas*."

"Yes," Marat said patiently or resignedly. You take your pick.

"The government should put him in the Olympics," I said, not to be deterred. "If he's climbing up these hills every day, he'd make any team he wanted."

"Yes," Marat said. "Then, with the money the government paid him for winning, he could raise the standard of living of every peasant in his province."

"Well of course he'd do that," I agreed. "He has to be an idealist."

"Or more likely," Marat said, "he'll put in a pool next to his luxurious mansion in Acapulco."

Now we sat down and ate some *tortas*, I massaging my legs between bites.

"Marat," I began, ready to unburden myself, and I told him about *Leticia*.

His response was simple and to the point. "Do not let your ego get the best of you." And that was all he said on the matter.

Silence followed my confession and his rebuttal for some time, and by then it was getting late in the day.

I kicked at a patch of dirt.

"Do you want to be up here for the night, Marat?" I asked. "Or climb down in the dark?"

Marat quickly got the picture. Standing, he said, "Yes. We should start down."

Now, Marat showed me just how incredible and intrepid an adventurer he was—he couldn't find the trail that had gotten us to this spot. I take no blame—I was just a follower.

"If we keep heading down, we'll find it," Marat said confidently, and then plunged downward into the brush and trees.

For the next hour, we would cross a path, take it until it stopped descending, head once more into the brush, find another trail and take it until it proved to go nowhere, then start downward again. Somehow, we were turned around and we never did hit one of the switchbacks we'd followed on the ascent. The next thing I knew, the path we were on ended. It was finished, cut off, and the only way downward lay against a sheer, fifteen yard drop. Peering over, I could not make out any handholds, finger holds, footholds or any holds at all.

Had we a rope, it would have been simple. Had we two parachutes, easy. I would've settled for a hang glider.

"I'll go first," Marat said.

"I'll go second," I volunteered.

He sat on the ledge with his feet dangling over the edge, then turned, pressing his boots into the rock, placing most of his weight on his arms and slowly lowering himself over. When all that remained in sight were his hands, he called up, "I've got a toehold."

I guess I missed something.

"There's a ledge here," he said. "I want you step down on my hands. I'll support you.

This was a trust issue—I don't like heights any more than I like snakes of the venomous variety. I weighed the Marat who went off with the *Federale's* wife with the one who came back for me in *Guadalajara* and spent thirty minutes massaging my legs so I could join him at the *Plaza de los Mariachis.*

"Do you want to spend the night up there?" he yelled. "Alone?" he added.

Decisions, decisions, decisions. I took my time. I wasn't going to let him pressure me.

"Ease your self down," he said, "and put your feet into my palms."

Letting out a huge whoosh! I got down on my ass and extended my feet over the ledge, carefully looking for the whereabouts of his hands. I was sweating. Marat was not that big of a guy, certainly smaller than me. Would he be able to hold me while balancing on the ledge, even if it was only for a few seconds? It's not that I'm an out and out coward, it's just that since the accident, I was a bit averse to pain, and falling down that cliff seemed to offer the possibility of a lot of it.

Turning around much as Marat had, I lowered myself with my arms. My toes extended out into the air, grasping for a docking port.

Success!

"I've got you," Marat said.

Now I carefully let my full weight down on his hands and he lowered me until I could get one foot on the ledge. The man was awfully strong.

He went down again, found another ledge and lowered me once more. He must've had a lot better eyes than me, because that vertical drop looked smooth as ice and these ledges he found were not more than three to four inches wide.

But the next time, he didn't go over so fast. As he bent down and visually explored the area right below us, I could see he was puzzled.

"I can see nothing this time," he said. "Nothing at all."

"Time to take off the shirts and shoes and make a rope," I said.

"No," he said. "Follow me." And then, he started to move horizontally along the edge.

God knows why, but as I started to move, my chest pressed as closely to the wall of rock as possible, a long, thin yellow and black wasp landed on my arm. First I blew softly on her, but she seemed to like me and didn't want to leave. Next I tried talking to her, but this too was to no avail. I really hate it when this happens. I was too close to the wall and there was too little room to bring my other arm around to flick her off anyway. Too much movement and we were both going to fly. Slowly, I brought my arm closer to my head and in my gentlest voice, I told the wasp I was going to stomp the living shit out of her if she didn't leave right then. She looked at me quizzically for a second, stung me to remind me who was the boss, then off she flew.

We kept edging along the ledge for another eight yards until it came to an end. Marat crouched down and peered intently along the wall below. It was late and we were now in total shade. The sky above the lake was a bright crimson and dusk was not far away. This time, there was more room, and he turned on his knees then lowered himself once more with his arms.

"Last time," he said before disappearing below the ledge.

This time I could see the foot holes and I didn't want to exhaust the poor fellow, so I came down by myself.

Wiping the sweat off my face, I looked up. It seemed even worse from down here. I've cliff-climbed, but with ropes and belays and good equipment and I couldn't believe we'd come down it. It was a good forty to fifty feet straight up. And as I scanned either side of it, I saw that that was the only possible way from where we had been, that we could have come down.

Marat had already moved off, as this ledge led into another path, and I scampered after him. The light was fading quickly now, and he ran into another trail and started sprinting down it. Adrenaline took over and I sprinted after him. Running down a close-in trail like that was exhilarating, jumping logs, going around corners of switchbacks. The scenery was so near and passing so fast it felt like I was moving a hundred miles an hour. By the time we reached the road, we were far from the city of *Chapala*.

We began to walk, keeping our eyes and ears open for a ride. I was exhausted.

"Hey, Marat," I said in a heartfelt tone of voice. Right then I really felt I owed my life to the guy—I guess I should say twice. "Thanks."

It wasn't long before I was limping worse than usual and Marat broke his usual rule, flagging down the first bus that came down the road.

It was a first class bus and I don't believe I've ever felt in so much comfort. We were the only two people aboard—that's probably the only reason the driver stopped.

I sunk into the cushy seat and fell asleep.

CHAPTER 10

Ajijic

"Crime doesn't pay" –Mom and Dad

By the time we reached *Ajijic*, I'd stiffened up so much, Marat had to help me down the steps of the bus. I could do no more than keep my legs straight, using my arms to sort of hop from step to step and finally to the ground. Damn first class buses sure had a lot of steps.

"We should find a place to rest," Marat said as he walked and I hobbled down *Avenida Colon*, the paved main street. "Then I'll find some food."

We had not walked far, when right there in the middle of the street we saw a herd of maybe fifteen cattle, completely unattended. They were dusty white Brahmas, easily recognized by the hump just behind the head and the dewlap neck. The odd thing about Brahmas, they all look like bulls, especially if you're used to plain old dairy cows and if you don't crouch down to examine them inch by inch. They have long horns and the hump adds greatly to the illusion of size. And this group *was* weird.

As Marat and I took our first step to cross the road, the whole herd shifted its attention in unison, blocking our path. We were bemused, but nonetheless, retreated. They followed our movement, then went back to simply standing, their heads turned to the sidewalk. Marat sprinted quickly across the street and they didn't have time to do more than turn their heads, but now I could see they were keeping a closer eye on me. I tried to cross again but I could only hobble, and the largest one, clearly the leader, moved into the center of the road between me and the other side and his mates quickly joined him. They looked like they were going to charge. I had to go back.

I guess Marat was pretty tired as well. I think this was the first time he lost patience with my injuries.

"Tomas," he yelled, "Come on. We need to find a place, and I'm hungry. *Vamos!*"

So I made another move. Unfortunately, this bull wasn't too slow for me. He checked me in every direction I tried, except for the one where I started, and his minions once more turned with him like a school of fish and backed him up. Then he stared long and hard into my eyes as if daring me. It was a stand off.

Now, I'm a country boy, and I've seen a lot of cows in my time, but never anything like this. I wouldn't say we mixed with cows back in northern Minnesota, but we certainly came into close proximity with them. There were rumors of cow tipping round about midnight during one summer and when I cross-country skied amongst cows on snow-covered pastures in the winter—none of them ever even bothered to look up. I didn't really have a problem with your ordinary, run of the mill, everyday type cow, but these were different. They were after me. I had to come up with a plan—either to distract them or make them pay in advance for mauling me or whatever their evil machinations would involve.

The first one, the bull...every time I made a move, he was in my face as if daring me to cross. The others...I could see they were just followers. But that first one, he made me do a double take. I swear, now that I looked closer at him, there, on his horns, my name was written in big red letters: Tomas on his right horn and Kardadasi on his left; and I hadn't even had a beer.

Marat yelled from the other side of the street, "You stay there. I'll find us a place." And he started down the street.

I watched him with one eye until he disappeared round a corner. The other eye was fixed on the beasts.

Was this to be the place I died? I harkened back to the scale of insignificance. How would this look? I didn't think being gored to death was too high on the scale or if they got together and trampled me—if I was in Pamplona I might have reconsidered. I guess it measured up to getting pegged at the net by McEnroe and shouting: "You cannot be serious" just before the pain makes you stumble forward into the net, become entangled and inadvertently strangle yourself; or if a coconut dropped fifty feet from a palm tree and squashed your head like a grape. Of course, fifteen people a year are killed that way in Thailand.

But here I was, face to snout with the Brahma bulls. If I tried going down the sidewalk they moved that way. If I backed up, they started forward and if I tried to cross the street, they moved to cut me off. It seemed as though they were only content if I didn't move at all.

Then, after about a half-hour, the big guy, the one with my name written on his horns, the one I was certain was the leader and a bull, started to yawn. As if it was a signal, another one came up, got behind him and started humping him. Now, confused, I bent over to look underneath the scoundrel and sure enough, he was a guy. I didn't know there was such a thing as a gay Brahma, but who was I to argue. This might be my only chance. I limped across the street as fast as I could. The big guy turned his head to look, but stayed put. I guess he was having too much fun. Soon, as I reached the other side, I looked back and could see a whole orgy had started. Consumed with their own interests, much as I was consumed with finding a place to cross that wasn't inhabited by bulls, they had forgotten all about me. And much as I wanted to watch, for scientific edification as well as instruction on new moves, I staggered down the road.

As I turned off *Avenida Colon*, I saw Marat speeding back toward me.

"I found a really good deal," he said. "It will cost hardly anything."

His words were to prove prophetic.

His vision strayed over to the herd. "Hmph," he said. "Gay Brahmas."

"Looks that way."

"This man builds a hotel but it is not yet finished," Marat said. "There is no running water in the room. We'll have to use an open air, communal bath, but there are two beds. We're leaving early tomorrow anyway..."

"It's a shelter," I said. "Lead on."

After making ourselves at home, Marat left our open-windowed shelter to find food, and I, still fully clothed, got under the covers and mercifully fell into a deep sleep. I don't know how long I was out, but the next thing I knew, Marat was excitedly shaking me awake.

"I have a surprise for you, Tomas," he said.

He went back to the door, opened it and said, "This is Petite Soufflé," or something that sounded like that.

"She's a psychic," Marat said as a little Indian lady shuffled into the room. "I thought she might cheer you up."

Marat the mathematician believes in fortune telling, I wondered? She looked rather familiar.

"What do you want?" she asked in a gruff voice.

Hmm, I thought as I sat up, if it looked like a Granola, walked like a Granola and talked like a Granola, it's probably a sister, so naturally I asked.

"Say, do you have a sister?"

"Do you have a sister?" she repeated.

"No, really, do you have a sister?" I asked.

"No, really, do you have a sister?"

"No, no," I said. "I don't mean repeat it, I mean, really, do you have a sister?"

"No, no," she said. "I don't mean repeat it, I mean, really, do you have a sister?"

Jesus, I thought. Again! Just like my little brother.

"Oh God! Give me a break," I requested.

"Oh God! Give me a break," she said.

Now, I decided to use my fierce intellect on her. "I am stupid," I said.

"You are stupid," she rejoined.

Damn! She was too quick for me.

"Yes I am," she said.

I slumped back on the bed. It seemed as though it was going to be a long night.

There was one thing I wanted to know, and maybe she could tell me, so I asked, "Are we safe?"

"Yes," she answered. "For the time being."

"What do you mean 'time being?'" Marat asked.

"You are safe right now," she said. "Ten minutes from now, I have no idea."

"No idea?" I repeated in wonder.

"No idea," she said and I hoped we hadn't got back to the repeating part.

"I only tell the present," she said.

"The present!" Marat exclaimed. "What kind of medium only tells the present. That is less than worthless."

"My kind," she responded. "And you better watch it. I can tell that you are thinking of not paying me. Now give me the *verstunken* pesos...you know, I can tell the future if I want," she added, tantalizingly.

Marat forked over ten *pesos*.

"But," she said as she turned and headed out the door, "I choose not to. By the way, you are still safe."

She was out the door.

"You're still safe," she said.

Then in the distance, I could hear, "Everything's still hunky-dory."

I closed my eyes, and hungry, grimy and sore as I was, once more fell back to sleep. I didn't wake up until the next morning when I was vigorously jostled by Marat.

"Get up! Get up!" he said in a hushed but urgent tone. "We have to go."

As my brain started realizing it was awake, I briefly wondered why he was talking in a loud whisper. There was this urgency about him that was surprising.

"Can I take a shower?" I asked, not caring if he approved or not. I needed a shower and I was going to take one. By now, I figured I could make it on my own. If he was in such a hurry, he could go.

"Be fast," he said, looking at his watch. "I want to be out of here. We've wasted too much time. We need to get to Mexico City."

As I showered in the cold water, my senses returned and so did my old suspicions, and I wondered if Marat had wandered the city and seen the *Federale* Chief, or, if he had cuckolded someone else. I might as well have been with the dead all night and I had no idea what mischief he had been up to. But I hurried and in five minutes I was showered, scrubbed, dried, dressed, packed and walking out of the hotel.

In the cool morning air *Ajijic* looked quite different. All I could remember from the previous night were Brahmas. Now I could see business establishments lining the main street: *cantinas*, other hotels, a police station, clothing stores, a market with artisan's kiosks and a couple of three-legged dogs. It took us a good ten minutes before we were out in the open, walking between grassy fields on either side of the narrow road.

"You know," Marat said as we walked, his pace faster than usual. "I want to go to Cuba. To work in the sugarcane fields with the people. You interested?"

"Well," I said, looking at him with mild surprise. There had been many times on the trip where I thought he couldn't wait to deposit me in Mexico City and wash his hands of me. That he'd have a better trip without a gimp or a conscience slowing him down. "It's illegal for an American to go there. Actually, I think we can go, but it's illegal for us to spend money there."

"So what," Marat said. "You go through Mexico, don't use a passport, which you don't have anyway, and it's *no problemo*. Nobody will know you are there and you hardly have any money left anyway."

For some reason Cuba had always fascinated me. I greatly admired *For Whom The Bell Tolls* and I always associated Hemingway with Cuba—he came up with the plot of the story while staying at the *Hotel Ambos Mundos* in *La Habana Vieja. Batista, Castro* and *Che* were history in the making and Hemingway was there. An older friend had a drink with Hemingway at a bar, and my uncle had been to Cuba in the fifties.

And throwing off the tyrant did have its romantic images; and in Cuba it was already done, a major plus.

"So you are a communist after all," I said with undisguised glee. I had caught him out, finally.

He promptly ignored me.

"*Castro* has taken that country, what, since '59, and look what he's done. He's stared down the United States, beaten back an invasion, arranged a friendship with Russia. Those are impressive in themselves. But the most important thing is that you look at this country, Mexico, and you look at the haves and the have-nots, no? Have you ever seen such a disparity between these two? The slums you visited in *San Luis Potosi* compared to *Tapatia*? Extreme, no? This is what I mean. As far as I know, it was much the same way in Cuba before the *Revolucion. Castro* has introduced universal medicine, universal education. His people are probably the best educated and well cared for in the third world. I know a man from Argentina who told me he'd go to Cuba if he had a life-threatening disease rather than be treated in his own country."

We were now out of the city and walking away from the lake. We had not yet stuck out our thumbs and it was getting hotter. Marat took out two bananas and handed me one as if he had read my mind. We peeled in unison and began to eat as we walked.

"I know a girl living in Peru, but from Cuba," he went on. "She had left Havana to visit relatives and had not gone back when she was supposed to. She liked the freedom, but said that if she got pregnant, she would go back for her baby, regardless of the consequences. For the medical care."

"The only reason the U.S. hates him is because he national-ized U.S. corporate holdings and they got nothing."

"The Cubans in your country…they hate him because they had the good life, and he took it away. He gave it to other people in a more equitable way."

"So you're saying he traded one group of people in power for another group of people in power," I said.

Marat paused in his soliloquy. He looked like he was think-ing. "Yes," he said. "I'd agree with that. The only thing is, the group of people thrown out were few, the group of people that have benefited from *Castro* are many. So it was for the good of the many that he threw out *Batista*."

"I am not an idiot," Marat said with rare emphasis. "Sartre knew what was going on under Stalin and he never said a word. Many leftists in the U.S. did the same. Most communist regimes have forsaken their promise, many becoming worse than their predecessors. *Castro* has killed people, yes, and jailed many, but he has actually worked to make the lot of the common man better."

"Perhaps I should worry about you," Marat then said.

"Why?"

"Look what happened to *Castro* when he could not have his baseball career," Marat said. "And now you…you can no longer play tennis."

That was it! Now I knew my life's calling: I would overthrow Nixon and the military-industrial complex.

It was a long walk out to the main highway. And sitting in a large grassy field to our left was a policeman's car. Just sitting there, no more, no less. Still, as I looked at him briefly, then changed my attention to the *Pemex* Station at the highway junc-tion where Marat wanted to start hitching, a bead of sweat began its short journey from the back of my neck to my waist.

"See the police car?" I asked Marat.

"Don't worry," he said. "It's a local cop."

As we put our bags down on the side of the road, across from the gas station, I asked, "How much do I owe you for the room?" We usually split the bills down the middle.

"Nothing. Don't worry about it," he said.

"What do you mean, nothing?" I asked somewhat surprised. "It was that cheap?"

"No," Marat answered. "I didn't pay for it."

"You what!" I exclaimed incredulously and that single police car now looked poised to strike. "You didn't pay for it?" So that's why he was in such a hurry. Images of dark, filthy, vermin-ridden Mexican prisons once more formed in my mind. Horror stories had made their way north for many years—the only good thing is you might be able to bribe your way out of minor offenses. If you don't like anything else about the U.S., one thing you have to like is the legal system. I'm not saying that every trial is just and everybody is exactly equal under the law, but at least our judicial system aspires to that standard.

Still, this was a crime anywhere and we'd be guilty anywhere, though it had to be a minor offense if there ever was one.

But then there's always tomas guy that wants to set an example for other wanton foreign lawbreakers.

The man who minutes before was talking about benefiting the many and helping the people had now basically robbed the guy who was kind enough to open his unfinished hotel to us.

"Do you have any idea what Mexican jails are like?" I asked Marat.

"I tried to find him," Marat answered, a little miffed. "But I couldn't find him and I wanted to get on the road."

"Why didn't you just leave some money for him?"

"If I left some money for him," Marat said, "and somebody else found it first, then we'd be in the same boat and less the money as well."

"Jesus," I said, shaking my head. "We could've at least taken a bus out of there. Then we'd at least have a chance for a getaway. We spent...he's had an hour to tell the police, and that guy's just sitting there waiting for us. And who knows when we'll get a ride. We're just sitting ducks out here. That guy," I said, nodding toward the police car in the field, "he'll end up being our ride."

"Don't be so nervous, Tomas," Marat said as if talking to a little child who was upset for lack of understanding. "If the police ask us, we just say we left money for him. And we tell them where we left it. And if it's not there, which it won't be, we act surprised and say somebody must have stolen it. Then we'll give him the money...finished."

Of all the lame-brained stunts.

For all his travels, I don't think Marat understood the helplessness of being completely in someone else's power. I only understood it from watching countless movies and from my basketball coach. You break the law in a foreign country, you have no power whatsoever. Plus, it violated one of my rules as originally formulated by Patrick, my brother. And Marat had the same rule: don't mess with the law in a foreign country. Go figure.

I was none too happy as we stood out in the open in the morning sun, waiting for a ride. Now the sun, for the first time on our trip, started baking us. The car in the field had not moved an inch. Well, I thought, at least it isn't raining. A cooling wind came up off the lake.

Every two minutes, I'd sneak a look at the police car, only a hundred yards away. I wondered what he was waiting for. Two hours passed. He must've heard by now of the two craven, *gringo* tourists who cheated a kindly old man out of his money.

Now it began to rain, and the wind turned from cool and refreshing to cold.

Soon, we were soaked to the bone. A nice warm prison cell looked pretty good right about then.

Then, a big Chevy station wagon pulled up with three young guys in the front seat and three more in the back seat. I guess in Mexico, the station wagons take up the role of the Volkswagens back home.

Marat and I were ushered into the rear of the wagon where we could only lie down, but comfort be damned. A few minutes and we would be out of there, and just possibly home free.

But as we started moving, I saw the cop car start moving as well, in a slow creep. Sure enough, he turned onto the highway and followed us, keeping the same speed and distance behind us.

Accelerating when we accelerated, slowing down when we slowed down, he never seemed to vary, always staying about a third of a mile behind.

Lago de Chapala was huge and always on our left as we continued down the road. As we reached a straightaway, the driver got the car up to around sixty, and all of a sudden, the police car's lights came on and his siren started blaring.

I guess he wanted more of a challenge—a moving stop. Probably hadn't dealt with more than drunks, chicken thefts or things like that. I could understand. *Ajijic* was a small town. The police in my hometown get excited when anything out of the ordinary happens. Usually, they only get summoned because Lena Knudson's house was broken into and her Dale Earnhardt autographed rug was stolen along with some deer antlers, or Ole Olson's wife hit a cow with her pickup, or Sven Johnson hacked off his toe while trying to butcher a pig. You can read all about it in the police blotter-accident report for the local weekly, The *Whiskey Creek Journal.* Then there were the assorted DUI's, speeding and going across the centerline offenses. Hell! These poor guys were bored. Yeah, I could understand. For him, this was something—two *gringos* and he got to nab them by himself. It would make a much better story for his girlfriend, buddies or mom if he had to run us down in a high speed chase, rather than just pull up to us with our thumbs out. Otherwise, his buddies would probably say he only caught us because we thought he was going to give us a ride.

Next thing I knew, we were back in *Ajijic*, in an eight foot-by-eight-foot concrete jail cell, complete with one barred window a bit above our heads, two rickety thatched chairs, one dark hole in the floor which I took to be the multi-sex *bano,* one dirt floor crawling with vermin, and one barred door, through which we had been unceremoniously tossed.

Marat's excuse hadn't worked, nor his attempted bribe—and here we were.

This was a pretty small town and there must have been only one cell in the jail, because it was already occupied when we

arrived. Crouched down in one of the corners of the cell, was a
man with black hair and smooth brown skin—I took him to be
an Indian. He didn't look too happy, so Marat went over to have
a conversation and perhaps cheer him up. After all, this was the
best of all possible worlds.

The only thought I could now retain in my head was when
earlier, Marat asserted he was not an idiot.

Maybe I wasn't too bright either. Why didn't I think of just
going back and giving the guy his money?

Walking out on a hotel bill in Mexico, that was probably no
more than a couple of pesos—how stupid was that?

I couldn't believe it. Of all the insignificant, ignominious reasons to get tossed in the hoosegow. At least if we'd done drugs it
might've been fun, or if we'd run guns or drugs to feed Colonel
Ratas' men in the mountains, it would've had the romantic, revolutionary feel to it, not to mention the adventure element. We'd
be like *Che.* But no. We walked out on a hotel bill. The grandchildren don't hear about that one. They'd think I was a moron. I
wondered if there were any charges for the bribery—that at least
might rate as a felony and give us some credibility.

Now, the turnkey, a skinny man with a pockmarked face,
came up to the door and rested his hands on the bars. With a
sleazy smile and fractured, accented English, it sounded like he
said, "Senors. *Manana* weel be *bueno* for you. The officer
Federale wants to speak with you. He looks for two *gringos.*" He
then revealed a larger gap-toothed smile and began a villainous
laugh like Peter Lorre in a B movie.

"Jesus Christ!" I exclaimed.

Even Marat turned a little paler than usual.

Why would a *Federale* be looking for two *gringos*, I wondered? I hoped it was because he had heard two *gringos* were
traveling together when his wife was rogered, and not because
he'd seen us at the massacre and didn't want to shoot *gringos* in
front of his men.

The news had caused the slightest bit of anxiety and I had to
lie down.

I looked at Marat's new friend in the corner and I could see a cockroach crawling up his pants leg and another, seemingly preening itself on his bare foot. There was a scorpion in the far corner near the hole, and it was small so it might be one of the real venomous kinds. I certainly hoped so. I gave up on the idea of lying down.

There were the two chairs, but Marat had one of them, which he'd pulled up to the hardened criminal of the cell to continue the conversation in relative comfort, and on the other was the biggest, blackest, ugliest, meanest tarantula I'd ever seen. I decided to usurp his position, but every time I made a move, the tarantula turned in my direction to fend me off. Remembering the Brahmas, I suspected a conspiracy. Whether I approached from the north, east, south or west didn't matter. Even if I feinted in one direction, he'd quickly recover—the little bastard was trying to intimidate me. He'd better watch out, or he was going down the hole.

So, I decided I might as well spend the night standing.

I leaned against the damp wall furthest from the scorpion and tried to close my eyes. Certainly we'd need our strength to contend with the torture lying ahead.

I'd been in jail a lot before but as a visitor not a detainee. I prefer my jails that way.

Boy, what I wouldn't have given for an old-fashioned jailbreak. I could imagine Errol Flynn tying a rope to the bars of the window. But then I heard something. I looked at Marat and the other evildoer and they were both staring up at the window, and sure enough, there were gnarled, grimy hands there, and they were tying a rope to the bars. Now I closed my eyes again and forcefully thought of Kirk Douglas outside planting explosives. No. Wait. Bad idea. Wall could come down on our heads. So I imagined Kirk tying the rope to a team of horses. I listened. Sure enough, I could hear the neighing of a horse and the braying of a burro—it was a Goddamned convention—and sort of a clippity clop sound, like a horse prancing about on the street right outside our cell. All of a sudden, I heard a whip snap and I closed my eyes as tight as possible and imagined Burt Lancaster shouting for the horses to gallop and the bars being pulled from the wall. Immediately, the bars were wrenched from their sockets and burst free of the wall, and I thought, I should try this positive thinking more often, especially with women and break point.

And the first one in shall be the first one out. The desperate outlaw on the floor jumped up, grabbing the chair from Marat and putting it against the wall below the window. There were shouts from inside the jail sounding like the pock-marked man, but the bandit was up and squeezing through the window in a flash.

"Come," Marat said, and he grabbed my arm and pulled me to the chair.

"Are you crazy?" I yelled, now coming to my senses. I was now holding the chair for Marat.

"You want to add jailbreak to our resume?"

Marat was halfway through the window. I was on the chair.

"We'll spend the rest of our lives in some stink hole like this," I explained, as I dangled halfway out the window.

By the time Marat was out of the window and thudding onto the ground, a swarthy looking Mexican fellow, heavily mustachioed and complete with poncho, sombrero, bandoleer and rifle, was greeting our new friend in an affectionate manner, kissing him on both cheeks. No Errol, Burt or Kirk. Just five of them looking all like the first in the dim streetlight, their horses turning and rearing as if they couldn't wait to leave. The leader swung our cellmate up onto his horse, motioned toward us and then questioned him. He looked us up and down, and now, we could hear more yelling coming from inside the jail.

The big man pointed his rifle at us. Another first. Nobody had ever pointed a gun at me, not a real gun anyway.

"*Senors*," he said. "You have a choice. You can stay here, or come with us." His horse turned in a complete circle then reared up. "But if you come with us, you must join us," he said as he regained control of his mount.

Now, the jailer's face appeared through the disbarred window. "You *chinga tu madres*!" he screamed in a frenzied voice. "I catch you and keel you!"

Turning back, I realized the jail keeper's words were directed at all of us but I took it personally. "Oh yeah," I yelled. "May you live in interesting times!"

It was the best I could do on such short notice.

Before he could escalate the trash talking a hail of bullets splattered against the jail wall, sending him to the floor.

Now, I was incredulous as Marat, like a rodeo cowboy, and with a loud "Whoop!" ran and jumped onto the back of one of the horses. One of the others, who was on a mule, held out his arm to me and I went for it, swinging up behind him. This pissed me off. Marat got a horse.

"*Banditos?*" I yelled to Marat as we began to gallop down the dirt street.

"*Banditos,*" Marat shouted back. "Or rebels."

I could hear the leader laugh as he called back to us, "We ain't no rebels! We are the *banditos*. We love *dinero*!" Then he began to sing, but it was more like a chant: "Gold, swag, loot, filthy lucre, silver, oil, platinum, *dinero*"—this is a rough translation. The men hummed along.

My first thought was Wow! Here we are, galloping down the street of a modern town as though it was sixty years ago. I felt like a cross between John Reed riding with *Pancho Villa* and John Dillinger (on account of the Minnesota connection). Considering my mount, I probably should've felt more like *Sancho Panza*.

Sirens began to sound as we turned down a side street. Here, off of the main road, it was completely dark and I had no idea where we were going—these guys didn't carry flashlights.

Now I could feel my mule heading downward so I speculated we were going into a riverbed or canyon, and the police sirens were nearer. Hell, of course they were. We were on horses and donkeys for crying out loud. But we were on a narrow path and I hoped no cars could follow us. Of course, if Marat's luck held, the path would probably widen out or the cops had jeeps with good clearance and four-wheel-drive.

As I leaned back with my hands braced on the mule's rump for balance, Marat, on a horse in front of me, turned around and shouted with glee, "Hey Tomas, this is getting to be a great adventure, no?" And he laughed.

I now reconsidered the order of my mistakes. Obviously the first big one was coming down here with him. This was my second thought.

By now, I decided the king of the *banditos* was not being completely frank with us. They were most likely kidnapping us and telling us we could join up so we wouldn't start a ruckus. But there could be another reason. After all, they had found us hardened criminals in a jail cell with their compatriot and did not yet know exactly who they were dealing with. In their eyes we might actually be nefarious lawbreakers, murderers, rapists, counterfeiters, drug smugglers or gunrunners. Perhaps we could even be of service in their greedy, wicked activities. Teach them a few new tricks. So he was biding his time until he had more information.

Anyway, our status with them was yet to be determined. But then it dawned on me. The bandits had us, not the police. Nor was the *Federale* head mucky muck going to torture us in the morning for the plundering of his wife or eliminate potential witnesses to his wicked deeds. So this was a good thing. This was my third line of thinking and now I decided I should quit while I was ahead, plus it looked like we'd made our getaway.

We now crossed a small stream and headed uphill. I still couldn't see further than the horse and rider in front of me.

CHAPTER 11

Banditos

"Life is hard. It's harder if you're stupid –John Wayne

We continued uphill for some time. There were gentle slopes where we stayed on mule and horseback, then more medium and steep slopes where we got down to ease the strain on our mounts as we proceeded upward, but almost always in a zigzag, switchback pattern. Except for the trail beneath my feet, I couldn't see a thing. It was so dark under the trees on the mountain that I could only hear the footsteps and hoof steps of myself and the mule, and the bandit immediately in front of me, who led our beast. There was little or no talking. The man who had given me a ride, had tried to make a little conversation early on but I couldn't understand him.

This continued for about an hour till we were far up on the mountain.

My mule was pretty sure-footed, but still, when I rode, I was glad for the darkness so I couldn't see how precarious the trail really was. Like I've said, though I've climbed before, I was no great fan of heights. I like the feel of the ground under my feet and every time we mounted, I was nervous. By now, I had decided to believe the leader—that these guys were *banditos*—and having nothing else to do, my mind wandered and wondered what it would be like to actually *be* accepted into their brotherhood—become a *bandito*.

Thoughts of Burt, Errol and Kirk came back to mind. Oops, I guess they mostly played lawmen or pirates, but there wasn't any open salt water nearby, and so these *banditos* would have to do as my new role models.

The smell of the horses, mixed with the grime and B.O. of the bandit hiking in front of me, and the pure musty smell of the brush and pine trees made me feel like I was in some old movie western. I wondered if this was going to be one of those from the frying pan into the fire episodes.

I could just see Marat lobbying them to change their operations to robbing the rich and giving to the poor. I figured these guys robbed from anybody and gave to themselves. Still, it was quite the picture to imagine Marat in his maroon alpaca sweater reaching down to his knees, bandoleers crisscrossing his chest, maybe an eye patch over one eye, and a black bandana wrapped over his hair, all under a sombrero. He'd have to have a thick mustache, if he could grow one (this had always been a question for him), and dye it black like the ones these guys sported—light brown just wouldn't be intimidating enough. In a fit of whimsy, I wondered if any *bandito* had ever uttered, "Aarrgg! Jim boy!" or what the translation would be in Spanish. Can't tell you why, but somehow—with apologies to all the *banditos* out there, pirates seemed more spectacular than mere *banditos*.

As I followed the mule around the corner of another switchback and started up again, I could see below the lights of what I figured was *Ajijic*, and I could just make out the still ringing sirens, by now quite faint. I could even see the little cherry tops blinking on and off as the police cars sped to and fro. I had no idea what they were chasing now. Maybe they thought we were still in the town.

We weren't that far as the crow flies and we heard the sirens for the better part of the next hour, whenever we were on a side of the mountain facing the lake. As we went further into the *Sierra Madre*, the sirens receded and once again, as we kept climbing, the only sounds I heard were my own labored breathing and the hooves of the mule against the dirt trail.

In another hour, it seemed a bit lighter—probably by then my eyes were more adjusted. At once, everyone's eyes turned to the northeastern sky, as a dim sound reached our ears. In unison, everyone of the *banditos* stopped moving, with all of us, motionless and silent, turning our ears in that same direction. It wasn't long before I recognized the sound of a helicopter, the blades churning the sky and sounding like Colonel Kilgore's AirCav swooping in on a Viet Cong village and killing everything in sight. I hoped these pilots didn't have the same tendencies.

Choppers! I certainly hadn't thought of that.

By this time, we had crested the first ridge and started down the other side of the mountain into a valley. As the ground was level, we had mounted and rode once more. Recollecting the other day's climb, and the hills and lowlands seemingly stretching out for miles, I figured we'd cross the valley and once more start upward. Of course, I had no idea how far into these mountains the *banditos* hung out.

We started moving again and the sound grew louder then fainter, disappearing occasionally, and then coming back fuller than ever. The helicopter must have been going back and forth in some kind of search pattern. Twenty more minutes had passed before we could see a far off light in the dark sky.

By then, the copter was heading toward us and we could see the search beam it was sending back and forth onto the trees and ground below it.

Great, I thought. If I'd gone to Nam, at least I'd have been the one in the air with the guns. To me, it looked like they were covering every possible hiding place, and we stood out like hunters in their bright orange jackets. Well at least they wouldn't mistake us for deer.

As soon as our fearless leader felt the helicopter had come too close, he ordered us to disperse and spread out in the underbrush away from the trail. Everyone quickly dismounted and led their horses into the brush and got them down on their forelegs—my buddy took the reins of his mule, another, Marat's horse—I guess they didn't trust us yet.

I started to go over to Marat, crouching down as I moved, but my companion of the mule grabbed my arm and motioned for me to get down.

I was quite aware of what an incredible expanse of ground we were on, but I still felt I was up on stage and everybody could see the spotlight was making its way directly toward me, and the audience would soon see I didn't know my lines. How could they have come even this close, I wondered? It must be a conspiracy. I looked at everyone of the *banditos* in view and tried to ferret out which one was the plant, the traitor.

Would we be rescued? Would that be good? Probably not. Back to jail, with the bad food and water that we had so far been spared. I'd probably have the touristas night and day—they might as well just inject me with dysentery or cholera. And let's don't forget *Federale Commandante* Assad.

I wondered how much time we'd get for jail breaking? We did have a pretty good excuse, and no doubt Marat would try to sell them on our being kidnapped, but then again, we all know how successful he'd been so far. Perhaps he should confine his haggling to sweaters.

The chopping of the chopper blades grew louder and the search beam drew ever closer, crossing a wide swath of territory, seemingly missing nothing and illuminating trees only yards away from some of the *banditos*. Then, from my vantage point, I could see light glancing off my new comrades, who stayed completely immobile.

Soon, the beam passed over me and the muleteer, and to my great relief, it kept going, continuing its search pattern, and there was no indication that they'd seen any of us. I closed my eyes as it passed and hoped the others were as wily as us *gringos*.

As the helicopter receded into the night air, soon crossing a ridge and disappearing except for the noise of its rotor blades, we all got up. Now everybody walked his mount along the trail and we headed in the direction that the chopper had left.

All the bandits seemed to be speaking nervously, as if they were as relieved as I was. But in another ten minutes as we reached the valley floor, the chopper came back over the ridge and resumed its search patterns.

I'm certain the same question crossed everybody's mind—was he just going back over the area he was supposed to cover or had he seen us? Immediately, we hurried into the brush and underneath the pines.

Once more the chopper seemed to be coming straight at us, but as it continued, I could see its line of flight had changed and it veered ever so slightly to the south, its beam crisscrossing the lakeside face that we had just been on. I guess he hadn't seen us, and our leader, now impervious to the threat, got up, leading his mount forward.

Marat came up to me as we made our way through the brush and back to the trail. I guess he thought I worried a lot.

"Don't worry," he said. "This is so vast an area the helicopter will never find us. Not at night. He would have a hard enough time finding us in the light." He patted me on the shoulder. "How are the legs?" he asked.

"Fine," I answered. I hadn't really thought about them in all the excitement.

Then Marat nodded and went forward to join his rider.

Now we entered into a narrow valley—pretty open and without much cover—so we mounted and walked them quickly across in a little less than a trot. Even with the night to cover any blown-up dust, the bandits didn't take any more risks than need be.

The rider in front of me kept his eyes on the southern sky for the whole crossing, and continually crossed himself for the whole time we were in the open.

Then we started uphill again. By now, the horses were quite fatigued and once more everyone dismounted.

It must've taken ninety minutes before we got to the top of the next ridge. Most of the time, when we were walking the horses, I'd only looked at the ground, making sure of my steps, but now I looked up and saw a sky full of stars. It was magnificent, stretching across the entire horizon, now unblocked by the ever-present peaks of the mountains, and unsullied by man-made aircraft and city lights.

Bringing up the rear, I could see the silhouettes of the *banditos* and their mounts against the sky, like some Remington painting from the last century.

As I caught my breath, I realized I could no longer hear the drone of the chopper blades. From this ridge, which was the highest we'd climbed, all evidence of civilization, of cities and police cars, sirens and lights, had disappeared. We were alone, and safe—if you discount our captors.

In another hour's time, we came down into yet another valley, this one thick with forests. After mounting once more, we set out over this plain just as raindrops began to fall. I held my hands cupped to catch as much as I could, drinking a few handfuls then turning my face skyward for a wash.

We then rode through a downpour, replete with so many bolts of lightning that I was glad I hadn't brought any golf clubs. It let up as quickly as it had come, when a heavy wind blew it toward the lake.

It was silent again for the next half-hour and we were still in the valley when I could hear voices in the near distance.

The next thing I knew, we were entering the periphery of a small camp. I wasn't very impressed as I peered through the darkness to make out branch-covered lean-tos and a few small dark-colored tents. I could count perhaps a dozen bodies strewn about on the ground, sleeping outside under ponchos and heavy blankets.

These guys didn't even have the sense to have pickets, unless their sentries had recognized us and let us by without a peep. I didn't think so.

My father was a war hero, at least to me he was. An army engineer, he had memorized the eye chart so he could pass his physical to become an officer. He had finished a twenty-five mile hike, with one boot missing a heel that had fallen off in the tenth mile. All this, so he could be one of the first on the beaches and receive two purple hearts in MacArthur's march back to the Philippines. I had been regaled with enough war stories during my childhood to know these *banditos* were second raters.

It was very obvious to me that if there were choppers looking for us, there were also soldiers on the ground.

It was getting cold up here as the evening grew later and we were drenched, Marat looking like a drowned beaver in his now dark maroon alpaca. There were not many people up and about—only a few men and women, but those who were awake all came up to our cellmate, Rafael, and hugged him and kissed him on his cheeks.

I could see that he winced with every hug and wondered why.

I also wondered if it was appropriate to strip out of our clothes, but remembered that I had gotten strange looks earlier on the trip just for wearing shorts. There was always the possibility they might shoot us for baring our bodies in front of the womenfolk.

The people pointed to Marat and me—I guess they were asking questions. Soon, many wandered over to Marat and patted him on the shoulder or shook his hand—those that hugged him got soaked. With me, they just looked me up and down as if they didn't know what to make of me.

I would've loved a steaming cup of coffee right then, but I didn't think they were stupid enough to light a fire with a chopper up in the air looking for them.

A woman brought over some stew that I found out had been cooked earlier that day, and began doling it out to our rescuers and then to us. The stew had been buried under sun-baked rocks during the day and was still lukewarm, though it was *mucho caliente* in spices. I took one bite and decided I'd be better off hungry.

After we'd eaten, Marat anyway, they ushered us into one of the dark green tents—at least they were camouflaged, which showed some sense—waved and left. Thankfully, the valley near the camp was sheltered from much of the wind. They had established it in a narrow slot between two low hills.

I quickly took off my cold shirt and wrung some of the water out in a corner of the tent.

"How come they were so friendly to you?" I asked Marat.

He laughed. "When they asked about us," he said, "our cell-mate pointed to me and told them that we became good friends in the jail. As for you, he said he didn't know anything."

Great, I thought. I seem to be winning all the popularity contests with the women, and Marat's winning all the popularity contests with the common man and the bandits. That's definitely a switch from my norm. Oops. I forgot about the *Federales'* wife so we were even on that score.

So, I hesitatingly asked Marat, "So, did he, the leader I mean, back there at the jailbreak, kinda mean now that we're here it's sort of, join us or die?"

"Probably," Marat said, gleefully. "You might want to prepare yourself mentally, like you would as an athlete for a lifetime of banditry."

I do believe he was enjoying himself.

And maybe I was wrong. After all, the police wanted us, the *Federales* wanted us, and now the *banditos* wanted us. We were in this together. As long as I stuck with Marat, I'd have no worries about being popular.

We stayed in the camp for two days and nights, and each of those days and nights, helicopters flew near or over the vicinity of the camp.

During that time, I found out that Rafael had been whipped and beaten. Neither Marat nor I had been able to see his features clearly in the dim light of the jail call, lit by its single low watt bulb.

We learned that they didn't stay in any one place very long and that helicopters and small planes were almost constant companions, but as long as they didn't get caught in one of the few treeless, open valleys, they were as good as invisible from the air. The constant movement was to err on the side of caution.

At this moment, the leader of the camp didn't want to move further into the mountains until Rafael had recovered from his ordeal. The cuts from the whip still bled from time to time and he needed rest to regain his strength.

Each man and woman of the group had his or her own unique, pathetic story about why they became *banditos*, except for the leader, who became a bandit simply because that's what he'd always wanted to be.

Orphaned as a young child, he learned his English from American missionaries. Originally encouraged to follow in their footsteps, he had read too much, seen too much and figured that the religious life would be too boring for him.

Reading about American "Robber Barons" of the last century, he thought this was his true calling. He readily admitted he was starting small.

"I am in business," he told us as we sat around an early morning campfire. "In business, you take other people's money, no?" he asked. "That is what I do. I take other people's money."

"Yes," Marat replied. "But a business usually provides a service for the people whose money they take."

"Yes, yes," said the bandit. "You see, I provide a grand service...stories to tell their friends, parents and grandchildren, no?" Then he laughed merrily. "You pay for a potato, you eat it, it is gone until it comes out the other end, and then it is gone again. You buy a house, it burns down, so it is gone. If it does not, you live in it and pay every day of your life for it. Something is always going wrong. A car breaks down. A horse, you pay and pay and pay to feed it, house it, groom it, then it dies and you have nothing to show for it. Ah, but these stories..."

A look of wistfulness, almost accompanied by tears, entered his eyes, or maybe it was an ember from the fire.

"*Senors,*" he said. "My stories, they provide a lifetime of service. If you live a hundred years, you can tell them for a hundred years."

Then, a sparkle appeared in his eyes and a broad smile on his lips.

"And..." He held up his right forefinger for emphasis. "And, you only pay once."

He was quite proud of himself that way and thought he provided a great benefit for all those people with their boring lives.

Perhaps, I thought, but for all the banditry he professed to, they all seemed to live a pretty meager existence. I decided not to bring up just how small he was starting.

On the third night, no helicopter came around, and on the next day we moved to a spot by a river and everyone jumped in, cleansing themselves and their clothes—even two *senoritas*, one who was maybe eighteen and another older woman who might've been close to forty. Surprisingly, they waded into the stream, got out of their clothes and swam, then washed their clothes while standing naked in the river. Later, they laid in the sun while their clothes dried, draped across the pine branches.

It hadn't taken long for Marat to notice the women in camp, though I quickly glared at him for a time till he got the message, and then practiced my glare on the young girl who kept sneaking glances at, and offering furtive smiles to the Frenchman. I guessed she was drawn to his light skin and light brown hair, which was so unlike any of the swarthy men in camp.

Unfortunately, there wasn't much to do in the camp besides reading or studying Spanish, and I couldn't keep an eye on Marat twenty-four hours a day.

Her flirting had gone from the random smile the first day, to winking on the second day, and the next day, the third, I'd caught her on one occasion, blowing a kiss through the air at him.

So, while keeping an eye on the likely lovers to stave them off, I realized that after all this time there had been no talk of kidnapping or ransom.

I knew Marat was interested in the girl, who I started calling *Dulcinea* when I first saw her, because she seemed so innocent and virtuous. Certainly, she would be free and that was probably a plus for him, but she wasn't a prostitute and Marat much preferred prostitutes. He liked to perform his task and then have no responsibilities or repercussions. The girl comes, he comes, and then she goes. Finished. He wouldn't have to see her again, unless he felt like it, and there would be no guilt if he didn't. He wouldn't have to buy flowers or candy or baubles, romance her in the time-honored fashions, or any of the other little details that are so important to an actual romance. He didn't even really mind having to pay, though he would always bargain. His favorite story was how he was staying in a cheap hotel in Laos, and the first night he heard a knock on the door. Opening it cautiously, he saw a beautiful Laotian girl, with long black hair, a perfect bronze complexion, about eighteen, and well versed in Laotian art, history, food, culture and music, as well as fluent in French.

Talk about your room service.

She traveled throughout the country with him for a week, teaching him about all things Laotian, plus cooking, doing his laundry, giving him massages with the required happy ending and sleeping with him. At the end of the trip, he gave her five dollars. I'm still not certain if he liked telling the story so much because she was an incredible woman or if he'd gotten all that for a fiver.

For all his intelligence, Marat certainly had his blind spots.

On the fourth day, I found out that I hadn't kept a good enough eye on Marat or the girl.

Right after breakfast, as Marat and I sat talking under a pine tree in the morning sun, me lying on my back and propped up on my elbows, and Marat lying on his side and appearing quite satisfied, the leader of the bandits—the one who'd rescued us—approached us, accompanied by three of his biggest, vilest, meanest looking men.

With angry expressions on all faces, they screamed at Marat with what I took to be curse-laced epithets, but ignored me entirely, except for a few sanctimonious glances. Then, they forced the Frenchman to his feet, tied his hands and carried him to our tent.

I have to admit, I wasn't too surprised. By now, I'd learned to take some of these things in stride, and casually wondered what luck of Marat would get him out of this, not to mention being quite satisfied that I was above reproach in the matter, and thus, uninvolved, untouched. Maybe I'd win the popularity contest after all.

The leader of the *banditos* was angry, but one of his companions was angrier—he was the brother of *Dulcinea*.

I let Marat stew for a bit, then round about noon, I slowly walked over to the tent not quite sure if it was allowed. There was a guard, but nobody seemed to care about me and no one tried to stop me. As I pulled back the tent flap and entered, I was surprised to see Marat bound up like a calf run down and roped in the rodeo, his hands tied together, his feet tied together and both tied to each other. Noting how quickly the bandits had left him in the tent, I figured they'd roped him in record time.

He did not look quite so satisfied at present, nor very comfortable.

"Let me guess..." I offered.

"Do you happen to have a Swiss Army Knife?" Marat inquired.

"Nope," I said. "What happened? The girl?"

I have to admit, he looked pretty funny, but I couldn't laugh because he kept groaning. He was bent over in two, lying on the hard ground and as I've said, not comfortable.

Now he came up with understatement of the century. It was like, "Hey Colonel Custer, there might be some Indians nearby," or "That Aussie, Rod Laver, has some potential."

"It was all my fault," Marat grunted.

Now, I don't want to be the type of person that takes pleasure in another person's sorrows or trouble—though I admit to occasionally using the word *schadenfreude*—so I only did it for a few minutes. I decided to hear his story and only then decide if I needed to come up with a plan for extricating us from the *bandito* camp.

"I knew it," Marat moaned. "I tell myself all the time, I should stick to prostitutes, no? It is all cut and dried. Planned out in advance. You know the cost. You know the result. Everybody gets what they want and then goes their way."

What'd I tell you?

"Whenever I go with a nice girl..." he said.

"A nice bandit girl," I helpfully interjected.

He grimaced and said, "Whenever I go with a nice girl, this sort of thing happens."

I wanted to ask, and so did, "Marat, what were you thinking? Are you out of your frickin' mind? You're in this small camp. There's only twenty, twenty-five people—everybody knows everybody else. Everybody's probably related...and you let yourself...let me guess, she seduced you."

"How did you know?" Marat asked excitedly. "You're right!"

Two PhDs., I thought.

"Still having a good time?" I politely inquired.

He groaned, as his demeanor darkened. "I'm not sure this will turn out well," he opined.

Two PhDs., I thought, *and* a flair for the obvious. Of course, having a flair for the obvious is better than not having a flair for the obvious.

"What's going to happen?" I asked.

"I think they will want me to marry her," he said.

Marry her, I thought, that's not so bad. They could've wanted to castrate or disembowel him, and maybe if they were pissed off enough, me as well.

"If I refuse," he added, "they will probably castrate or disembowel me and then kill me. I doubt if it would be a very pleasant death."

As if there are any, I mused and wondered where this one would place on my scale.

I was having a hard time finding sympathy for him. He knows this, that they might kill him, but he didn't know enough to keep Marat Jr. in his pants. He violated his own damn rules. I was only here because of him. Now I wondered how I would be affected by his indiscretion. After all, a man is considered by the company he keeps. I was not even counted as a friend by Rafael, so they might have no interest in keeping me around—perhaps ransom would raise its ugly head again—or death by Bunga Bunga.

"Any idea when all this is going to take place...your decision, I mean?"

"Three of them and the girl's mother are journeying to a village to get a priest they know," Marat said.

"To perform the service?" I asked.

"That or the last rights," Marat groaned.

I could see the shadow of the large guard on the canvas of the tent. He was close by and I wondered if he could hear us and understand English.

Regardless of how moronic and thoughtless I figured Marat had been in this situation, we were friends. We had come a long way and I couldn't just leave him to his fate.

"I think you should marry her," I said loudly.

I'm not going to say that I'm a man of action, but I was an athlete and I knew a little bit about strategy, bluffing, intimidation, ferreting out a weakness or two, and most importantly, deceit.

Quietly, I moved closer to where Marat was bound.

With one eye on the shadow, I examined the knots. I had been an Eagle Boy Scout and as such, had a passing familiarity with knots. Unfortunately, mostly we learned to tie them. In the movies, the hero usually manages to undo the ropes himself, and here Marat had a willing accomplice so this should be easy.

I tried to slip my finger in between the knotted strands to see if I could stretch them at all, but they were way too tight. I couldn't budge them and anything I did seemed to make them tighter. These were done well and I developed a professional appreciation for the complexity with which they were fastened. This was going to take some time, and if I couldn't come up with something sharp, we were sunk.

"They're on pretty tight," I said.

"They were tied by a big, fat man," Marat said, his face in a perpetual grimace. "They called him *El Gordo*."

Worried the guard would hear us, I started speaking the little French I knew in fits and starts.

"Did they say how long they'd be gone?" I asked in my meager French, admonishing Marat to speak slowly so I could understand.

"It sounded like it was a day trip," Marat answered. "They could be back as late as tomorrow morning, or as soon as tonight."

"Did they say they were going to kill me too?" I asked, thinking it was pretty strange to hear those particular words coming out of my mouth whether in French or English.

"No," Marat said. "They don't care about you...as long as you go along with the band's decision."

I stared at him for a second, pondering whether if I let him hang for a few moments it might help him reform. But I couldn't.

"They did say something about you being stupid for traveling with a man like me," Marat added, laughing for the first time, though this quickly turned into a groan as his movement further tightened the thick ropes.

I would've laughed, but I was busy trying to come up with a plan.

"I'm going to get us out of this," I said simply.

There was a look of surprise, then genuine affection on his face.

CHAPTER 12

Gagool

"Her hair is like a flock of goats descending the slopes of Mount Gilead." –Song of Solomon 4:1

There was a third lady, much older, who I had taken to calling Gagool on account of her weather-beaten skin, scraggly hair and hunched over back, the fact that she looked to be over two hundred years old, possibly had been friends with the Aztec rulers and was only three upper teeth short of an empty mouth, who then entered the tent, bringing two bowls of hot porridge. She was accompanied by a contrite *Dulcinea* (though now I was thinking of changing her name to Jezebel) holding two cups of coffee.

Dulcinea was allowed to hand me my cup, then the old crone shooed her from the tent, apparently thinking she and Marat could still get up to mischief even in Marat's waylaid condition.

Then Gagool walked over to the prone Marat, knelt down and slapped him hard enough across the face to leave a red finger-shaped welt on his jaw.

Next, she motioned for me to come over, which I did, warily, and then we helped sit him up to eat the porridge and sip the coffee.

"Ask her if I can go outside," I told Marat, and I found out there were no prohibitions whatsoever regarding me.

When we had finished eating, she laughed, said something in Spanish and left with the bowls and cups.

Marat told me she said she didn't want to treat her future grandson-in-law *too* badly.

The Frenchman could be stubborn. And even though I hadn't really asked if he was going to go through with the marriage, I could see him saying no and just walking out and being shot on principle.

"You know," he said, as if reading my mind. "I could marry her, then wait till all the suspicions and anger died down, and then just leave, but that would not be right. If I marry her, then I have to assume the responsibility, no?"

Another surprise, another principle. Nothing like taking responsibility. I threw up my hands in exasperation and went out of the tent. It looked like I'd have to save him before the wedding. That gave me one day and maybe a night, and I had no Spanish with which to form an allegiance (bribe) with any of the *banditos*, and I still was pretty slow on my feet, though by now I could feel that wisps of strength were finally returning to my legs.

I needed to think and I needed to warm up, so I went to the campfire, got another cup of coffee and walked to the river, found a nice spot in the sun, sat down, got comfortable and begin to ponder the vicissitudes of life and banditry between sips of scalding hot coffee.

I hadn't been sitting for long when *Dulcinea*-Jezebel walked up behind me, and I swear, gave me the same kind of grin she'd given Marat at the start of their dalliance a couple of days before. Very discreetly—she was discreet in some matters—she knelt down, and dropped a small wrapping by my feet while in the action of putting her hands in the water to wash. She winked at me, then blew a kiss and then got up and left.

Oh oh, I thought. She's accelerating the process. So nervous about this prospect, though I knew I'd have the fortitude to resist her, I forgot the package at my feet for a few seconds.

Recovering, I looked down at it. Then I looked around as I moved it closer with my left foot. Now it was between my legs and hidden under them. No one was close. I started to reach for it when I heard a crack of a twig coming from the direction of the camp. I slowly reclined against the riverbank, making certain the package was covered. It felt hard under my leg and my curiosity was up.

The guard from Marat's tent emerged from the pine trees, came down to the creek and washed his dishes. Looking over at me suspiciously, he then waded in and bathed fully clothed. I wondered if all the bandits were now prohibited from bathing nude around the *gringos*—even the males. Who knows what evil lurks in the heart of a *gringo*?

As he got out of the stream and left, I bided my time, casually looking back toward the camp at random intervals.

Then, another bandit appeared, also coming down to the creek. This one splashed water on his face, looked at me, grunted something unintelligible and left. Five minutes later, yet another man came, then another. None of them coming in pairs but always alone. They must be keeping an eye on me, I thought, but at least they're doing it with fairly consistent timing. I checked my watch— every five minutes a new man arrived at the river. This was going to be easy, I thought. Then I remembered, in a tennis match, as soon as you started to think you had it in the bag, you were doomed. I became more cautious.

When the current *bandito* left the stream, I looked at my watch. Following his retreat, I saw that he didn't look backward at me. Still, I waited till he had disappeared into the trees. Then I looked at the time again. I had maybe a minute if they kept to schedule and I was definitely not at all certain they would do me that courtesy. Keeping my eye on the trees, I slowly pulled the package closer using my leg. When it was close enough, I reached down, grabbed it and brought it up to my crotch, lifted my rear and sat on it.

The next person appeared like clockwork. It was Gagool, the old crone. I reckoned they were running out of men that wanted to wash.

She smiled at me and went into the stream. Dipping herself up to her neck, she then came nearer and stood up, her water-soaked dress now exhibiting her scrawny, tube-like sunken breasts. Then she placed her hands under her breasts and raised them seductively, if you could call it that. Now I knew where *Dulcinea*-Jezebel learned her tactics, though I could see she still didn't have a thing on the master.

Well, I knew from long experience that "Hell hath no fury like a woman scorned," so I was going to have to be very delicate in getting out of this. I couldn't move without revealing the package, which had begun to feel like a knife under my butt.

A knife. I guess *Dulcinea*—I decided I should return her generosity with my own, so I dropped the Jezebel from her name— either didn't want to marry him or she wanted to escape with us and see the big city. Or maybe Marat was like James Bond and once a woman had made love to him she was forever enraptured. Maybe I should ask for tips.

But right now that was the last thing I needed. Gagool was moving toward the riverbank. Holy shit! Was she actually going to try to seduce me? And I thought 007 used to get in horrifying predicaments! I figured my only chance was to play dumb, by now a piece of cake. But how? Then I remembered Kerouac. What if I got up and took a whiz in the river?

Jack Kerouac mused about a rose thrown into the Hudson drifting all the way to the sea and all the wonderful places it would pass and I had to wonder about pissing into this river and all the wonderful places I could befoul. Of course, that had nothing to do with saving my ass, but random thoughts are a trademark of mine. Oh my Lord, I bet Gagool's doing it all the time. She's over two hundred years old—probably couldn't control her bladder if she tried. Now there's an image I'm gonna have to put out of my mind.

And there she was, right in front of me, now lifting her skirt as she waded nearer. This is what one does when one wants to keep a skirt dry, but hers was already wet. I couldn't tell what from.

I expected the worst. Was she going to pee in the river thus contaminating hundreds of miles of pristine drinking water for countless innocents, or was she going to try to straddle me?

Who'd have thought I'd spend my vacation trying to not get laid or look at naked women?

She stumbled over some loose rocks near the shore and plunged headfirst into the water.

Quickly, and in one deft move, I jumped to my feet, shoved the package into a front pocket and turned to walk back to the camp. I was in the shelter of the trees, before she up-righted herself.

Making certain no one else was around as I walked through the thick woods, I felt the small parcel. It was a pocketknife. I carefully shifted it to the further side of my pocket and tried to look natural as I entered the camp.

After letting myself be seen around the campfire for a half-hour and eating a plain corn tortilla, I leisurely made my way back to the prison tent, nodded to the guard and entered.

I walked over to Marat.

"If you're ever asked," I said. "Tell the hag that I'm a virgin, have little or no knowledge of women and thought she only wanted to take a swim."

He strained to look up at me, confusion in his eyes and I could tell the long period of non-movement was taking a toll. The poor man looked downright disconsolate.

I carefully put my body in a direct line between the guard and Marat, then knelt down by the Frenchman and pulled out the package and showed him. I gingerly put it back in my pocket.

"Don't say a thing," I whispered. "Don't even try to move. Just listen...your girlfriend...she gave me a knife."

I guess I also should have warned him against pricking his ears, because they moved visibly. And his face lit up—if a face can do that. Still, I was confident I blocked the guard's view. I slowly snuck a glance and there he was in his usual position of leaning against the tent, trying to make out what we were saying.

"Repeat after me," I whispered. "But speak in Spanish."

"I think these people have treated us fairly and the food this morning was very good. Say it loud," I suggested.

He did so. I figured a little brown-nosing couldn't hurt.

"You think they're gone until tomorrow?" I whispered conspiratorially, going back to French.

"I hope," Marat replied.

"Then here's the plan," I said, beginning to massage his legs to get some circulation going. "I'm going to wait till this guy falls asleep tonight, then I'll start cutting your ropes. If he doesn't fall asleep, I'll find a rock to knock him out...something."

I really did hope that he fell asleep. I hadn't hit anyone in anger since I was a kid and two older kids spit on my little brother. I went after both of them, both of them were bigger than me, and I hoped tonight turned out better for us than that fight turned out for me.

"What if they get back with the priest earlier?" Marat asked.

I admit I liked leading the show for a change. I was getting downright arrogant. "Then I'll club then too," I said with what had to be the most false bravado ever uttered on this or any other planet.

"I guess we'll worry about that later," Marat said.

Except for his inability to resist women, he was one tough son-of-a-bitch, I thought. That whole day, he didn't complain once about the ropes or his excruciatingly painful contorted position.

I went out to have lunch. Now both Gagool and *Dulcinea* were giving me furtive, lascivious looks. Well, at least Gagool isn't mad at me, I thought. We couldn't afford any more complications before the break.

The day went by all too fast. In tennis, I'm big on practice and drills but here I wasn't at all sure I was ready, not having practiced whacking guards, cutting prisoners free and then escaping *bandito* camps and hightailing it through mountainous jungle terrain with much regularity. I guess it would soon enough be on my resume, no?

I needed to go off by myself and meditate to calm my nerves, but I didn't want to be caught alone by Gagool. My main fear was that looks or actions would give me away and I tried to put on my best game face.

The plan was simple enough, but I wondered how Marat would even be able to move after being bound up like a calf for some twenty hours. And then we were going to run across the mountains with *banditos* chasing us. I started thinking about cutting the ropes earlier, if it was feasible. After all, we'd only get one chance, and if we were caught, it would no longer just be him in trouble. We'd both go down.

Back in the tent before dinner, I massaged my own legs for a good twenty minutes. I had my own mobility problems as well.

"Marat," I asked, hopefully. "Are you sure you don't want to marry her?"

"I can't marry her, Tomas," he said. "It would be a lie, because I would just leave."

So let's see if I've got this right. He had no problem sleeping with this girl, who was under the protection of her brother, mother, great, great, great grandmother, and who was just possibly an innocent on hormones, but he did have a problem with marrying her and running off in the process of saving his life and that of a friend, who was now going to risk himself to extricate him from his folly.

Brother! Maybe I was the one making the mistake here.

Didn't I say it was always about a woman? I contend that both Paris and Agamemnon would've had less tsuris if they'd only had better dating strategies. I might as well add Clytemnestra and Marat.

I blew out a long breath and sat down to think this through. After an hour Gagool entered the tent to bring Marat food.

She looked my way and this time made a weird face. I almost thought she was going to stick her tongue out at me. Then, she went over to Marat, boosted him up, spit in his face, took her skirt in hand to wipe him off, gave me a knowing look as she examined his bonds, and began to spoon feed him.

I wondered if she'd also spit in the food, but didn't bring it up.

"Should I untie you now?" I whispered after she left. "You're going to be awfully stiff."

"I don't think we can risk it," he answered. "We only have one shot. If someone comes in, finished. You as well. I think we wait...until they go to sleep."

I didn't agree. I could see he was exhausted from the strain and stiffness of his position, mostly mentally, but was he thinking more clearly than I?

Then I went outside to scout around. It was already getting dark, and I could not see the leader anywhere. This relieved me greatly—we still had a chance.

Realistically, one never knows how long these visits to the village priest take. You have to get there, convince him to return with you or kidnap him, then you have to return with him. And what if he's old or just slow or refuses to leave or refuses to travel on a horse or wants a wagon? Needless to say...so I won't say it.

I now tried to remember how late the guards of the camp usually stayed up, but wasn't sure if I'd seen the present guard before. They all looked rather similar to me, except for Gagool and *Dulcinea*. They all had those long drooping mustaches, they were all dark-haired and dark-skinned. Was this man one of the guys that fell asleep early on previous nights? Or was he one of the ones that stayed up and talked into the night with his amigos? I wasn't sure.

I also didn't know if they took turns at guard duty or the shifts lasted all night. After all, this was the first night he was guarded and held like this and the more I thought about it, the more I thought we couldn't take the chance that the leader wouldn't be back until the next day. When you add to that the fact that Marat would need some time to stretch and get limber, the sooner I cut him loose the better. The fact was I couldn't stand the waiting; butterflies were in my stomach just like before a big match.

Retrieving a bowl, I took some rice and beans and sat down near the others. As usual, it was only lukewarm, having been cooked earlier when a fire wouldn't stand out. They used only dead, dry wood to cut down on any smoke.

Eating a platain, I secreted a few away in my pockets for the journey ahead, then walked down by the creek to be alone.

It was late December by now and the night came early. I looked at the stars and wondered what my brothers were doing, so far away. Had they crossed into Iran yet? Visited Persepolis? Susa? Kabul? Were they faring any better with *banditos* than I?

Oh brother! I just realized I haven't called my mom since I've been down here. Hope she's not worried. She doesn't even know I'm in Mexico. She's gonna kill me. Maybe my brothers will call our parents from the Khyber Pass. That would be pretty cool. They'd be the only mom and dad in town to get a call from there. As for me, first big city I reach I'll look for a phone. I wouldn't want to get in trouble.

I watched the stars for a few moments then returned to the tent.

Gagool was departing just as I approached. Marat had been right. She checked the ropes again. As I walked past her, she sneered and spat off to the side. I took that to mean she didn't want me anymore.

"How are you doing?" I asked Marat.

He coughed. "Could you wipe the spit off my face?" he asked.

Uh oh, I thought. An escalation. Last time she wiped it off.

"Is she the only one that's come in to check on you?" I whispered, as an inspiration hit me. No, I wasn't going to bonk her on the head. She was an old lady.

"Yes," Marat answered as I wiped his face.

"Not even the guard?"

"No," he said. "She's the only one besides you. The girl sometimes comes with."

"Wake me in an hour," I said, and quickly dozed off beside him.

Exactly one hour later, Marat nudged me awake. My eyes opened like a shot and I stared at the ceiling of the tent, taking a few minutes to get my bearings.

"Did she check on you again?" I asked.

"Yes. And this time she kicked me."

This was not going to get better. I looked up a few words in his Spanish book. I got up and left the tent, waving to the guard with a smile.

He grunted in return.

Now, I had no idea if this was very intelligent or if it would work, but I had to give it a try. Looking around, I couldn't believe my luck. There, sitting a little away from the others, were Gagool and *Dulcinea*.

Walking up, even in the darkness, I could see a hint of a smile come to Gagool's face. I hoped she thought I was coming around. Walking right up to her and smiling, I suddenly turned, looked at *Dulcinea* and motioned for her to stand.

Gleefully, and with a smirk-like sound directed at her great, great, great, great grandmother, she did. Then I embraced her and kissed her on the mouth, keeping on eye on the soon-to-explode Gagool.

Her expression turned from expectancy to surprise, to anger, rage and then frothing at the mouth anger.

I stood back and said in Spanish, "Tu, yo, tentio. Dos horas, no?"

Dulcinea looked at Gagool guilefully and then back at me and said, "*Si.*"

Then I walked away slowly, backing up just in case Gagool attacked.

Sure enough, Gagool rose up, spittle dripping down her leather cheeks, grabbed the girl's arm in a death clench and dragged her away.

On my return to the tent, I nodded to the guard, who was now sitting with his back to the opening, and went in. Kneeling down by Marat, I waited to see if he turned, but he didn't move. The watchman was obviously tired of all this and I wondered if they ever did take the trouble to spell him. Then I took out the package and slowly unwrapped it and began to examine the knots.

It was dark and hot in the tent. Marat had been sweating and his shirt was soaked.

"What are you doing?" he asked in a whisper.

"I don't think Gagool will come anywhere near me for a few hours," I said.

"Gagool?" he asked.

"That's what I call the hag."

"Why?" he asked.

"H. Rider Haggard. *King Solomon's Mines.*"

"You should call her Madame Charlotte," Marat wheezed.

"Why?"

"It was Madame Charlotte, who assassinated Marat," he said with quite good rhythm.

I know you're thinking that "t" in Marat should be silent, but you have to take poetic license once in awhile.

And if you're thinking the "t" is pronounced, well it's French. What do I know?

"There once was a Charlotte from Nantucket..." Marat continued. He was on a roll.

"Now just sit still and don't talk," I said as I began sawing through the ropes binding his feet and hands together. "This is going to take awhile."

He was facing me and I could see the grimace on his face. I don't know how he bore the pain so well. I would've been whining hours ago.

Of course, it sounded so loud to me that I thought everyone in the camp, not to mention the guard at the doorstep, could hear my every cut, but I continued as deliberately as possible.

I did this very slowly at first, constantly looking backward and listening to see if the guard had moved.

It was around eight P.M. by now, and soon, both Marat and I grew impatient. I increased the pace.

Still, it was another ten minutes before the first rope snapped, and Marat couldn't help but let out an "Aahh!" of relief. I stopped and looked at the tent flaps. There was still no movement. I went behind Marat and began to knead the muscles of his lower back, as he slowly and painfully tried to straighten out for the first time in some twelve hours. It was almost comical as he bent both his elbows and knees and straightened his back at the same time.

Where was a good chiropractor when you needed one?

"Quit moving so much," I whispered, as I turned him around. "Give me your hands."

Sighing quietly, he extended his arms so I was able to begin on the ropes binding his hands.

This took another fifteen minutes and then I moved down to his feet, as he massaged his wrists and then his back.

"Are you going to be able to move?" I whispered, again looking back at the front of the tent. Good. Everything was still.

"Don't worry about me," Marat whispered back. I heard both gratitude and relief as his soft voice cracked. I hate to say it, but he sounded almost like a frog had caught in his throat.

"How about your legs?" he asked me.

"I'll be fine," I answered. "You know, this life of the *bandito* has grown stale with me."

It was then I realized, I had cut the "Gordoan" knot. Granola had been close, only missing by one letter. Boy! She was good!

"Now," I whispered. "Watch what I do." And I slowly got up on all fours. "Ok," I said. "Do what I do. This will help your back recover quickly."

Marat quietly got up on all fours.

"Now arch your back," which I proceeded to do and he proceeded to imitate.

"Now thrust your pelvis forward," which I proceeded to do and he tried to imitate, but I could see he wasn't getting it. I needed a better analogy. I kept doing the movement while I thought. Probably the language barrier.

"Ok. I got it," I whispered. "Pretend you're doing *Dulcinea* doggie style."

"Ah, yes," Marat said, now getting it easily.

So the two of us humped side by side for a good two minutes, then he continued till his back started feeling normal, and I was grateful none of my friends had been around to see.

Around nine, I silently crawled over to the front of the tent and then came back.

"The boredom got to him," I said. "He's sawing z's. Let's go."

As we crawled to the rear of the tent, Marat grabbed my shoulder.

"Tomas," he said. "You know you can stay here. They don't want you. They are after me."

"Who knows," I said, starting to dig up the ground at the rear. I didn't want to have to lift up the flap too much, as I didn't know how stable it was. "Maybe to them one *gringo's* as good as the next. If you're not here they might want me to marry her and I'm too young to get married."

A smile came to his features. I think he was really touched and appreciative that I was standing by him.

While I dug, Marat took handfuls of the dirt and formed it into piles. Once he got enough dirt and folded up one of the blankets, he was going to put the second blanket over it so it looked like he was still there...I never said the plan was complex with a lot of twists.

I snuck my head under the side of the tent to see the lay of the land. It was clear. I went back in, saw that Marat was finished with his dummy, and motioned for him to come. Holding the tent material up, I let him go first, then followed.

Soon, we were walking quietly through the forest and away from their camp. After a few minutes, Marat stopped and looked up at the sky. He must've been taking bearings, because he turned. From what I could gather, we now skirted the camp and headed south, back toward Lake *Chapala*.

Fifty yards after circling the camp, he stopped again.

"You know," he whispered. "They're going to expect us to head back down to the lake, to civilization, where we'll find safety."

"I don't know," I said, scratching my now bearded chin. "What if they expect us to expect them to expect us..."

"Yes, yes," Marat interrupted.

"Besides," I said. "They found us in jail. So will they think we want to go this way and risk capture again? Remember. They think we're outlaws too."

Boy, now this was getting way too complicated.

"Do we want to go that way," I said pointing to the south, "and risk it? By now it's probably all over the news about the two renegade *gringo*s on the lam."

I sincerely wished I'd earlier spent some time thinking about the aftermath of the breakout.

"And you're as pale as ever, man," I said. "You look like such a *gringo*. You're going to stick out wherever we go."

Marat sat down and thought for awhile. I turned my attention to the direction of the camp, listening for any movement or sound.

In a few minuets, he walked over to me.

"Perhaps you are right, Tomas," he said. "Perhaps we should go further back into the hills."

Now we turned once more and headed back on our original path.

"I brought some platains and a few tortillas," I said. "And I'm sure we'll run into a stream up here so we won't go thirsty. We'll be ok for awhile."

"And we are bound to come across a road sooner or later," he added.

"Wait," I said before we'd gone more than a few yards. "What kind of trackers are these guys?"

I took the knife and pierced part of my t-shirt sleeve, then ripped off a thin strip. Then I broke a few low branches off, walked south, breaking a few more, and placed the cloth on the tree with the most southerly break. I now felt like a combination of Natty Bumppo, Daniel Boone and of course, Fess Parker.

Then we turned and headed north, but slowly, sacrificing speed for quiet, and in a direction away from the camp.

After a bit, Marat put his hand on my shoulder and he stopped walking. "Tomas. Whatever happens I want you to know how much this means to me. You are a true friend."

"Well it's been my great pleasure to assist in your excape." Just then I remembered the "join us or die" part of the *banditos'* creed. So I guess I was in as much trouble as Marat anyway.

CHAPTER 13

The *Commandante*

"This is the best of all possible worlds." –Voltaire

We had only gone a few hundred yards, when I no longer felt like the trailblazer-frontiersmen type, as a lithe figure ran out of the dark and up to Marat (she gave me a smile and a wink), jumped up into his arms, wrapping her legs around his loins, hugged him, kissed him, and finally began speaking in a high-pitched, excited voice.

Marat quickly put his hand over *Dulcinea's* mouth—she was so loud I thought Gagool, the police, the *Federale's* and any helicopter pilots in the vicinity would hear her—then unwrapped her and set her down.

Apparently, she had managed to ditch Gagool and had been waiting for us to make our break. It was bittersweet to learn she hadn't outguessed us but had followed us from the beginning.

"So now I suppose we have to kill her," I said sarcastically to Marat.

But Marat, literalist as ever, said, "No no no. That would not do. She is an innocent. I would never kill anybody."

"Just kidding, Marat," I said slowly, hoping it would sink in.

Now Marat tried to convince her to go back to her camp and family, but I could sense that she wasn't up for that.

Every time he'd uncover her mouth, she'd go off on a diatribe, loud and in Spanish, and we soon got the idea.

"If she goes back," Marat said, "she will tell the whole world where we are."

"So...we kill her," I said with as much innocence as possible.

Marat furrowed his brow and glared at me.

"You should just marry her and settle down," I told him. "You'd have your hands full, cause she's a real party girl, but after a time of adjustment, you could raise a family of *banditos* to take from the rich and give to the poor."

Marat furrowed his brow and glared at me.

So we had a third member in our party. As soon as Marat assured her she could come with us, she smiled gleefully and put her finger to her lips to signify her undying silence.

By now, we had lost a good part of our head start, so we moved off at a rapid pace, north, away from the lake and deeper into the mountains.

After an hour of walking, *Dulcinea* suddenly told Marat that we didn't have to worry. Her mother, brother and the *bandito* leader would not be back till the late morning, and the others in the camp wouldn't come after us without orders from their leader. It was a long haul to the priest's village, and she even wondered if the priest's village might be watched by the *Federales* or *la policia*. This priest was a suspected sympathizer with guerrilla and rebel causes. All good for us. She even speculated they might be caught, and as far as she was concerned it was good riddance for her brother and mom. She wanted the freedom to be in a city and go dancing and drinking, listen to music—she'd had enough of the rustic life. In fact, she then intoned in Spanish, "I want to see New York, Paris, London, Chicago (she mispronounced it, but didn't everybody)? I want to sing. I want to dance. I want to Cha Cha Cha." Marat translated. I was certain I heard a "Reech Frenchman, no?" in there somewhere.

I guess she'd waited the hour so we wouldn't reconsider sending her back.

And there was an advantage for us. She actually knew her way through these mountains.

"*Mi abuela* might make the fuss," she said in Spanish. "But nobody listens to her unless she threatens a curse."

Then she giggled and sat down. She had a coarse burlap bag with her and now she pulled some tortillas, *platains* and uncooked beans out of it, but it was plain she was rummaging in there for something else. Soon, she extricated another bag, made of soft, black-dyed leather.

Laying it on the ground, she carefully untied a piece of string binding it. The look on her face was strange, almost as though a combination of awe and dread—the kind of dread you get when you go into a cemetery. You think there may be something there to hurt you, but you're not sure, but you also think you'd be considered a simpleton if you believed there was and didn't go in.

Spreading the four corners of the leather cloth on the ground, she looked at the contents in wonder, pointing at them.

There was a dead bat, a tongue of something or other—large enough to be human, and I sincerely hoped that wasn't the case—a yellow powder that glowed in the darkness, and other animal body parts, like sparrow wings, bits of antlers, something that looked like Oscar Homulka's eyebrows and squirrel nuts.

"Double, double toil and trouble," I intoned. "Where is the eye of newt?"

Damn if she hadn't stolen the old hag's curse bag! Whew, I thought. What if Gagool had put a potion in our porridge, to make Marat stay and marry the girl, and MAKE ME FALL FOR HER! God! Talk about your lamentations! It was too much to even contemplate. Of course, if I *was* under a spell, how would I know the difference anyway? So, I guess, who cares?

She wrapped the whole kit back up, stowed it in the big bag and got up, still smiling.

Now, with *Dulcinea* out in front, Marat in the middle, and me bringing up the rear, we once more started a gradual ascent of the mountains, as she quickly found a path. Again there were switchbacks of steep incline, then straight paths up dusty, overgrown trails, crowded between sheaths of dandelion-like flowers and tall weeds which swept across our bodies and faces. We might descend for awhile then start upward again, but we were definitely going higher and higher into the mountains.

To my surprise, and *Dulcinea* was full of surprises, she stopped when we reached a promontory and sat down. Digging into the burlap bag, which by now seemed to contain tenfold more than the average woman's purse, she produced a bottle of hooch which made the strongest arak or rotgut taste like sweetened water.

After a few gulps, we continued on the path, which now dipped toward a new gully, all three of us stumbling, joking, laughing, belching and coughing like frat boys on Spring Break.

And thus we walked for five hours. Up switchbacks, down and across valleys, up more switchbacks, down switchbacks until it started to grow light. By then, the affect of the alcohol wore off and I began to feel the blisters.

We trekked another hour before I just had to stop, take off my boots and survey the damage—on both feet, in almost exactly the same spots. There were three of the bastards—one apiece on the big toes, one in the middle of each foot, just below the toes, and the last on each heel. They were big and white and puss-filled. *Dulcinea* looked like she was going to vomit just inspecting the poor bastards, and I couldn't walk on them anymore.

Now this would have counted as a really ignominious way to get nabbed, so I took out the knife.

"Marat, do you have any matches?" I asked.

"No," he answered, but turning to the girl, he asked her.

Once more, she dug around in her carryall for a few minutes, pulled out the liquor and took a few swigs. She belched, reached in again and came up with a big grin and some big wooden matches.

I put two matches together, lit a third to ignite the first two, then held the tip of the blade over the flame until it grew red on both sides.

Against all medical advice, I took the cauterized blade, made a slight puncture in each blister and kneaded out the puss, or filling, if you prefer, until they were drained. Don't try this at home.

"Tell her to give me the whiskey," I said to Marat.

Pouring it over my feet, it burned so badly I wondered if I should've just continued walking on the damn blisters.

My mind tends to wander on the best of days, and now, for God knows what reason, I wondered if Marat left his notebook behind again and we were going to have to go back to the *bandito* camp or the *Ajijic* police station to retrieve it.

I decided not to ask.

Just then, as I was about to put my socks back on, there was a scurrying sound coming from the woods.

Marat looked at me and I hurriedly tossed him the knife.

Then we heard a horrific, unearthly screaming like a Banshee from hell, and Gagool emerged from the bush, her eyes popped out and bloodshot, and strange, indecipherable invective streaming from her mouth along with foam and bile. Waving a hatchet above her head with one hand, she sported a machete with the other and a direct bearing for me. Hastily I assumed she was most angry with me—see earlier reference to a woman scorned—and she charged headlong up to me. Much to my mother's protests at the time, my father had taught me a little of the "sweet science" and as she got close, I noticed that her arms were spread wide above her head and there was an opening up the middle. I popped her with a left jab to the nose.

Dropping her weapons, she fell to the ground, but my blood was up. I picked her up and put her in an airplane spin while Marat and *Dulcinea* stood by wide-eyed. Then, I remembered the many times I'd watched the Crusher on All Star Wrestling and the moves that worked on everyone except Verne Gagne. I turned Gagool on her back, brought her in front of me, dropped to one knee and brought her down across it—the famous backbreaker. Now I looked around for vegetables, like carrots or broccoli, that I could stuff in her mouth. This might not sound related, but one time when Killer Kawalsky was wrestling one of the well-thought-of guys, the Crusher, knowing full well that

Kawalsky was a vegetarian, walked around the ring throwing vegetables into it and taunting "Wabbit, wabbit!" Needless to say, but I'll say it this time, Kawalsky went crazy and started stuffing carrots into the mouth of the guy he was trouncing.

I didn't have time as Marat and *Dulcinea* pulled me off. I strutted for a few moments. I think she only weighed about seventy pounds—it had been child's play.

I wiped the sweat off my brow and looked down at Gagool's motionless body. "All right," I cried out. "You want some more? Huh?"

"Tomas!" Marat said.

"Ok ok ok. What do we do with her?"

Dulcinea was already moving her bag far away from the hag. I guess she was frightened what would happen if Gagool got her black magic tools back.

"Don't worry," I said, full of sound and fury. "I can handle anything she's got."

"We can't just leave her," *Dulcinea* cried. "She'll turn us into toads."

Marat translated that nicely.

Now, Gagool, coming to, looked at us, mostly me, with an unfathomable hatred. "I have left a trail for my band," she sputtered. "They will come and kill you."

Marat translated that nicely as well.

Marat then shrugged his shoulders and motioned for *Dulcinea* to bring over her bag. This she did, but reluctantly and never taking her eyes off her great, great, great, great, great grandmother.

After searching through the bag, Marat came out with a coil of rope. Gagool struggled mightily until I threatened to pop her once more in the nose, then she stopped flailing with arms and legs, preferring to hurl invective which *Dulcinea* was certain would change us into porcupines.

I looked into the bag.

"Got any duct tape in there?"

I held Gagool up to a tree while Marat wrapped the rope around her. So you won't think we were entirely unsympathetic, we tied her quite high so that no animals might get her before the *bandito* trackers showed up.

Then, to make certain she knew what she was up against, I said, "If you tell your buddies which way we've taken, I'll show you a few more of my professional wrestling moves." Marat translated but she just hurled more curses and bile our way.

"Let's go," Marat said, and he started to move off into the brush. Socks and boots went back on and I followed. We had not gone more than a few steps, when we saw that *Dulcinea* had not moved.

"What is wrong?" Marat asked.

"That is not very nice," *Dulcinea* said. "Back at the camp, most of the guys cut her down after awhile."

We started hiking again, taking the trouble to go east for a bit and making our trail very apparent so even those guys could find it. After an hour, we found a river, walked along it for another hour and then cut back towards our original direction. We kept going all day, without running into a single person. My treatment, that I'd learned from my dad worked. After a few minutes, my feet were fine.

The air was brisk and felt good in my lungs. There was a sense of freedom in these hills that you could not get in the city, made more so by our escape. I hadn't even thought about the *banditos* more than once or twice since the girl joined us.

And I could see that Marat had begun to get a little tan, we were so high up. The sun felt good on my skin—I figured it was about seventy degrees.

"Well, let's see," I said to Marat. "We've done the irate husband bit, we've done the murdering *Federales* bit, we've had our stint in jail, we've had our jailbreak, our being shot at bit, our *bandito* bit, and our being chased by *banditos* bit. We've only been down here a little more than a week...What's next? I wouldn't want to get bored."

Marat just grunted as if he did not appreciate my sense of humor.

"Rebels," I shouted. "*Lucio Cabanas* is next."

"Be careful what you wish for," Marat said with utmost seriousness.

We walked another few minutes under pines, amidst chaparral and tall grass on a level, winding trail that narrowed to a few feet in width.

I guess I should've remembered the jailbreak and had more respect for my own conjuring powers.

"Oh shit!" I exclaimed ten minutes later, when from both sides of the path, springing forth from the ground and brush like the spawn of dragon's teeth in militia fatigues, were armed men looking every bit like clones of *Fidel* and *Che*.

There were twenty that I could see, and I reminded myself not to be too conspicuous in the reckoning. I quickly put my fingers at my sides. They were not wearing the uniforms of the *Federales* or police, so at least they weren't looking for us.

Who were these guys and what was their beef? What was our new bit?

At least twenty rifles and AK 47s were now leveled at us, and out of the corner of my eye, I could see *Dulcinea* smiling and winking and sidling up to the man who looked like he was in command. I wondered if I should warn him about her brother?

I also figured I'd go back to calling her Jezebel.

By now, I was seasoned, and having a rifle leveled at me was no big deal. Nothing like a little arrogance to get you in real trouble.

Just at that moment, Marat came up with an aside to me that he had not wanted anyone else to hear.

"Looks like you get to meet *Lucio Cabanas* after all," Marat said in a whisper.

"If he hasn't been killed since the last time he was killed," I responded.

But with this, one of the rebels who must've been closer than we thought, excitedly approached Marat.

He spoke to Marat in Spanish, but the only words I could make out were "*Lucio*" and "*Cabanas*." Throughout this conversation Marat nodded his head a lot as though in agreement.

Soon, we were brought up to the leader, the rebels' guns were shouldered, we were patted on the back by all and sundry, and we started out on another trail, replete with the usual switchbacks, ups and downs, steep inclines, sharp drops, and straight paths up dusty, overgrown trails, crowded between sheaths of dandelion-like flowers, nettles, and tall weeds which swept across our bodies and faces. This time, however, we were being treated royally.

"They overheard us talking about *Lucio Cabanas*," Marat said, now not bothering to keep it quiet. "They think I know him so they're taking us to their camp."

"You are not going to believe this," Marat said, patting me on the back. "But he is the leader of their camp."

Yeah, so the "royally" wouldn't last for long. I guess it escaped the holder of the two PhDs., that as soon as they found out we weren't really amigos with their fearless leader, we were either back to the captive scenario, the ransom gambit or the "join us or die" number.

"I thought you said he operated in *Guerrero* State," I muttered hopefully.

"I thought he did as well," Marat said. "Perhaps it got too hazardous for him there and they moved north. We are not that far from there."

"Should we tell them about the professor who told us to come and fight with them?" I asked Marat.

"I think it is much better to be closed-mouthed," Marat said. "Wait at least till the topic of killing us comes up."

Now, the drone of a small plane was heard.

Jesus. I thought. Can't anybody get any peace up here?

It seemed to be coming from the north, in the direction we had been heading. Evasive action ensued, as all the rebels faded back into the brush, disappearing even from my view. They had forgotten something. Marat and I were gawking up into the air when two of the rebels grabbed us and took us to ground. No sooner did I hit the ground than I made out the wings of the biplane, a two-seater, topping the ridge in front of us. It flew so low over the trees I thought of hitching a ride.

We would've surely been spotted if we'd been in one of the valleys, possibly even if we'd just remained on the trail. Marat's famous luck still held...but for how long?

As soon as the plane was out of sight, we resumed our hike along the mountain trail.

"Still looking for the *banditos*?" I asked Marat.

"I don't think so," he said. "The *banditos* are like gnats, troublesome but drawing little blood. The rebels, they threaten the regime, the way of life."

"Besides, I recognized the markings on the plane," he said. "Clearly army. Looking for these men."

Within an hour, we began another long descent into a lush green valley, so thick with trees, vines, shrub and grasses I wished I had taken Gagool's machete. Had the guerrillas not known the whereabouts of this trail, we would've needed machetes to cut through.

It was almost like a rain forest—the only things missing were the howler monkeys and the leeches. Nope. I looked down and there weren't any.

Little sun made it through the trees. It was almost as if we were walking at dusk.

As we reached the level floor of the valley, the column stopped and I could hear a shrill whistle, sounding indistinguishable from a bird and coming from the front.

It was soon returned by a fainter whistle off in the distance. The guerrilla in front of me waved for us to move and so on we went, under the canopy of a huge forest of pines. I guessed we were totally invisible from the air in this place.

By now, the column stretched out over seventy yards, with Marat and I around the middle. Somehow, Jezebel-*Dulcinea* had managed to squirrel her way to the front, walking with the leader of the group.

When the file of rebels passed an armed man that I took to be a sentry, he waved and smiled and gabbed with everybody until we came abreast of him. Then he looked us up and down, seemingly confused till his amigos explained, then he smiled and waved.

In another half-hour, we stopped again. It was the same procedure with just a little variance in the birdcall. I had seen other sentries back off the trail, their rifles leveled. These men were much more professional than our *bandito* comrades.

As we continued on, the trail narrowed and the column, perforce, compacted into a single file. The occasional branch would snap back in your face to keep you alert, and the path zigzagged like a switchback even though we were now on level ground. Here and there were false branches off the path to confuse anybody who wasn't familiar with the correct trail. It would be pretty easy to get lost up here. At any given point I could only see ten yards in front of me to the next turn. Marat found out later that they'd patterned it after the labyrinth, all the better to lay out ambushes against the government forces. I bet we were at least 4000 feet above sea level, and though my breath was still labored, it was a lot easier now that the ground was flat.

The guy in front of me was a little playful. He moved forward, holding a branch like he was going to keep it back when I passed. Then as I got near, he snapped it right in my face, making me duck or get lacerated. I contemplated doing the same to the guy behind me to show I had entered the spirit of the brotherhood, but figured he might just shoot me.

Already, I could tell these rebels were jokesters, along the same lines as Marat.

The trail finally straightened out and we then came to three sentries, one of whom spoke with the commander then took off running. I no longer had any idea what direction we were heading in.

We walked another half-hour when the smell of smoke from a wood-burning fire hit my nose. I guessed these guys were so far from civilization that they didn't worry about the army or unfriendly peasants coming upon them or reporting them. Even if they were spotted, it would take a long time to move an army up here—maybe they hadn't heard of the AirCav. Still, they had hidden from the plane, so apparently they didn't want to take too many chances. I later learned they knew the schedule of the overflights—probably some ex-Nazis in the army making the planes run on time—and so, waited till they passed before starting any fires.

Now, another ten men came down the trail, hurrying by us. I guessed they were to take the place of the men we accompanied in their early warning system.

I caught up to Marat just as we entered the outskirts of a large camp.

"What if they ask us to join or die?" I queried earnestly. "We're kinda all ready under contract with another group, you know."

Marat looked at me as if I was crazy. He declined to answer.

Soon we were in the middle of the camp, all under the canopy of trees and hidden away by the impenetrable forest. Of course, maybe I shouldn't say that, because we penetrated it.

Small wisps of smoke billowed up from low trenches, but dissipated in the leaves of the trees. I could hear the chopping of wood from outside the camp, the playing of children. A *mariachi* band played music in the background—this was a large camp.

Women were cooking, others washed clothing, three were entering the camp with buckets of water balanced on a pole over their shoulders. Men were checking and cleaning weapons. All looked up at us as we were escorted further into the camp, but most of the attention was short-lived.

There was a boy picking lice out of a soldier's hair, and women picking lice out of little children's hair, and young girls picking lice out of women's hair. I knew right away the rebel bit would be a great experience. I spontaneously felt my own scalp to see if anything was moving.

Marat saw this and smiled grimly.

"Lice can carry disease, *Senor* Tomas," he said.

We were marched up to an olive green tent on the farthest side of the camp.

Well, I thought. The jig is up. We're going to meet *Cabanas*. Won't that be a hoot?

As we got to the tent, the leader motioned for us to stop, said a few words in Spanish to Marat, and entered by himself.

After a few minutes, he returned and ushered us inside. There, sitting cross-legged on a mat, maps spread out on the ground before him, was the legend himself, *Lucio Cabanas.*

I could see Marat's eyes light up. Here was a true revolutionary fighter. Marat had confided to me that he sought to model himself on Andre Malraux, the French tomb robber, antique smuggler, warrior and author, and his own travelling was providing the content of his journal.

"You read Malraux," Marat had said, "And it's like being at home with an old friend sipping sweet Vietnamese coffee. I can read a book like *Anti-Memoirs*, and never finish it. That would be too much like losing a close companion, a lover. I don't even want to finish it, the book I mean."

Marat could 'wax' quite a bit when it came to Andre.

Now, he whispered, "I have never felt more akin to Malraux, than at this instant." Malraux had not just robbed Angkor tombs, he had also started a newspaper in French Indochina criticizing his countrymen for their treatment of the natives and even asking why the French were there.

During the Spanish Civil War, he organized a squadron of French flyers to fight for the Republic, and flew missions himself.

Serving in a tank unit during the French debacle in the early days of World War Two, Malraux then fought with the Maquis for the rest of the war. He was even captured by the *Gestapo*, but escaped. How he was able to be this man of action yet write books like *Anti-Memoirs*, *Man's Fate* and *Man's Hope* was certainly beyond my ken, though I could certainly see why Marat idolized him.

The *commandante* was not tall, actually a bit shorter than me. His chest seemed to bulge a little, like he did pushups but nothing else. Somehow, it was out of proportion to the rest of his body, which was quiet skinny—I guess that was to be expected living the life he did. He was slim at the waist, even looking a little feminine to me, though I was not about to comment on it. I was surprised. I had expected him to be as macho as they come.

Dressed in olive green fatigues and wearing the same colored kepi, he wore a red bandana over his face so only his eyes were visible, and they were a piercing dark brown. Occasionally, he would slightly lift the bandana enough to put a cigar between his lips and take a puff, and he must've been smoking it for some time because the butt was almost down to his fingers. I casually wondered if I would laugh if he burned himself with the butt. Alas, no luck, he took one more drag then rubbed it out on the dirt floor of the tent. There was less than a half-inch left. Then he coughed and spoke to us in a voice most likely raspy from too many cigars and cigarettes.

Marat told me later, in a loose translation, that he asked, "What the hell are you two doing here?"

And then I saw Marat put on the most charming act I've ever seen, even without the benefit of knowing what he was saying— I guess he figured he might as well pull out all the stops, so if we *were* put to death, at least he might qualify for a posthumous academy award. Gesticulating wildly, his voice moving in tones up and down, sometimes piercing, other times low and calming. He made them laugh, he made them cry—I swear tears came to some of the soldiers eyes (though their guns were never quite put at ease) as he continued his soliloquy. Perhaps there was some truth to his performance. After all, he did feel Malraux's presence.

Unfortunately, the *commandante* now turned to me and all I could say was, "*No comprende*," and he didn't seem to like this.

In this fashion we whiled away the hours, and then he told Marat to leave. Marat said, "Let's go," to me and got up. I stood up as well, but then the *commandante* moved between me and the tent flap, putting his hand roughly on my shoulder and barring the way. Quickly, he barked out some orders to his men, who then escorted a protesting Marat out of the tent.

Oh God, I thought. Don't tell me this guy fancies me.

When everyone had left, he motioned for me to sit back down, went over and tied the tent flaps together, then turned to go back to his original seat.

Oofta! I thought. This was a famous Norwegian expression of exasperation, surprise, discontent, disappointment—you name it—that one could not help but learn if one hailed from Northern Minnesota, and that, in addition to a Norwegian version of Rockaby Baby, was the extent of my Norwegian.

The *commandante* then turned to come over and stand above me, putting his hands behind his head to take off the bandana.

And at the same time I was wondering what miracle of Marat's unfailing luck—hoping the transitive principle would apply since I was travelling with him—was going to get me out of this one.

As he untied the bandana, he crouched down next to me and spoke softly in English. He understood English, I realized, and the raspiness was gone from his voice.

Aio! (pronounced eye-yo) I thought as he removed the faded red bandana. This is a famous Singalese expression of exasperation, surprise, stupefaction, wonder—you name it— that I learned from a Sri Lankan Montessori teacher that had taken tennis lessons from me the last summer. Yes! I was going to be saved by the transvestite principle. He was a she, and gorgeous as well, though she did smell a bit gamy, but I guess that was to be expected from her job.

I couldn't believe it.

My eyes grew wide and my backside felt very relieved.

She now started to unbutton her shirt, revealing a soft copper colored belly, and a muslin cloth tied tightly against her chest to hide her breasts. Turning around, she asked me to unwrap it, as she undid the snap to her pants, and who was I to argue. Soon, standing before me was one of the most unbelievable bodies I'd ever seen. What did they say about Marilyn? She had curves in places where other women didn't have places. So did *Lucio*.

After I undid the cloth, freeing her breasts, she put the shirt back on, though she left it unbuttoned. Unzipping her pants, which she left up, she said in a whisper, "Well?" and motioned to me as though she could not quite understand why I hadn't started to undress as well. Hell, I was still in shock.

"None of these men in camp knows that I'm a woman," she said, now pulling my shirt over my head. "I trust that you, being a *gringo*, and having no interest in our affairs, will keep our secret."

I wondered if this came under the join-or-die clause all these groups seemed to have.

I started to get out of my pants.

"They are *muy macho* and would never fight for a woman, or die for a woman," she said, in between small bites of my chest.

"Where is *Lucio Cabanas*?" I asked, trying to make small talk.

"Oh," she sighed, pulling me over to a blanket on the dirt floor of the tent. Unfortunately, my pants were only part-way down, caught and sent me hurtling in a one-and-a-half gainer to the floor

She laughed and jumped on top of me and sighed again.

"There are many of him. *Lucio*, I mean," she said. "He has set up over twenty groups—I do not even know how many—and each leader covers himself like I do, to be unrecognizable, and tells the people he is *the Lucio Cabanas*."

Spread the wealth, I thought, as my hands eagerly slid down to her rear, inside her fatigues and cupped her cheeks.

"So that's why they kill him so often," I mused, then kissing her.

"He does not mythically rise from the dead, no?" she said, stifling a giggle.

In between kissing and various other movements and gropings, she told me the story of how he had saved her from the rapine of the *Federales* when she was a young girl. I didn't think she was much older than *Dulcinea*, and that made me wonder what would happen if *Dulcinea*, social climber that she was, tried to attach herself to the *commandante*. That might be funny, and in any event, both Marat and I would want to watch.

So, *Lucio Cabanas* had saved her, taken her in and trained her to be a fighter. He had this idea, but very few people he could trust implicitly. It obviously wouldn't work if everybody knew the secret, so only the "*Lucios*" were in on it. No one else. All the followers in every camp actually thought they were with *the* one-and-only *Lucio Cabanas.* The peasants, their constituency, didn't get much news out here in the countryside, so every time they heard that *Lucio* was killed they just laughed and wrote it off to government propaganda. As for the other *Lucios*, they would cry for their lost comrade and be more determined than ever to strike back so the people knew that *Lucio's* "death" was another perfidious lie.

Continuing her story in the throws of our lovemaking, she whispered, "I haven't made love to anyone in the six months I've led this group. I am bound by the fiction. I am the only woman in all the groups masquerading as *Lucio*—that was one part of the plan I don't think he thought through." Then she stifled another giggle.

She had never taken off the kepi, and now, as I lay on my back, she sat up and straddled me, and pulled the bandana back on. Though her pants were down to her knees, looking up, all I saw was the bandana, the kepi and the eyes—her shirt had closed—so it seemed like I had *Fidel Castro* on top of me. I was happy she didn't start smoking the cigar again. I can't go out with women who smoke.

"Just in case," she cautioned, motioning to the bandana, "one of the men should wander in."

I tried to remember what her features really looked like and thrust my hands into her shirt just to make sure.

She started to breath harder, and soon started to moan, then came down and lifted the bandana to kiss me.

"Put your hand over my mouth," she said breathlessly. "I am loud in sex and they should not hear us and wonder what is happening."

So we gyrated and pushed and pulled, sucked and blew, kissed and climaxed, rested and started all over again. This lasted, and I estimate, the better part of two hours, then this brave rebel commander snuggled up beside me and fell asleep.

Well, this is a strange turn of events, I thought as she started

snoring. Definitely the most interesting sex I've had. Her appetites were voracious. Then, I casually wondered if she had a
brother.

Paranoid as I'd been on this foray into Mexico, I knew that she
could not reveal her identity to any of her men, or screw any of
them because nobody else could be allowed in on the secret, but
now I knew. What did that mean or portend? That she wanted to
have sex with me because she could get rid of me without a problem or any embarrassing questions? Double Oofta!

Like Marat said earlier, she couldn't let us go, because if we
came down from the mountains and the police got us and started questioning us, we'd spill our guts in seconds. And now on
top of that, I really had to worry about my performance. Back in
the States if it was none too good, the worst I had to worry
about was a breakup. Here it was perform or die. I'd better be
good. Then I started wishing she'd fancied Marat instead.

At this point I wished I had an oracle bone, or I could get
back on one of those buses, find a goat and perform my own
divination by entrails. I needed answers, even from a Granola or
Petite Soufflé.

It was dark by the time she woke up, and she immediately
got on top of me and we started all over again. I guess she really
liked being on top—of course, I had to consider her position.

Naturally, I rose to the occasion...sorry.

She then said the magic words: "Reech American?"

I looked at her eyes staring lustfully above the red bandana.
Brother, does every woman I meet want a green card?

I thought that now was as good a time as any to change my
story, so I answered, "Yes, rich American." Then innocently,
"Why do you ask?"

I could see a smile forming under her scarf as she bent over
to kiss me, then leaned a bit more forward placing her left boob
in my mouth.

"It is perfect, no?" she asked in a little girlish voice.

I knew better than to speak with my mouth full, but I did
nod.

"You marry me and bring me to *Estadios Unitos*?" she asked, as she sat up and freed my mouth.

"Do you have a big brother?" I asked nonchalantly.

"No," she answered, puzzled.

"But of course," I said, lying through my teeth. "But why do you want to go there? I thought you were here to liberate the people of Mexico, to bring justice?"

"*Si, si,*" she said. "We free the people here, then we go to *Estadios Unitos* and free the people there. We kill Dicky Tricky."

"Tricky Dick," I corrected her, but gently.

"Then we get a nice car and a three bedroom apartment with a convertible den and lanai, a big grassy back yard and I make six babies for you." She hesitated, thinking. "As many as you want," she then added.

Well, that was a relief. At least I didn't turn her away from her ideals.

She buttoned up her top, pulled up her pants and went out and got us some food. No sooner had we finished the beans and rice, when she hopped back in the saddle. Then we fell asleep, her from satisfaction, me from exhaustion. This went on the whole night.

Finally, at four in the morning, I put my foot down. "This has got to stop," I said, "or I will be dead by morning."

"Don' you like me, Mr. Tomas?" she whined, again, almost like a little girl, and making my name sound like that of a Brentwood hairdresser.

"Oh yes, I like you," I reassured her, "but Tomas junior needs a rest right now, or he'll be out of commission for a week." I would've let them kill me right then and there rather than exercise my prerogative anymore. I was plum worn out.

Then she surprised me. She just meekly buttoned up her shirt, and lay down, nestling herself against my shoulder. For one brief moment, she lifted her bandana to show me her lower lip stuck out in my direction, giggled, fell asleep and started snoring.

That was easy, I thought. Maybe I could take over this whole operation. I wonder how much they bring in, in a given year.

After all, my mom had been starting to pressure me to get a real job. Maybe this is the best of all possible worlds.

I wondered if I could put it on my resume.

Of course, with me, paranoia is never very far from optimism and vice versa. I wondered if she had some Gagool-like talents and had put some type of spell on me so I would consider going into business with her, not to mention she was going to keep me here indefinitely. I decided to call her *Circe*. I fervently hoped she wouldn't turn Marat into a pig—we'd grown close.

Early the next morning when I went out of the tent, the brisk air and smell of cooking fires was invigorating until I noticed the amused stares coming from a few of the rebels. I guessed that they had caught the muffled sounds of some of our sessions and they were snickering as I passed. I realized I was walking with my legs wide apart because I was so damn sore. I think they were expecting me to be sore on the other side. Probably would look the same either way.

This would indeed have to be our secret.

CHAPTER 14

Oops!

"In order to avoid being called a flirt, she always yielded easily." –Talleyrand

B reakfast was beans and tortillas with a few slices of mango and washed down with strong black coffee—I really missed reading my Minneapolis Star sports page over breakfast; I need-ed to know how the Vikings were doing—then came a frenzy of activity, as all fires were smothered, laundry was hauled down, anything that could possibly be seen from the air was hidden, animals were gathered and herded into camouflaged tents, and rebels hurried into their tents or under thick branches and stood motionless, while looking into the air, their guns ready.

Like clockwork, a slight drone was soon heard coming from the northeast. I stood surveying the now empty grounds and occasionally looked toward the sky to the north as though I was a complete idiot and unaware of what was at stake.

As the drone grew louder, my brain finally woke up to the realization it was another army plane, searching for us.

Two soldiers ran out of the brush, swooped in, each grabbing one of my arms, and hurried me off to the bottom of a huge ficus.

I changed my position, which was, thanks to the soldiers, originally one of face flat in the dirt, and I looked around for Marat. This was the first he'd been out of my sight for so long a time. I wasn't too worried though. I knew it would be pretty hard for him to get into trouble here, especially since I had a friend in the umpire's chair.

Kind of wired from lack of sleep and sex—when I'm tired like that, my mind and thought processes seem to race—I was restless, and I've always been one to make use of every minute of my time. So I took off my backpack, which I'd had on every second since we'd left the *bandito* camp—with the possible exception of the previous night—and unzipped it to get out Marat's Spanish book, which I had requisitioned during his captivity. Just as I ran the zipper down, a single ray of sunlight—and looking around the camp and up at the canopy, it was probably the only ray of sunlight that did—broke through the trees. Maybe the only ray to break through during the entire history of the rebel camp. Damned if it didn't break through the canopy of ficus and pine, penetrating down just as the military plane flew over. And I looked in horror as it sparkled brightly, in what seemed like an atomic light off the zipper tab. I quickly put my hand over it, but feared the damage was done.

I was in a panic for a second, but then thought there was no way in hell that one split second of light could've been seen from above. The plane would've had to be at the exact right angle, the pilot would've had to be looking at the exact right instant, and he was flying so close to the trees at the time, he had to keep his eyes on the horizon or risk crashing. Besides, if he saw that one glint, he might think it was a rock anyway. I guess the proof would be if he returned. Then, another fear entered my fevered, fuzzy mind. I surreptitiously looked around to see if any of the rebel soldiers had seen my faux pas. I wondered if all this paranoia would've been with me if I hadn't been up all night screwing, when I should've been sleeping so my mind wouldn't be like mush.

The rebels closest to me were engaged in an intense game of cards, and others were still watching the sky. It seemed I was secure from that quarter and I breathed a sigh of relief. Damn! In this camp, I was bent on getting us in more trouble than Marat.

We were given free run of the grounds and I learned to endure the occasional gibes, as men, women, children and goats stuck out their tongues in lewd, suggestive manners. We weren't bound and gagged, we had our freedom of sorts and I'd always wanted to feel part of something larger than myself.

It was pretty nice out here in the woods—it reminded me of those days in Black's Grove, and how I guess I was kind of doing all those adventure type things my brothers and friends and I always dreamed of. We weren't responsible for anything, didn't have to think about anything in particular, except the nature of existence, and I, in particular, sex.

Circe was busy doing *Lucio Cabanas* things so I hoped I'd been given the day off. In the meantime, I figured I better get some of those tips from Marat. Being discarded by an unhappy lover out here could be worse than heartbreaking.

I spent a good half-hour bathing and soaking in a cold mountain stream, and that went a long way toward soothing any aches and pains I still had, and the solitude helped me gather my thoughts and settle my mind.

The rest of the day was spent in studying and memorizing, brief flirting with the *commandante*—very subtle of course—and to my surprise, training with the ever-present AK-47, the weapon of choice for revolutionaries everywhere.

About mid-afternoon, Marat came up to me and put his hand on my shoulder. He looked at me with compassion and maybe a little guilt as he said, "I'm sorry, Tomas. I did not want to get you into such a situation."

"Don't worry about it," I said with more cheerfulness than he was prepared for. Of course, I couldn't tell him. I was sworn to secrecy, and if I told him, it would be out. Better I was outed, than her. I decided to just keep my mouth shut and let him think the *commandante* was a guy. I didn't really care just then, and that meant, at least while we were in the rebel camp, Marat would look at me differently. Maybe it would even make him feel guilty enough to stop getting us into all this trouble.

As dusk approached, the *commandante* seemed to be giving

me more and more amorous looks. She was quite adept at this even though only her eyes were visible above her bandana.

Soldiers sang around the campfire as the evening meal was being prepared, and they told stories of which I could only glean the smallest of references. But the sound of the songs themselves told everything about lost love, family, injustice, the good fight, political struggle, honor and heroism. They were stirring, galvanizing as only folk songs can be. The most uplifting music for me was always music that sprang from or became synonymous with a cause. To hear French ex-pats and exiles sing the *Marseillaise* in defiance of the Germans, Israelis singing the *Haveinu Sholom Aleichem* to bolster their spirits during the fight for Jerusalem or the myriad songs of the Spanish Civil War, brought a swelling to the chest, a choked-up feeling in my throat, an inability to speak.

In a darker vein, in *Guadalajara*, Marat and I spent the better part of an evening in a café listening to Chileans singing about the "missing" after the overthrow of *Allende*.

The songs this night had a similar effect on me. I almost felt like joining them for real and not under duress or the threat of death, and fighting for rights and justice for the poor who had ultimately done nothing worse than be born into the wrong family or the wrong situation.

Does not one have an innate desire to become part of something greater? Or find a calling that is meaningful? Whether it is a cause or a spiritual quest? Something more meaningful than who has the nicest car, the biggest house or hottest girlfriend— not that those are totally bad things. Why are we here? Where did we come from? Where are we going to? Right now, the only place I was certain I was going to was to find another mug of hot coffee. It was getting cold up here and I was certain I'd have to be limber for the night ahead.

Most revolutionaries, it seemed to me, just wanted to trade places with the people in power, and most revolutions wound up with governments not much better than the ones they ousted.

I had a feeling, call it an intuition, that these people Marat and I were singing with simply wanted a level playing field. And I began to think of my own country and its violent beginnings and violent expansion, and all the criticism and rage directed against its latest war, and I realized one thing I had downplayed or maybe taken for granted: there is probably no place, no other country in the world, where one can rise so easily. Maybe the field in the U.S. isn't completely level, but I'd be willing to bet it is the most level playing field in the world. And that's another reason I loved tennis and sports in general: sport is the most level playing field.

We sang till late in the night, Marat joining in easily. I hummed along. The men passed around homemade sangria fermented from mangoes and wild berries that soon had us laughing and slapping each other good-naturedly on the back and arms and heads.

Jezebel alternated from singing along with Marat to slipping over to the other side of the campfire and holding hands with the rebel leader who had brought us in. Nobody seemed to mind, and when I asked Marat about it, he posed the question: "Does the sun shine any less bright for having shone on another man?"

This night was one of the happiest moments in my young, still unformed life, and I started to think of my brothers and wondered where they were and what they were doing and thinking, even what they were reading, because I always think of them when I'm happy.

A little after midnight, fires were extinguished, drunken sentries poured cold water over their heads and went out to relieve other sentries, others went to their sleeping places, whether a ground cloth, blanket or tent, and the *commandante* grabbed me by the hand and led me to her boudoir where another night of passion would soon ensue.

After an hour or so I was beginning to think she really liked me, because she started talking in low tones and alternating this with higher pitched baby talk, and if I did anything that displeased her—like wanting to take a rest for a second or two—she'd come close to me, stick out her lower lip in a comic, childish way, break out in a grin from ear to ear and stick one of her boobs in my mouth again, not that I'd complain.

"Perfect, no?" she'd query.

"Umph, umph," I'd say.

She curled her lips and wrinkled her forehead as if thinking. "I know nice girls should be married first and I'm a nice girl...but this charade is *muy muy* stressful...and I like the sex." Then she giggled some more and became even more passionate in her lovemaking, though always keeping quiet enough that she wouldn't be caught out by the others.

She'd barely dozed off in my arms, and hadn't even had time to start snoring, when I heard shouting around the camp. I could hear an occasional "popping" that had to be gunshots and sprung up like a bolt and shook her awake.

"Something's going on," I said, handing her the chest cloth and helping her wrap herself up. Within seconds she was dressed, grabbing for her AK-47 and checking it to make certain it was loaded.

"Where's Cassandra when you need her!" I asked rhetorically.

"*Que?*"

"You know. Cassandra. Warning the Trojans."

"*Claro,*" Circe said. "Nobody'd believe her anyway."

"Wow!" I exclaimed. "Athletic, gorgeous and well read too."

Circe put her hands on her hips adopting a defiant stance. "You know," she said. "I had to take a test for this position. They don't take just anyone off the street."

And a bit of an edge, I thought. I like that.

She stared at me for a second, then rushed for the tent opening. As she brushed back the tent flaps she stopped in mid step.

"*Vamos,* Tomas!" she said. "*Des pues termino aqui* I meet in Mississippi."

"Minneapolis," I corrected. She *was* close.

She hurriedly rushed back, kissed me and turned once more. At the tent flap she hesitated again. She pointed at me.

"Your last name," she cried.

"Kardadasi," I answered.

"Tomas Kardadasi my love," she said. "I will find you." Then she flew.

I had barely opened the tent flap to look out at the hubbub, when Marat swooped in and grabbed my arm, virtually pulling me through the pandemonium that now was the camp: men, women and children were running to and fro, carrying weapons, some with grenades; animals were herded out of camp to the north and up precarious mountain slopes. There was a general screaming and shouting permeating the darkness, and no matter how hard I looked as Marat dragged me toward those same precipitous slopes, I could not see the *commandante*. By now, we could hear the constant snaps and cracks of rifles and the staccato of machine guns. The rear of the camp was already devoid of people as we ran in the opposite direction from the gunfire.

"Where are they?" I asked Marat.

"They've gone to try to stop whoever is attacking them," Marat said. "Probably army."

Damn! The first time I've ever had that effect on a woman and a whole damn army intervenes. I was ready to bet Assad had a hand in this.

Then we heard the now familiar drone of helicopters filling the air above us.

"Mortars," Marat said as two explosions rocked the tops of the trees. "Hurry. They are close."

As we struggled up an incline, a flare exploded in the sky and the whole camp lit up.

"*Merde*!" Marat exclaimed. We were now hiding in thick foliage on a ridge directly north of the camp, and silhouetted against the moon, we could see soldiers shinnying down ropes through the trees that hid the camp. I looked up at the nearest chopper, where a man was standing at the door looking out. Now it was my turn to exclaim.

"Jesus" I said to Marat. "It's your buddy Assad."

Then, I received an even bigger shock. Now my eyes literally bugged out. There, in the helicopter, standing in the open doorway leaning out, his pink eyes, pink skin and pale white hair for all to see, was the albino. God Almighty! He had teamed up with Assad. How the Hell he knew I was here I'll never know. And just because I owed him five bucks! What that guy wouldn't do for a fiver. Geez! You'd think if he was so hard up, he wouldn't have loaned it to me in the first place. And it'd only been a couple of months anyway, the bastard.

Not wanting to make eye contact, we both huddled down, hugging the earth.

"The only way we'll get away from that guy *is* to go to *Cuba*," I said. Marat didn't know anything about the albino and I thought it best to keep it that way.

Marat put his finger up to his mouth, motioned to me to follow and then began to crawl over the ridge on his belly.

And thus we crawled for a good twenty minutes. The next thing I knew we were sliding down steep inclines on our rear ends. Soon as we hit level ground we were up and running through the briar, bramble, brush and bush of the jungle-like terrain. I really should have taken Gagool's machete.

We sprinted up hills and slid down others and it seemed as though the gunfire would never stop, like we'd never get away from it.

After another half-hour, we stumbled on a trail and even though we now ran along switchbacks, we made better time. After an hour of running, we stopped to catch our breath. By then, the gunfire had subsided and we only heard random shots and no big explosions. I couldn't help but wonder what had happened to *Circe* and the rebels. In horror, I wondered if my pack zipper had been responsible for bringing the army down on us. Then, of course, I wondered if anyone had seen my mistake, in which case, the rebels would be after us for revenge. The way I figured it, if that was the case, we'd now have the *banditos*, *Federales*, rebels, albinos and cops after us, not to mention one love-sick, cross-dressing revolutionary. I wondered if we could add anyone else.

I also cursed that I'd never get to see *Dulcinea*-Jezebel and *Circe* get it on and wondered if it would that be a twosome or threesome? I must have been a little less uneasy of the road ahead by then, if I was having thoughts like that.

Through the scant light, I could see that Marat's face was streaked with blood. His arms exhibited the same types of marks. I then felt burning sensations on my arms and face, intermixed with sweat, and realized I had been on so much adrenaline I hadn't even felt the cuts till then. Thankfully I wasn't in my usual uniform of tennis shorts.

Marat stood up, took a deep breath and said, *"Vamos,"* and then started moving again. Soon, we were cruising through the mountains as though we were on auto-pilot, only stopping occasionally for Marat to get our bearings from the stars.

Another chopper made its appearance, flying directly overhead with its shining beam trying to ferret us out. This happened half-a-dozen times, as if to catch any stragglers, but we could always hear them coming early and had time to search out good hiding places.

I could just imagine Assad, twirling the ends of his mustache and yelling to his men, "Find the adulterer!" and I unsheathed my middle finger, thinking find this, you bastard.

By dawn, we were obviously exhausted, having run-walked all night, up and down myriad hills, through myriad valleys, even swimming across the width of what Marat thought was the *Rio Grande de Santiago,* and the sound of the choppers had long since diminished, then disappeared.

We kept moving north, and figured that sooner or later, we'd stumble into a village or maybe even *Guadalajara.* Whatever this mountain chain was, we'd by now crossed its highest point. Even though we kept going up and down, we were now gradually getting lower. By midday, we found ourselves in a wide, open valley covered with tall bushes. They seemed to have a uniformity to them, as if they were planted by farmers in neat rows; they were spread out over a huge area, as far as I could see.

We had just finished an hour run—I guess my legs were finally healed and strong—or it might've been the adrenaline, or both. As we started through the plants, I was breathing pretty hard and so was Marat. And, as I breathed in, I thought this smelled familiar. Somehow, I couldn't place it.

"I know this smell," I said. "What is it?"

Marat started to laugh. "Tomas," he said. "You don't recognize this?" He chuckled some more. "It's grass, marijuana, pot, weed, ganja, Mary Jane..."

"All right. All right," I said. "I get it."

A field of ganja. Drug growers. Drug dealers. Why can't we run into some nice, respectable people?

Now, of all the drugs in the world, I'd always thought of grass as a rather benevolent, sort of a coming-of-age drug, that wouldn't addict you or hurt you too much, not like cocaine or heroin or alcohol. I disagreed with the people who said it would lead you to more powerful and more dangerous drugs and thought it should be legalized. What do they say? That seventy per cent of crime is drug related. Well, legalize the harmless types like ganja and you get rid of some of the crime. If you even got rid of ten per cent, it would certainly ease the workload of the police.

None of my friends who'd tried it or smoked it regularly had gone on to the stronger stuff, failed out of college or screwed up their lives...so far anyway.

I know I'd rather meet someone on the road who was smoking pot, than someone who was drunk. The pot-head would probably be going twenty miles an hour and be very mellow, in search of a Snickers and a pizza, while the drunkard would probably try to ram you, then get out of the car and challenge you to a fight because he ran into you.

But it was a bit different running into a field of grass and possibly, the guys who grew it, smuggled it and sold it.

We seemed to have the propensity for running into businesses where death and gunplay were part of the corporate plan. And if they saw us, they'd most definitely figure we were narcs. How could we even begin to explain how we got to this place? I went through it and still didn't believe it.

Once more, we left a bad situation only to find ourselves in a worse one. I was not too happy.

Marat was unfazed. While I was back to being my paranoid,

pessimistic self, he had been gathering leaves. He had sat down and ground them up, found some loose paper in his pack and rolled a super-sized joint.

He still had one of *Dulcinea*-Jezebel's matches and struck it against the zipper of his pants to light it.

So, he smoked.

"This is really good shit," Marat said, taking another hit and holding the joint out to me. "Here. You have to try it. I hate smoking alone."

"Nope. Not my thing."

"Just one toke."

"Nope."

After much cajoling and extolling on his part I agreed to take one puff. I gingerly took the hit and started coughing.

It wasn't long before 1) I wanted a pizza AND Snickers AND Coca-Cola; 2) I began to talk a lot; and 3) I began to lament. I also took another hit.

"I miss her," I said to Marat.

"Miss who?" Marat asked. "Do you have any food?"

"No," I answered. "I miss the *commandante*, of course." Now that we were no longer with her people, I didn't feel like I had to keep the secret. Besides, by now I was in an altered state of consciousness and I would talk about anything and everything.

"Anything sweet?" Marat asked. "Like sugar, anything...wait a minute. The *commandante's* a man. I'm really sorry I got you into that one, Tomas. I don't know how I'll make it up to you. I'll feel guilty about that the rest of my life. I'm so sorry."

He looked so abjectly forlorn I thought he was going to cry.

"The *commandante* is a woman, Marat," I said.

"The *commandante*," Marat said incredulously. "That guy that raped you? What are you smoking?" Then he looked at the big joint that was in my mouth as I took another drag and began coughing uncontrollably.

"This is good shit," I rasped out.

"Oh," Marat said. "That's what you are smoking." Then he began to laugh uncontrollably.

I handed the joint back to him. Laughing, I asked, "Do you think it's wise for us to make so much noise, seeing as though we are obviously in the territory of ruthless drug lords?"

"What did you say about the *commandante?*" Marat asked. "I forgot."

"He is a woman, *senorita*, babe, doll, broad," I said. "And pretty hot too."

"I think you are stoned," Marat said.

"He was a she," I said. So I told him the whole story, at which point, he laughed even more hysterically than before.

"And I was feeling so sorry for you," he laughed loudly. "And so guilty."

I pushed him down on his back and put my hand over his mouth, before he brought down on us every drug trafficker in the world.

"There could be smugglers all over this place," I said in a staccato fashion, allowing for bursts of my own idiotic laughter.

"Are you serious?" Marat asked in much the same fashion. "This field is immense. Remember when we were up above it? Did you see buildings of any kind? No. Of course not. They're not going to have anything like that. They could be seen from the air. Probably the only time people are here is to plant or harvest."

He ended this fine speech with, "I think we should take some of this with us."

I could see that Marat was very logical when stoned and laughing hysterically. And as long as we weren't buying it from anybody, I guess there was no one that could turn us in and get his money back.

However, I did see one problem. Though I'd never actually seen a marijuana plant before, these plants looked pretty tall and harvesting season couldn't be that far off.

"Take all you want," I said to Marat, thinking we could not possibly get into more trouble. I think this falls under the "famous last words" axiom.

So, we smoked and coughed and hacked and became restless

and thirsty. So, laughing like hyenas, we got up and started to wander around the field. Soon, we stumbled onto part of a sprinkler system and we were able to tend to our thirst. Next, I spied a huge operation and building project and got down on my belly, my head held above the fray with my hands.

"Don't get too close," Marat warned. "Fire ants."

Hmm, I mused. These ants in your pants could be a problem.

I got up, waved goodbye to my little fire ant buddies—I felt we had bonded during this short time—and we began to walk.

The scent of the air, the grasses, the nearby pine trees, the grass, the sun on our faces, a cool breeze that seemed to come up whenever the sun got a bit too hot—everything was perfect. The only things that could've made it better would've been that pepperoni pizza, Snickers, Coke and either a front row seat at the Cooper watching *Lawrence of Arabia* or a "Dead" concert at the Indoor Met in Minneapolis.

The better part of an hour passed as we walked, each lost in his own thoughts—the giggle stage had evolved into a meaning-of-life stage—when suddenly, we heard some voices and stopped dead in our tracks.

Now, Marat, with the experience of his brief army training, and myself, with the experience from long days of playing a lot at war and cowboys and Indians when I was a kid, crouched down and inched forward very quietly through the plants. It wasn't long before we reached the edge of an open field—a rectangle no more than a hundred-and-fifty yards long, and maybe a tenth as wide.

"This is strange," I whispered to Marat. I could no longer hear any voices and there was no one in sight.

"An airfield," he whispered back. "They have to get their product to market."

"Maybe we should make friends," I said jokingly. "Maybe hitch a ride outa here."

"With these guys?" Marat asked, literal as usual. "These guys would slit our throats as soon as look at us."

"I was merely thinking professional courtesy," I said. After all, we were affiliated with both a bandit group and a band of rebels.

With the smugglers about, it wasn't wise for us to move around too much. Neither of us could think of a plan, other than to wait for nightfall to circle around the field and then continue north, so we crawled backward about twenty yards, sat down and waited for a plan to fall from the sky and hit us over the head, or for Marat's famous luck to kick in.

After an hour of sitting, I began to hear men talking again, and this continued on and off for the next few hours, though the voices never seemed to draw too near.

Bored, I crept back out to where I could view the field. Now there were a few men placing things around the landing strip—I guessed these were signals for a pilot.

One thing about being stoned—besides wanting to eat or screw or see an epic movie or hear a rock concert—is that time passes very slowly.

So we waited and the time passed very slowly. The longest period of time would elapse, where it would seem that the whole of my life transpired before my eyes, and so I'd look at my watch and see that only five minutes had gone by. I guessed I'd missed something.

We didn't dare talk above a whisper, but every once in a while, Marat would break out giggling, then I'd start to giggle and we both did anything we could to stop. I'd think of death and torture and maiming, but somehow, even these morbid thoughts would bring forth a laugh.

"That was really, really good shit," I said. "Maybe if we bought some..."

Of course, Marat's response was a stern "Do not be ridiculous, Tomas."

This made me burst out in laughter and I had to hit myself violently on the arm to stop. That made Marat laugh again, so he grabbed a handful of dirt encrusted weeds and stuffed it in his mouth, which in turn, made me laugh again.

"Does that taste pretty good?" I asked, digging my nails into my arm to cause enough pain to stop me from giggling again.

This seemed to go on for a couple of hours, but when I looked at my watch, only twelve minutes had passed. We figured it would be safer to move further away from the landing strip for safety and laughter purposes.

Then, we remembered that we still had food in our packs from when we left *Dulcinea*'s camp. Ravenously and pathetically, we dug through our packs, but only came up with one banana, which we duly split. If only I'd had some peanut butter to give him.

Then, of course, we fell asleep.

CHAPTER 15

Aero Marat

"If I had some ham I'd have some ham and eggs if I had some eggs." –Tom Boice

Around midnight, I was shaken awake by Marat, who put his hand over my mouth to make sure I didn't scream out in surprise. He pointed to the sky and I could hear a drone which by now I immediately recognized—another damn airplane.

We moved closer to the landing field and soon could see lights popping out in two vertical lines on the ground. Lucky for them they didn't light up a night earlier or they would've had Assad as a guest; by now it wouldn't have surprised me if he owned part of the business.

The plane must have been flying without lights and there was no moon. We couldn't see anything as the drone grew louder. After a few tense minutes, a little Piper Cherokee, about a six-seater, brushed the plant tops to come in for its landing. It turned and taxied right by us as it came back down the field. Immediately, the signal lights were put out and men ran to catch up with the plane. When it came to a stop, just abreast of where we were hiding, two men, each carrying dark suitcases, jumped down and greeted their comrades.

Five men emerged from the nearby field, carrying two duffel bags apiece on their shoulders.

From what I could see, the men from the plane briefly examined the bags, nodded as if satisfied and handed their suitcases to a sixth man on the ground, who set them down and opened them. I couldn't see what was in the suitcases, but figured it was *dinero*. Then, after the pilots took a more detailed look at the duffel bags, both sniffing the contents and thrusting their arms into each bag and pulling out leaves and examining them—I guess to be certain the good stuff was not just on the top of ordinary leaves or real grass—they signaled approval and motioned to the others who began loading the plane. Then everyone walked across the field opposite from us and disappeared into the tall plants.

It was so dark, we could barely make out the plane sitting unattended and only some seven or eight yards away from us at one end of the runway.

Marat stood up.

"They did not even leave a guard," he said. "And I did not see any weapons."

"So?" I responded. No, I thought. Marat doesn't know how to fly. He wouldn't even dream of something this foolish.

"Come, Tomas," he said as he walked onto the field to my almost complete surprise. "We must check this baby out."

Then, as he walked, he surprised me again. Still moving forward, he turned so that his upper body was facing me and lit another joint—turning, I guess, so that the smugglers couldn't see the flame. He took a long inhalation and passed it back to me and I quickly cupped it in my hand.

"I love to smoke when I fly," Marat said as he blew out the smoke from his mouth.

Now I turned and took a big drag, figuring that I was going to need to be stoned to get on that plane. Besides, if I was going to die, I might as well get the rush from the crash.

Handing the joint back to him, I knew I had to make the attempt to reason with him, no matter how feeble.

"What are you doing?" I asked.

"What more perfect way to get back to civilization?" Marat asked as he climbed up on the wing and opened the driver's side door. He turned back to look at me. "Go get up on the other wing and keep a lookout."

"Besides, we'll be able to put some distance between us and all the people you said were after us."

"I was just speculating," I protested. Lucky I still hadn't told him about the albino.

I climbed up and stood on the wing, minutely scanning the part of the field they had disappeared into for any movement. I'd flown stand-by before but this was ridiculous.

"*Bien*," Marat said. "Come on," he whispered. "Get in."

First I prayed to every God I could think of, then I did a meta meditation just in case I was killed so I would be reborn into a good birth for my next life, then I stepped inside and asked the million dollar question. "Do you really know how to fly this thing?"

I asked hopefully.

"Let them eat cake," he said merrily.

"Do you mean piece of cake? I again asked hopefully.

He looked at me as though I did not have a flair for the obvious. "Yes," he said. "I learned how to fly in the army...because Malraux learned how to fly."

Of course I should have known that. What was I thinking? Or as my dad used to say, "Will the wonders of the world never cease?"

As soon as I got in my seat, Marat flipped the ignition and we started to taxi down the field.

"I should mention," Marat said casually, "that this runway is pretty short, which means we do not have room for error, and I've never taken off at such high altitude, which means we do not have room for error..."

"Anything else I should know?" I dutifully asked. By now, I was looking forward to the rush.

"Well...I doubt these smugglers will be too happy about us stealing the plane," he said, his eyes intently focusing upon the myriad gauges.

The field was bumpy, but we were gaining speed.

"And if you look to our rear," Marat continued, sounding every bit like a flight attendant or airline pilot. "You will see men with guns chasing us."

I turned to look just as the first shots went off. We were not yet airborne.

"Dump the duffel bags, Tomas," Marat said.

I looked at him in confusion.

"It will make us lighter," he said. "So we can take off more easily." He took another drag from his joint, passed it to me and laughed. "Besides, they won't be quite as mad if they get their weed back."

Now there's a real question of degree.

Quickly, I scooted to the rear of the plane and hauled one bag back to the front and tossed it out my door, then watched as it tumbled over and over, finally bowling over one of the smugglers. I hadn't realized they were quite so close.

"Ah, Marat?" I said in the manner of a question.

"Yes, Tomas," he answered.

"Do you think we can take off pretty soon?"

"Whatever you like, Tomas."

And he jerked back on the throttle. Nothing happened except for the tracers that were whizzing by, some even finding their mark in the fuselage and wings. I went back to get the rest of the duffel bags.

Now, as I noticed my own high set in, I wanted to see how many of them I could knock over.

"I already got one," I said to Marat who now took on my earlier look of confusion.

Throwing out the second bag, I was disappointed by quite a big miss. The smugglers were falling too far behind the airplane.

"Marat," I requested, "Could you slow down a bit?"

"I have to," he said. "We have come to the end of the field."

"You're turning around?" I asked. "Heading right into them?"

"Yes," he answered, as he slowed down the plane to come around.

"Good," I said, and hurriedly went back and lugged up another bag. I reckoned my problem was that there was too big an interval between throws. It's like a second serve. You don't want to take too much time between the first and second serve or it throws your adjustment off. So, instead of throwing the one bag, I left it there on my seat and went back to retrieve another, then another, but that was all the room I had. It would have to be three at a time.

We were gaining speed again and heading straight for the bad guys.

"Do you have headlights on this thing?" I asked.

"Let's see," Marat said, and then fiddled around with some of the controls.

"*Voila*," he said as head beams came on, highlighting my targets.

Holy cow! This is too easy. Those tracers sure looked cool.

"Marat," I asked. "Could you turn the lights out?"

"Soitainly," he assented in a high-pitched Curly voice.

I hadn't realized he was a Three Stooges fan. Accordingly, I now had more admiration for him, though he later confided he only "got" them when he was high.

The airplane was rapidly gaining speed and the front end of the Piper Cherokee was actually off the ground.

As we whizzed by the bad guys I tossed out the first bag and missed, but as I tossed out the second I could see I was right. The first miss helped me gauge the second throw and I got one right in the gut and he tumbled over onto the field. It also helped with the third as I scored again.

This is why the second serve is the most important shot in tennis.

I could see Marat pulling back on the throttle as I went back for the rest of the duffel bags.

"Do we have to take off now?" I asked. "Could we turn and make another run at them?"

"They are shooting real bullets at us," Marat said. Then he coughed, hacked and laughed.

"Yeah," I said. "They're pretty cool."

"No. I think we need to go," he said.

I fired two more bags out the door.

"Do you think we should keep one?" I asked.

"No," he said as the plane left the ground and headed straight up. "It is against the law. We could get in trouble."

"Well," I said, thinking out loud. "How about circling the field once?"

"Soitainly," he said.

Banking the plane to the right, he came in fast, right over the plants. I aimed the bag at the big man who had taken the suitcases. I let it go. Bam! Right on top of his head. It was funny to see his Uzi spray bullets into the air as he crumpled into a heap. I was pretty good at this. I went back to see what else I could find.

Now I could feel the Piper Cherokee climbing again. There was hardly any light so I just felt around. Ah ha! Another suitcase. I'd watched a lot of spy movies as a kid, and looked the case over pretty carefully to make sure it wasn't booby-trapped. It looked larger than the ones the pilots had delivered, and when I opened it, I saw three Uzis, each fitted carefully into its own slot of Styrofoam.

"Holy cow!" I said as I took one out of its slot. I'd never even seen one of those except in the movies.

"What?" Marat asked.

"Three Uzis and ammo," I answered.

"Good," Marat said. "We'll probably need the firepower."

Whatever for? I wondered as I returned to my seat and buckled in.

Marat banked the plane once more and we turned to the east.

"When the seat belt sign is on," Marat said, "you will please remain standing and unbuckled. You will also notice that this is the smoking section and all passengers will please toke up."

Then he laughed again. "I notice you are still buckled in," he said. "Don't you trust me?"

I gave him the finger and he proceeded to laugh.

"Our destination is Mexico City and we have an ETA of hopefully tonight."

Marat was certainly good at cracking himself up.

"Oops," Marat said. "They only left us half a tank of gas."

"Damn," I said as I rubbed the barrel of an Uzi. "I wanted to go back and strafe them. I've always had this dream, ever since I was a little kid, to strafe some bad guys."

"Next time," Marat said.

Then we both started laughing.

"Can't they track us?" I asked.

"Who? The smugglers, the *Federales*? " Marat asked. "You know, you worry too much Tomas. In fact, you worry all the time. What is with all this worrying all the time?"

"Don't worry about it," I said. But what I was thinking was what would you do if you had to keep an eye on you all the time?

"How do you know where we're going?" I asked. "How can you see? What about mountains?"

"Ay yi yi! Stop worrying! I found maps," Marat answered in a tone of exasperation. "And there are no mountains in this range higher than 2300-2400 meters," Marat said as he fiddled with the altimeter.

"Look at this. This is perfect," Marat said, seriously. "Nobody will claim this plane. Nobody will report it stolen. They cannot. It might be stolen already or at least not registered. It is hauling drugs, no? They did not see our faces. They do not even know whether or not we are Mexicans from a rival drug smuggling gang. We will leave this plane on some field near Mexico City, disappear into the city and be done with it. They will never have any idea who did this. There is no way for them to find out."

"We will fly very low. I doubt if Mexico has advanced radar. Who do they have to worry about attacking them?"

"This is 1973," I said to caution him. "They aren't in the Dark Ages. Mexico is very advanced."

The argument became heated, and I went off and argued this and that about Mexico and drugs and *banditos* and rebels and all his costly actions and all the trouble we were in that would probably keep us in Mexican prisons for three generations. Then I noticed that he hadn't responded for quite some time. Looking directly ahead of me out of the cockpit, I noticed a mountain that was very close, then I looked over at Marat.

You know how you're driving and it's late and you're tired and you let your eyes close ever so briefly and your head nods just a little bit off to one side. You actually fall asleep at the wheel, but only for a half-second or so and you're up in a flash. And it might happen two or three times in the space of a minute, and if you are lucky enough to not crash in that time, you'll probably wake up. Well, I looked over at Marat and that's what he was doing. Then I looked in front of us again and saw we were even closer to the mountain. In fact, we were about to crash into a mountain that must have grown above the 2400 meters he talked about—maybe it was an old map. "MARAT!" I yelled as loud as I could and shook him out of his stupor. "LOOK!"

Marat snapped awake, yanked back at the controls and the Piper Cherokee lurched upward. It seemed almost straight upward to me. I could hear the scraping on the bottom of the fuselage as we struck one of the taller pines.

"Oops!" Marat said. "That mountain is taller than I thought."

So on we flew through the night.

I finally was too tired to worry about crashing, said my prayers once more and fell asleep, drifting in and out for the next hour.

When I woke up, I don't know why, but the first thing I did was lean over and look at the fuel gauge, then I made certain Marat was awake.

"We're getting pretty low," I said hesitantly, not wanting to be accused of worrying too much. "Don't you think?"

He seemed to be pretty alert.

"A little bit more, Tomas," Marat said. "We should go as far east as possible. It is still an hour to the dawn, Mexico City is near and we will have to land soon enough."

"Do you know where we are?" I asked.

"Hell no," he said and started laughing. From the smell of the cabin and the pervasive smoke, I reckoned he'd been smoking the whole time. In fact, I felt pretty buzzed from the contact high. I wanted some buttered popcorn.

"While you were asleep," Marat said slowly, as if he wanted to make sure it sank in, "I have considered a few things and I think it only fair since we have gone through this together, that I should ask your opinion before making a decision. I will lay it out for you, my thinking."

Well, I've got to tell you, I was honored.

"First," he said seriously, "I believe we are in much trouble in this country."

I loved it when he used his mathematical logic.

"Second. I do not have to tell you why," he continued, "but it is better for us to leave Mexico."

"Third, we have this plane." He exhaled as if coming to the point, even though it was still a bit off in the future. "But we have little petrol."

"I have an aunt and uncle in Mexico City, and I would like to spend Christmas with them, and possibly New Year's as well. I was in Mexico City before and I love it. The museums in Mexico City are splendid, and so are the palace and the grounds of *Chapultepec* Park.

"I really wanted to show you the pyramids at *Teotihuacan*," Marat said. "Many compare them to the Pyramids at Giza. The Temple of the Sun is the third largest pyramid in the world...and the Temple of the Moon..."

Trim the fat, I thought. With remarkable patience I said, "Yes."

"But if we can find petrol," he continued, "we could do both, then go all the way to the *Yucatan*." Now he looked intently at me. I could see he was torn.

Let's see. We were hitchhiking down to Mexico City and we'd hardly hitched a ride. Now we were going to skip our own designated destination. I wasn't sure. "If we could find petrol, yes, but we haven't."

"But think of all the churches and museums," Marat added. "All the murals by *Orozco, Siqueiros, Tamayo* and *Rivera* we could see."

"Oh yeah," I said. "I'd *really* hate to miss them. But if you think we should, easy come, easy go. If you think we should go right on through to the *Yucatan*...Maybe we should just go all the way to *Cuba*?"

"No. They would probably shoot us down. But Mexico City," he said wistfully, "and the pyramids. If we only had more petrol..."

I briefly interrupted. "And the *Federales, la policia* and the *banditos* weren't after us..."

"We could see them."

Sometimes there is room for compromise.

"You know, Marat," I said. "I was in a similar quandary once upon a time."

"Yes," he said hopefully.

"I was a Boy Scout, with my troop in Washington D.C." I said. "We'd spent the whole day in the capitol and had seen everything except the Washington Monument and the Smithsonian. We wanted to see both, but we only had an hour-and-a-half left before we had to leave for the train station."

"Would it not take months to see everything in the Smithsonian?" he asked.

"We were kids. What did we know?"

"Our scoutmaster asked for a decision," I continued. "We voted and told him we wanted to see both."

"How?"

"Our bus took us to the monument and we sprinted up the stairs, looked out at the city for a few seconds, sprinted down, and then went to the Smithsonian where we spent about fifty minutes."

"Did you see much?" he asked.

"Funny," I said. "Who writes your material?"

"Just landing the plane and getting into Mexico City would take most of a day," Marat said. "And then we would be on foot again."

"Right," I said. "This is where we compromise. The difference is we'll only do one of the two."

I could see he was interested.

"When I was in high School," I said, "I did a paper on *Teotihuacan.*"

"You did?" he asked with surprise.

I guess I neglected to mention to him that I was an archeology nut.

"There is a place called *Calzada de los Muertos,* The Avenue of the Dead, that runs right through the city," I said. "It's straight and level, and I think it's pretty clear. Over a mile long."

"Let me see if I can find it on the map," I said.

Marat handed me the map. I found the site in short order and pointed it out to him.

"You think we can land there?" Marat asked.

"Why not?" I said. "You're pretty good with this thing," and I had my prayer routine down by now.

"So," Marat said as if getting it straight in his mind, "we skip Mexico City, but we go to *Teotihuacan.*"

"Right," I answered. "But if you want to imitate *Malraux* and steal one of the pyramids, I think you'll need a larger plane."

He didn't laugh. I guess *Malraux* was one of those sacrosanct subjects with him.

"It will be dawn by the time we get there," Marat said, and as I looked to the east, I could see the sky beginning to lighten.

"Look over there," Marat said, as the outline of *Popocatepetl* came into view.

I looked, but something was bothering me, and try as I might, I couldn't remember it. Dang, I hate getting old.

Gradually we started to descend into the central highlands and soon we were racing over the treetops.

It was getting lighter and I could just begin to see the outlines of low-lying hills. Well, that was one thing I forgot.

"*Teotihuacan* is surrounded by low hills," I warned Marat.

"Roger," he said.

We banked up and over a section of the foothills, came around to a southerly heading and just about ran into the Temple of the Moon.

Hopefully, that was the only thing I forgot, but I pondered as Marat gunned the engine, sending us back up as the bottom of the plane came within a foot of the pyramid which formed the northern boundary of our proposed runway.

"There's the Avenue," I said innocently.

He now slowed our speed and brought the plane down in a perfect landing, taxiing right up to a position abreast of the third largest pyramid in the world. The sun had not yet risen and everything was still shadowy.

"Well?" Marat said. "Now what?"

"Follow me," I said, and I opened my door, climbed out on the wing and jumped to the ground. I walked around to his side and yelled, "*Vamos.*"

Then I turned and started sprinting up the 248 steps of the Temple of the Sun. I loved to run the steps at Memorial Stadium on the U of M campus. Sixty-four of 'em, steps I mean. They start out at about five inches high on the bottom and gradually get taller—by the time you got to the top it was almost a yard jump. Call it a character flaw but I loved it. After two weeks of sprinting up those steps you couldn't get a ball past me. Anyway, at least the 10 and unders couldn't. And this was great. I really needed a type of exercise where I was running for the pleasure of it, rather than to escape a bullet.

I was a third of the way to the top when I heard it. Damn! What idiots some tourists are—and they were probably Americans. Here I was, communing with a temple that was almost two thousand years old, trying to imagine being with the ancients in that long ago time, and some moron had left his radio on the steps, and it was still on and playing "*Your Mama Don't Dance.*"

It kinda wrecked the mood.

So, as Marat labored to catch up, I ran over and gave the radio a good kick and smiled as it crashed to the ground, seventy feet down. Ah, silence.

We got to the top, sprinted back down, revved up the plane

and were in the air. The whole break had lasted fifteen minutes. My scoutmaster would've been proud.

By now it was light enough to actually see more than shadows on the ground. We were still flying low and suddenly Marat banked and headed down.

"That was pretty cool," Marat said. "Want to do it again?"

"Huh?" I answered with my usual keenness.

"Our flight path takes us right past *Cholula*, the largest pyramid ever built. Larger than Cheops," he said excitedly.

"Naw," I said. "You seen one pyramid, ya seen 'em all."

Boy, that really took the wind outa his sails. But I didn't worry about Marat. You can't keep a good man down for long. Plus, I hadn't used a cliché in some time.

"*Pemex*," he shouted excitedly.

Damn. Too bad there wasn't a station at the pyramid.

We landed on a two-lane blacktop and taxied up to the *Pemex* lot and the gas pump.

Marat got down and looked around the plane for the gas tank opening, while, on the other side of the plane, my feet hit the ground just as a Mexican man, maybe the owner of the station, walked toward us with a confused look on his face.

He and Marat spoke for a bit, then the man left and returned with a ten-liter container of aviation fuel.

We refueled, paid the man and off we went.

We flew eastward, keeping low as the sun came up. I was ambivalent about the daylight. It was easier to see where we were going, but it was also easier to be spotted. I hoped Marat had his instrument's rating, because some of the time we were flying through clouds and mountain peaks piercing up out of the haze looking like great shark fins. When I glanced over at him, I could see he was intently looking at the gauges, then the map, a travel book that I hadn't even known he possessed, and occasionally, the altimeter.

The fuel gauge didn't register much more gas than when I had woken up before we got to *Teotihuacan*.

After a few hours on the eastern heading, we started to descend.

We were finally through the mountains, which Marat identified as the *Cordillera Neovolcanica*, a range of volcanoes. Soon, we could see the Gulf of Mexico glimmering on our left and we plunged even lower to follow the coast. Strangely, the sky to the northeast looked darker than the sky in front of us.

Now I looked at the map to see how closely it represented the coast. I immediately realized I needed a bigger map in larger scale or a smaller coastline.

By now the strange dark sky to the northeast was being punctuated by streaks of lightning. The sky was almost pitch-black. Great cumulonimbus clouds were dark with rain and we were heading on a collision course.

"Maybe we should leave the coast," I suggested to Marat.

Without a nod or verbal assent, he pulled on the throttle and we banked to the south, just as the first raindrops fell on the plane.

Soon we were cruising over ground that was flat and lush and green. In front of us we could see undulating hills, but below us, between the hills and the coast, everything looked like jungle. There were no roads, villages or anything like civilization, only swamp, forest and mangroves. We flew across a large river and smaller tributaries, and on these saw a few small boats plying the waters, some looking like people were fishing from them, others carrying cargo. We were so low, we couldn't see much more than what we directly passed over.

Occasionally, we would see rock jutting out of the jungle and Marat said those were probably the remains of Mayan temples and cities, some not yet excavated or even marked on the maps, there were so many of them.

"We are just south of *Veracruz*," Marat said. "The storm is blocking our path to the *Yucatan*...but look at this."

Marat handed me the guidebook, which of course was written in Spanish. But I could make out three words his fingers were pointing to: surfing and *Puerto Escondido*. Then I found it on the map in *Oaxaca*.

"Aren't we trying to get to *Cuba*?" I asked.

"The guide book says there are gnarly, hollow tubes at *Puerto Escondido*," Marat said. "And they break right off the beach."

"You're a surfer?!" I exclaimed, once again caught by surprise.

"But don't we need to get to *Cancun* to get a boat?" I asked. "So we can finally ditch Assad?"

"I have never surfed in Mexico," Marat countered. "And it is one of my lifetime goals to surf in every country in the world."

Well, I was certainly happy that I could help fulfill one of his lifetime goals.

"Are you going to surf in Liechtenstein?"

"One should not make light of another's lifetime goals."

"Do we have enough fuel?" I asked.

"And that Assad," Marat continued. "He definitely did not look like a surfer."

Ahead of us now loomed the foothills of the *Sierra Madre de Oaxaca*. We would have to cross this chain of mountains and the *Sierra Madre del Sur*.

Well, I thought, if this is truly the best of all possible worlds, then Marat's famous luck will show up again, and there is probably a good reason for us to go to the Pacific rather than the Caribbean. For one thing, I could make out enough in the guidebook to see that the surfing was certainly better. Maybe we could make our escape to *Guatemala* instead of *Cuba*, but then we couldn't work in the cane fields. Decisions, decisions, decisions.

"And we can keep the plane," Marat said, as if reading my mind. "After we surf, the storm will have passed and we can fly to *Cancun*."

Sounded good to me.

"We are heading up again," Marat said. "I hope we have enough fuel."

I now took the opportunity to take the palm of my hand and slap it up against my forehead.

So on we went. No lightning bolt came closer than about one hundred yards as the storm chased our Cherokee all the way to the mountains, but we certainly bounced up and down a lot with the turbulence.

We crossed the *Sierra Madre de Oaxaca* then Marat veered east to avoid flying over the city of *Oaxaca*—the only major city in the state, and as the sky was clear and blue in front of us, he kept the plane close to the ground, flying between peaks so that for much of the journey, we were lower than the tops of the mountains. By then it was only a hundred miles from *Oaxaca* to the coast, so it didn't take us long to cross through the *Sierras.* Marat kept our altitude so the ground was soon far below us.

"I really like the fact that we have so much altitude," Marat said as he rolled down his window, stuck his head out and began looking downward.

"Why?" I asked.

"Start looking for places to land," he yelled to me, as I began to see jungle once more in front of us, and far off in the distance I could make out a shimmering light blue which I took to be the Pacific.

"Why?" I asked.

"Because we are almost out of petrol," he yelled back.

I frantically rolled down my window and started to look forward, backward, to the side, and up—wouldn't want to miss anything.

"There have to be villages around here somewhere," Marat said. "Even in the jungle. Look for openings in the trees. We will find a soccer field or parade ground. Possibly a road."

Ever the pessimist, I asked, "What if we don't?"

"Then look for a river or lake," he said in all seriousness. "Preferably a wide one. I don't think we have enough petrol to make the ocean."

I had landed in a lake once with a friend of my father's. We had pontoons on that plane. I closed my eyes and searched my memory if I had seen any pontoons on this one. I opened the door to a sudden rush of air, then leaned out and looked below. Nope. Didn't think so. Pulling the door shut, I decided to content myself with looking for a landing spot, preferably very soft, something like mud or even quicksand.

CHAPTER 16

Marat Perkins

"Will the wonders of the world never cease" —Dad

It seemed as though we were peering out of those windows for half an hour. Though the wind felt good on my face, it would feel better when we spotted a straight, level landing spot.

"There is a small city near here," Marat said as he searched the map. "*Rio Grande*. It is the nearest, but it is very small."

The engine fluttered. I'd run out of gas in a car before. It isn't a real big deal. One of my tennis buddies had an old Carmen Ghia that had a broken gas gauge. He'd just drive it till it ran out of gas. He was late a lot. But then again, I'd never run out of gas before in a plane.

Five more minutes passed. Then, through the canopy of trees I saw what looked like a curvy brown line, snaking through the green.

"Down there, Marat," I yelled excitedly. I pointed. "There! It looks empty."

He dipped the plane slightly to the right so he could see. As we got lower, the brown line started looking like a dirt road. If we could go another mile, the road straightened out and appeared to be level. Marat then throttled the engine, gaining height with the last fumes and heading it toward the road. We got up to about a thousand feet.

"This is as good a place as any to ditch the plane," Marat said.

But now something else occurred to me.

"If we don't have the plane," I asked. "How are we going to get to Cuba?'

"We will take a boat," Marat answered. He laughed. "Then you won't have to worry about being shot down."

No, we'll be sunk instead, I thought or eaten by sharks or swallowed by whales. Maybe I do worry too much.

Now the engine sputtered. The prop came to a complete, dead stop and we were gliding downward toward the road. By then we weren't more than two hundred yards above the trees.

I went in back to see if there was anything else I could throw out to lighten our load.

Once more I said prayers to Ahura Mazda(not to be confused with the car), Allah, Buddha for last minute enlightenment just in case, Cronus, Ganesha (for good luck and prosperity), Hades, in case we wound up visiting him rather soon, Hanuman, because I was a long time fan, Hecate, Isis, Jesus, Jove, Jupiter, in case we wound crashing into the sea, Loki, Mars and Poseidon(some I prayed to by their different names so as to cover all bases. Besides, would it hurt to ask any one of them twice)? Then I included Quetzalcoatl in a nod to the home field advantage, Ra in case he might lend us some solar power—you see, this was well thought out—Shiva, Vishnu, Yahweh, Zoroaster (cuz I still like to have it both ways. Besides, his name sounds Spanish) and Zeus—and I did it in alphabetical order so as to not play favorites. I wondered if I should include prophets, but decided I only had time to entreat with the big guys, and I did try to stick to equal opportunity. Then I remembered I better include Bud Grant and Rod Laver to really cover all bases. I'd finished with this mantra-like invocation when I heard a voice coming from what seemed like the beyond.

It said: "We are now descending at a rate of one hundred and forty miles per hour. Our landing speed will be approximately seventy miles per hour. There is presently a fifteen mile per hour tail wind. The temperature on the ground, I believe is about 30 Centigrade. This is your captain. I hope you had a nice trip with us and when you think of flying you will try us again. Yes. We are Aero Marat. Oh, and our crash speed will be about fifty miles per hour."

"Marat," I said, as I returned to my seat. "We still have two bags of grass."

"*Merde*! I am busy right now," Marat said, his eyes focused on the fast approaching ground. Then he looked at me. "We won't have time to smoke it."

By now we were right above the treetops and the road was making one last bend.

I closed my eyes and began my meta meditation one last time. There was a lurch. Then I could feel the nose of the plane go up and seem to be at an angle to the road. I opened my eyes just as there was a bump, then another and the Cherokee came in for a perfect three-point landing.

The plane glided for ninety yards before finally coming to a stop right before it would have crashed into an old man riding a hay-filled cart pulled by a donkey. I swear if the propeller would've still been rotating, we would've given him a heart attack and a trim. As it was, the man's beard and hair seemed to turn from gray to white as we got out of the plane, and when I got on my hands and knees to kiss the dirt road and offer thanks to all my benefactors, I noticed the donkey now looked like an albino. I guess neither of them had almost been part of a plane crash before.

Marat walked over to the peasant and started speaking to him, I supposed to calm him down. The next thing I knew, the old man went over to the plane and started feeling the exterior with something bordering on reverence. After running his hands over the length of the Cherokee, he looked over at Marat, who gave him a nod of approval, and then climbed up into the cockpit. I could see him rummaging though the back of the plane.

He came back to the pilot's door and stuck out his head.

"Marijuana?" he asked.

I looked at Marat, who was smiling. He gave me a nod.

"*Sí*," I said.

The peasant got down, winked and shook my hand.

"Deal," he said. Then he followed the same procedure with Marat, who grinned as wide as a crescent moon and shouted to me, "We are now the proud owners of one burro and cart."

Taking our bags and an Uzi apiece, we hopped up onto the cart seat, Marat grabbing the reins while I buried the Uzis in the hay. Then we started down the road.

"If he gets caught," I asked, "Won't he tell about the two *gringos* that fell from the sky, almost decapitated him and traded him the plane and the dope for the donkey cart?"

Marat pulled out another joint, lit it, took a drag and handed it to me. "The police will look at him, think he is loco and say, 'Why do you think they call it dope?'"

"Seriously, Tomas," Marat said in the tone of fatherly advice, "You need to lighten up. To smoke more dope. It will stop the worrying."

I didn't agree. All it took was to remember stealing the plane. I figured I'd smoked pot for the last time. I'd never really been a drinker or smoker. I liked to have my senses about me, especially every time I was being chased by *banditos, Federales,* rebels, *la policia* and drug smugglers.

"I think we should go back and hide the plane...or sink it in the swamp," I said, as the donkey amiably pulled our new cart down the road.

"Tomas, Tomas, Tomas," Marat said with the utmost patience. "Everybody in this country probably knows about the two desperate *gringos* by now, so what difference does it make? The *Federales* know, the police know, the drug smugglers probably know, the *banditos* know, and do not forget the rebels and your *commandante*."

The bastard. How could he be so calm? And he hadn't even bothered to get a pink slip for our new rig.

Maybe at this time I should've mentioned the albino. That would get anybody a little bent out of shape. Marat needed more edge.

"We might as well enjoy what we have and stop worrying,

no? I think I would rather hear you lament about one of your old girlfriends." Then he started laughing.

The point was well taken.

We rode on for a while and I could tell he was deep in thought. After about an hour, he blurted out, "You are not lying about that *commandante* being a woman are you?"

Now I burst out laughing. I had thought his rumination was concerned with chastising me again about worrying, or telling me *Circe* put me in a trance and she was really a he.

"No. I'm not lying," I said. "In fact, she was probably the hottest woman I've ever seen. A go getter too." I even wished I had asked her to pronounce Chicago.

I took a hit.

Now content, I pulled a piece of straw from one of the bales and put it in between my lips. Then I leaned back, placing my hands behind my head and feeling like Tom Sawyer. This mode of transportation suited me. Nothing could've gotten me to get up right then. If all our possible pursuers showed up I'd just give them the finger and let them do their worst. Who cared? Not I. Hmm. This was really good shit.

Though I was drifting in and out of a relaxed sleep, I still noticed how closed in we were by the jungle on both sides of the road. There were no shoulders, and the road had become barely wide enough for the cart. But we were at sea level—no worrying about going over cliffs down here. I was very pleased with myself that I wasn't worrying about anything. What could possibly happen on this quiet, peaceful road, where all we could hear was the rhythmic, soothing clippety-clop of the donkey's hooves and the calls of tropical birds and monkeys?

And nothing did, that is, until toward dusk, when we reached a low part of the road that was covered with water, and in the middle of which was the biggest, slimiest, meanest, fattest, hungriest crocodile I'd ever seen.

As our donkey brayed and came abruptly to a stop, the croc raised his head out of the water, turned it our way and let out a loud noise that sounded like a grunt.

"Mating call," Marat said. "He's trying to get laid."

So add horniest to my aforementioned list.

I looked at the croc, pointed at Marat and raised my eyebrows up and down suggestively; after all, imitation is the most sincere form of flattery. The crocodile looked back amorously at Marat. Maybe he was a she—Marat had a way with women you know.

"Don't let me stand in your way," I said, extending my hand in the direction of the lovesick crocodile.

"No," Marat said. "This is serious."

"I think she likes you," I said. "Maybe if you nuzzle up to her, sort of let her have her way with you, she'll let us pass."

Marat was deep in thought. His brows were furrowed.

"Well. Do we just turn around?" I asked after awhile. I wiped sweat away from my forehead. Even though it was now dusk, it was so hot and humid I also had to wipe the fog from my glasses.

Now Marat turned the tables on me. He was fiendishly clever.

"Do you really want to do that?" he asked. "What if we go back and the police have already discovered the plane? Perhaps you were right, and we should have destroyed it, or hidden it in the jungle or dismantled the pieces and spread them across the marshes."

"If they did that," I said in a none too polite rejoinder, "they're probably following our cart tracks as we speak."

"Would you rather get caught sooner or later?" Marat asked. "I do not think our friend Mademoiselle Crocodile will move an inch. So I think we abandon the cart, turn the donkey around and let him go back to his master. Besides, then our trail will end here and throw off the police," he snickered. "They might even surmise that the croc ate us."

Returning the favor for past criticisms, I said, "Stop worrying. There aren't any police or *Federales* within a thousand miles of us. At least not the ones chasing us."

"And the surf is up that way," Marat pointed out and pointed with his hand.

Suddenly, I heard the faint but now unmistakable sound of chopper blades. The croc looked up. The donkey looked up.

Marat and I looked up. Jesus, I thought. Not again? I felt like reaching in the hay, retrieving an Uzi and showing them what for.

But the helicopter just flew right on by in a straight line. Lucky for them. My blood was up again. Maybe I should try croc wrestling. What would the Crusher do?

"What do you think?" Marat taunted. "Are they looking for us?"

"Too bad they didn't send 'em out to lift the crocodile from the road," I said. "They do that in Florida all the time."

"They are probably heading to the beach," Marat said. "To surf or look at women just like us."

I laughed. "Now what do we do about the croc?" I asked. "Those guys can move pretty fast. Are you sure you want to be on foot? We'd be in more danger, no?" I had caught some of the Latin syntax by now.

Marat got down from the cart and looked around, after a bit finding a few stones and pebbles.

"According to the map," he said, "this must be *Laguna de Manialtepec*. That means we are getting close. Here. Take a few of these."

He handed me a couple of the small stones.

"You want to peg him?" I asked.

"I want to give him incentive to move."

Marat would have made a good politician.

So now we threw out stones. Then we threw twigs. We hurled invective in Spanish, English, Thai and Nepalese. We even launched one of the smaller hay bales. The crocodile's response was to look moon-eyed and grunt louder for a mate. I had sympathy for the croc. Love can do that to you.

Marat reached into the hay and pulled out the two Uzis.

"No, Marat," I said. "We can't do that. It's against my upbringing."

Marat then hung his head. I could see he felt bad. It looked like he was going to go up to the croc and apologize, but I would've stopped him if he tried.

"What if we just shoot in the air?" he said. "No," he quickly reversed that thought. "That would only serve to give notice of our whereabouts."

Then, with the most serious look I'd ever seen him give me, Marat said, "We will have to go around him. Through the jungle."

"Great," I said. "I propose we give him an exceedingly wide berth."

It was getting dark and we didn't want to waste anymore time. Turning the donkey around and setting him on his way, we backed up till we were out of sight of the crocodile, then plunged into the thick grass and jungle.

The crocodile's plaintive protestations of undying love and yearning rang through the mangroves and trees as we tried to move quietly. Happily, those groans kept coming from the same approximate direction, so I reckoned Marat wouldn't have to prove his manhood yet.

By the time it was dark, we started to circle back to the road, but were halted by a swift flowing river. It wasn't wide, but it certainly had more crocodiles (maybe even our friend), piranas, and I was pretty certain fer-de-lances could swim.

"You first," I whispered. "Tell me how it is on the other side."

"All right," Marat said, undressing and putting his clothes and Uzi into his pack and wading into the water. When it got too deep to walk, he turned on his back and swam holding the pack above him.

It probably wasn't fair to let him go first to see if it was safe but Marat certainly had *sang froid*. He'd already done this in the *Yucatan*. Then I realized if I went in with him, my chances were better, up to fifty-fifty. I quickly undressed and waded in. Then I remembered something else. There's a little fish in the Amazon, the *candiru*, that swims up the hole in your penis, extends barbs and lodges itself. I wasn't sure if any got this far north, but just to be on the safe side, I left on my underwear, and when I had to swim, I held my pack with one hand, covered my crotch with the other and kicked with my feet, as I anxiously waited a chomp, bite or even nibble. Nothing got me, except that, on the other side, I observed Marat beginning to painstakingly pull off leaches. I got off lucky. Only twelve of the suckers had found me. Now, I heard a tick, tick, ticking sound.

"What the hell is that?" I asked in a whisper.

"The mating call of the bushmaster," Marat answered.

Brother, I thought. Another horny animal. Crocodiles, bush-masters, fer-de-lances, *Dulcineas*, Gagools and *commandantes*—the only one we couldn't make love to down here was *Leticia* the prostitute.

After getting rid of our fellow travelers, we dressed and headed off through more jungle, our intention to catch up with the road on the other side of the big crocodile.

It wasn't long before Marat stopped and crouched down on a swath of soft mud.

"*Sacre merde.* Look, Tomas," he whispered.

I was surprised he could see anything it was so dark by now.

"Look at this, Tomas," he said. "It is the track of a jaguar."

"Are you sure it's just not a big cat?"

"A very big cat," he said.

"He is going our way," Marat said. "Should we track him?"

"I wonder if it's horny?" I mused.

"And look here," he said excitedly. "The print of a tapir."

He carefully followed the tracks. Right then, we heard the chopper again. Marat and I looked up; I can't speak for either the jaguar or tapir. This chopper was shining a search beam, but he never approached our side of the road. From the sound of it, he hovered for a while north of us.

"The jaguar is tracking the tapir," Marat said as he examined more tracks. "This jaguar is young and stupid."

"Huh?" I said, sounding quite intelligent, I might add.

"The jaguar likes to attack its prey from the rear."

"Thank you Marlin Perkins," I said. It was too dark to see a facial response and he was only interested in talking about the jaguar and tapir.

"If the jaguar attacks a tapir," he continued. "Once it gets its teeth into the back of the tapir's neck, the tapir hunches its shoulders." He hunched his shoulders to illustrate. I dare you to try telling this story without hunching yours. "Its neck is very thick. Now, the jaguar cannot break free. The tapir then runs under low hanging branches and the jaguar is hammered. When it tires of this, the tapir jumps into the water. A tapir can stay under water a long time. Not so the jaguar."

"This jaguar is about to have a bad night," Marat said.

"Ok," I asked. "Can we go back to the road now?"

Right about then was the time when a python would probably drop from a tree within an inch of either Marat or my head. I looked up. Yup. Right on cue. Good, it landed closer to Marat. I tapped Marat on the shoulder causing him to jump a second time.

"I think we should move on," I said, nodding toward the reticulated python. He got my drift—after all, he had two PhDs.

In another half-hour we were back to the dirt road. Our foray into the jungle had covered over a mile, and by the time we reached the road, I could no longer hear the chopper. But we'd barely walked a few yards when we heard a ruckus coming from the bush. Ducking down, we saw a really big tapir crash out of the jungle and dart across the road, the jaguar hot on his tail. They were less than three yards in front of us. My heart was beating loudly, and as for Marat, I could hear his over mine.

In an instant, the jaguar leapt and sunk his claws and teeth into the back of tapir's thick neck. Stopping for a second, I could see the tapir hunch up his shoulders just like Marat said, trapping the jaguar.

Stupid jaguar. He was in for a ride. They disappeared across the road and back into the jungle. I wondered how long it would take before the jaguar said, "Oops!" or "Oh shit!" Nevermind. His mouth was full.

Getting up, we started to move fast. Going down the road was a lot easier than tramping through the jungle and marshland—see flair for the obvious.

Within ten minutes, we started over a wooden bridge. About halfway across, I heard a loud crashing sound. Marat cried out, "Look, Tomas! Look!" The tapir, with the jaguar still aboard for the ride, jumped into the river and disappeared from sight. We stood and watched. After another few minutes, the jaguar surfaced, swimming for its life in the opposite direction.

"That jaguar has learned a valuable lesson," Marat said solemnly, as the jaguar made the riverbank and shook off its anxieties and excess water.

We continued down the road for an hour. The only things I could hear were our steps and heavy breathing—it was quite muggy here, even at night. But then, a different sound reached my ears. It was a very soft rumbling. At first I couldn't make it out. We kept going. After another ten minutes I stopped to listen. Then I knew.

"It's surf! The ocean!" I yelled out, and I started running toward the sound, leaving Marat in the dust.

I was so ecstatic when I reached the beach, I threw off my boots and ran up and down the wet sand, my arms spread out and waving, looking much like the twit of the year. I could see a very starry sky from the beach, and in the distance to the east I could see the sky was a touch lighter and that meant a town, *Puerto Escondido*. We had made it. We had left all our pursuers in the dust. We were home free.

Then I peeled off my clothes and waded out into the ocean. After swimming back and forth for a bit in the cooling water, I came out and Marat was standing on the beach, grinning from ear to ear.

"I did not know you liked the beach so much, Tomas," he said. "It is about time you enjoyed yourself on your trip."

And he was right. It was about time. We walked along the cool sand, boots off and wading in the surf, and heading east toward *Puerto Escondido,* the surfing Mecca of Mexico, according to Marat.

The sky was dark, but there were so many stars that we could see the landscape clearly. After an hour of walking, the jungle had receded into the distance and there were cliffs and outcroppings of rocks to our left. Here the beach became narrower.

The roar of the surf on the sandy beach and the calls of seagulls (probably for a mate) drowned out all other sounds. I could not stop gazing up at the clear night sky and all the stars.

After awhile, the surf began to grow louder, finally crashing onto the beach in thunderous proportions as we came to *Playa Bacocho*—we were very near the city.

It was already one in the morning. It would be another hour before we got into town.

"We will stay here tonight," Marat said in the tone of a royal edict.

Neither of us wanted to spend money on a place to stay—Marat out of principle and me because I figured I must be running pretty short by now. I figured I might have to give some tennis lessons just to be able to afford to get back to the States. Besides, by my reckoning it was Christmas Eve. I didn't think anything would be open anyway. According to Marat, *Puerto Escondido* was little more than a fishing village, probably like *Puerto Vallarta* before Liz and Dick made their film.

Then, Marat led me back up to the rocks where we looked for a place of shelter, somewhere we could hide while we slept. *Jorge* had told us about hitchhikers that had their throats slit while sleeping on a beach.

I hadn't had a good night's sleep since the next to the last night at the *bandito* camp, so I just followed along. Any place was fine with me.

It seemed like I had barely gotten to sleep when I was jostled awake. I swear Marat was tireless, the bastard. I liked to sleep. My father swore it had taken ten years off his life just to get me up in the morning for school.

"Cowabunga, dude," Marat said in a French accented imitation of a California surfer. "Surf's up."

Walking back down to the beach, we headed for the town.

"Dude!" Marat exclaimed as we reached the outskirts of *Puerto Escondido*. "I don't have a board!"

"Cut the surfer jargon, Marat," I said. "Ok? I could've told you you didn't have a board when we started this trip."

"Duuude!" he said, drawing it out for at least ten seconds. He started to smile. The thing about Marat, I never really knew when he was having fun, that is, except when he was feeding me hot chilies.

For some reason, I started to think about the date again. "Merry Christmas," I said to Marat.

"Merry Christmas," he said back. "I wish I had something I could give you."

Christmas, I thought. We've only been gone twelve days. Unbelievable.

"Me too."

Now, all of a sudden I had a pressing need to know how much money I actually had. I'd only taken two hundred dollars for this trip, and I figured to be gone a month. I had no idea how much I'd spent. I might be begging on the streets pretty soon. In my pockets were a hundred pesos. About the equivalent of nine dollars. Looking in my pack, I pulled out thirteen ten dollar bills, one twenty, one five and four ones. I'd only spent thirty-two dollars? Boy, was I thrifty or what! I guess it helps when you don't pay your hotel bill or when you stay in jails and *bandito* and rebel ranchos.

"Tomas," Marat said as we began climbing a switchback footpath that led up onto the rocks. "I want to see the lay of the land. It is always good to know what is going on before we go into a new place."

It was the first town we would be entering since we were in *Ajijic*, so I was glad he wanted to be cautious for a change. It was a first and it was welcome.

When we got to the top, Marat got down on his belly, pulled out a small pair of field glasses and started to scan the area.

"*Encroyable!*" he said and then handed me the binoculars. It was early dawn.

It was a sleepy little village just like I had imagined. Most of the dwellings and buildings were on top of the rocks across from us, maybe a half-mile away, and below was the beach where you could see the waves crashing to the shore. There were already surfers riding them in.

"Heaviest sand bottom tube in the world, dude," Marat said.

"These are pretty good glasses," I said to Marat.

"Yes," he said. "Army. French Army. The best."

I didn't comment.

I could see over twenty people already down there surfing the waves. They looked like mere dots with the naked eye, but through the binoculars, I could see amazing detail. I picked out a scar running down one man's leg. Many of them had mustaches. They wore Speedos or regular swim trunks and were bare-chested, but there were six that were wearing olive green, long-sleeved shirts, almost looking like soaked army fatigues. One of those men was wearing an olive green kepi and surprisingly had a stick or something sticking out of the left side of his mouth. He looked familiar. It was a cigar. No, I thought, it couldn't be.

"Marat," I said, handing him the glasses. "Look at the big fellow just coming out of the tube. With the hat. Do you recognize him?"

Marat scanned the waves. A smile came to his face.

"That's *Fidel*," he said excitedly. "*Fidel Castro*. Duuude! I've always wanted to meet him. This is great. He must be a surfer dude too. Very few people know about this beach."

"Didn't he hang out in Mexico for a bit?"

"Yes," Marat said as he handed the binoculars back to me.

Sure enough, the hat, the cigar, the beard. *Fidel Castro*. This was like celebrity spotting. He was pretty good down there too. He was hanging ten and walking up and down his long board. Needless to say, both of us were impressed.

"I'll be damned," I said to Marat.

"If you stick with me, probably," Marat said.

As I scanned over the rest of the surfers to see if there was anybody else I'd recognize, my vision strayed to the beach where two small pick-ups were pulling up. More surfers, I thought. Let's see if they're famous.

"*Vamos!*" Marat cried, grabbing me by the arm before I could look. "I have to eat before I attempt the pipe."

We got up and headed toward the village.

"Well, Marat," I asked. "Are you going to teach me how to surf?" I'd never surfed in my life.

"Of course," Marat answered as we walked. "But not on this

beach. I cannot. You could die. These waves kill people. This is for expert surfers."

"Damn," I said.

"Just west of *Playa Zicatela* is *Playa Principal*," Marat said. "It is much milder. I will teach you there...just give me this one day on *Zicatela*."

"*No problemo*," I said. "I'll just lay in the sun and sleep." Or maybe I could find a place with a TV. I thought it could be the first week of the playoffs and I hoped the Vikings had the home field against the Redskins. Whether or not they carried it down here I had no idea.

"Maybe I will catch a wave with *Fidel*," Marat said, a light shining in his eyes.

We found a meager restaurant. In this place, all the restaurants were meager even by our standards.

While we were sitting over our eggs, beans and rice, I saw Marat's ears prick up at someone's conversation.

"Well?" I asked.

His mouth full and laughing, Marat translated. "The man says to his friend 'Did you hear about that crocodile on the road. Biggest one this year. They had to send a helicopter to move her back into the swamps.'"

I laughed so hard I spit out my food, but I still had the presence of mind to aim some of the particles on his beans. Like I said, I never hold grudges.

CHAPTER 17

Masala Dosa

"Even a blind hog finds the acorn once in a while." –Dad

We paid and then went to look for a surf shop. Sure enough, Marat's luck held out. There was only one such shop, and it was down to its last rental board, only turned in five minutes earlier by the friends of someone who was stung by a sting ray. I began to wonder if Marat's luck was the kind where if he got some boon, it had to be taken away from someone else. And it then occurred to me that as soon as I got him a place to stay in Tempe, I got trampled by a car.

Marat signed for the extra liability and collision insurance and we headed down a dirt road that went from the heights to the beach.

By now, the waves were more crowded. The tubes were gigantic—you could have driven a semi through them—and deafening as they crashed on the sandy beach. While we walked I saw two bodies tossed into the air like rag dolls. Marat was right. I could wait to go into the wading pool version of the surf.

Tossing off my boots when we reached the beach, I ran the sand through my toes and took my shirt off.

"Let me see the binos," I said to Marat, who was busy examining his board. Holding the board up with one hand, he reached into his pack and gave them to me.

I looked through the glasses. There was *Fidel*, coming through another tube about to exit. The guy was good. This was cool, dude. Oops. Sorry.

A little further out was another group, just about to catch a wave. Something looked strangely familiar about them. As they stood up, I could see they were all in Speedos, and, "Oh my God!" I shouted. One of them had white hair...and pink skin!

"It's the albino!" I said in shock. "What the hell is he doing here?"

Marat looked at me as though I was crazy.

I looked down the line of surfers. One was Assad as certainly as I stood there. I thought he'd put on weight—too many *cervesas* and burritos in drowning his sorrow.

Now, a light of understanding went off in my brain. Marat!!!

"So," I said casually to Marat as he stood on his board getting a feel for it. If there was one thing my coach had pounded into my head, it was "Don't get mad over a bad shot and don't get happy over a good shot." In other words, I didn't show my fast rising anger; I had on a poker face. "This surfing passion of yours...you don't seem to talk about it a lot. In fact, I was surprised when you told me."

"No," Marat said. "You know I like to be discreet about things."

"Well," I went on. "Did you by chance tell anyone else about your surfing passion?" I asked, handing him the binoculars and motioning for him to look out to sea. "You know, while on the trip?"

"Well...I told the one you call *Dulcinea*," Marat said as he got the idea that I wanted him to look. He was trying very hard to sound innocent.

"And?" I asked. "Anyone else?"

He hemmed and hawed for a minute or two, then sputtered out, "I might have mentioned it to some of the rebels," he said, drawing it out as though he hoped I would lose interest.

"And...?"

"Just possibly, I might have talked about surfing with Assad's wife."

I didn't want to but I had to ask, "You didn't happen to mention any particular beaches?"

"I might have mentioned *Puerto Escondido*," he said sheepishly. "It's the surfing Mecca of Mexico. I had to mention it to show I knew what I was talking about. But, you know, I did not think we were coming here."

Nothing like discretion, I thought. I took some consolation in the fact that I didn't think he had time to tell the police or the Army. And somehow, I couldn't imagine Gagool, the *banditos* or the rebels surfing.

"Do you see anybody out there you recognize?" I asked. "Besides *Fidel*, I mean."

"*Vamos*!" Marat cried, jumping four feet in the air as if he's just stepped on a snake. "He has seen me!" and he started to run back to the dirt road, carrying his board.

I grabbed the binoculars and sure enough, Assad had seen us. He automatically reached for his pistol with his hand, but didn't find it because all he had on were Speedos. Then he wiped out. I could see the others in his party snickering and pointing. He was pissed. There he was, pummeling the surf three hundred times with his fists, like some modern day Xerxes smacking the Dardanelles with three hundred lashes for destroying his bridge of boats. This is an estimate, I didn't have time to count.

Catching up to Marat, I shouted, "Where are you going?"

I figured we should be running down the beach, not back into town.

"I have to return the surf board," he said. "Or I'll lose my deposit."

Boy was he cheap. I didn't know whether to roll my eyes or once more slam the palm of my hand against my forehead. Either way, I was going to get screwed. I decided to not waste the time.

Like I said before, Marat was fast. Before I could stop him, he was halfway up the hill.

As I ran after him, I took various occasions to glance back at the beach to see if Assad and the albino had made it to shore.

What the hell did they have in common that they would form this unholy alliance?

I caught up to Marat at the top of the hill where he had stopped to look at the bad guys. Crouching down, I said, "Marat. Go! Return the board and get back here as fast as you can. Use your *Chihuahua* speed. I've got an idea."

He started running again.

"And don't waste time bargaining," I yelled after him.

I watched as *Fidel* made it to the beach. He seemed to view the *Federales* with much interest as Assad, his men, and the albino all surfed in to the beach, lugged their boards up to their vehicles, grabbed their sandals, ran back to the water's edge, each dipping one foot into the water to wash off the sand while hopping on the other like a crazed flamingo. Putting a sandal on the rinsed foot they then repeated the process with the other— maybe they were more like synchronized swimmers without the pool—and only two of them managed to keep their balance on the first attempt. They then sprinted up to their trucks, toweled off, dressed and piled in. Then I saw *Fidel* shake his head, take off his shirt and start wringing out the water. He was wearing bright red Speedos with a hammer and sickle logo under the long shirt. His five buddies all did the same.

I was startled by footsteps and turned to see Marat.

"All right, Tomas," he asked, breathing heavily. "What is the plan?"

"Just wait," I said as I continued to look through the binoculars. They were backing up and turning around. Then I saw them head up a tarred road—the one I'd seen them come down on earlier. Too bad I hadn't recognized them then.

"Let's go," I yelled as soon as they were out of sight. I had figured they couldn't take the dirt path we were on. It was so soft they would've gotten stuck.

We sprinted back down the trail to the beach and our course to the east took us right by the Cubans.

"*Senor Castro*," Marat said as he came to a stop in front of the Cuban leader. Marat was breathing hard but beaming. "I am honored to meet you," he continued as he stuck out his hand and shook *Fidel's* before his retinue could get between them. "I have admired you for a long time. You are fighting the good fight."

"Are you *Norte Americano*?" *Castro* asked, his tone registering complete surprise.

"No," Marat answered. "French." He pointed at me. "He is American."

I waved while sporting a sheepish grin on my face.

"Howdy," was all I could think to say. Later, I thought of all sorts of clever things, but you know how it is.

"I'm also a great admirer of *Che*," Marat said.

"*Che*!" *Castro* exclaimed. "Always *Che*! *Che* this, *Che* that. *Che* did this. *Che* did that. *Che's* wonderful, the greatest thing since sliced bread. Everybody only wants to talk about *Che*! *Dios mio*! I'm *so* sick and tired of hearing of *Che*. What am I, chopped liver?"

"You know he's dead," I said.

There was complete silence for a minute while this new info roiled through his brain.

"*Que*?" *Castro* finally said, completely surprised and also surprising us.

I thought I should fill him in. "In Bolivia, a few years ago. You know, CIA, Bolivian military, the usual."

Tears of anguish began streaming from his eyes as *Castro's* hands reached for the sky as if beseeching an uncaring God. "*Oh Dios mio*!" he wailed. "Why *Che*?" He tore at his hair and beard, then bent down and hit the ground with his fists. "*Che*! You were the best!"

I tugged at Marat's sleeve. "Shouldn't we be going?" Then to *Fidel*, "We'd love to chat," I said. "But the *Federales* are after us. *Adios*."

"Would you like me to help?" *Fidel* offered.

"Thank you, but no," Marat said. "We believe in taking personal responsibility."

My jaw dropped so low I had to spit sand out of my mouth.

"Well let me know if you change your mind," *Fidel* said graciously.

"Will do," I said.

"Not necessary," Marat said.

"*Via con Dios*," I said, then we started once more to sprint down the beach. There weren't many roads here and I figured the best Assad could do was come back down on the road he had taken into town, and then he'd have to run down the beach just like us, so we had a pretty good head start.

"Do you still have your Uzi?" Marat asked as we ran across a rock-filled spring.

"Yeah," I answered. But now I was shaken. It was something new to contemplate. How could I fire a gun at a fellow human being?

A lot of people in Minnesota hunt deer. It's huge in Minnesota. It's only a two week season, but in those two weeks it's total mayhem in the forests. Most of the hunters wear bright red or orange but the bloodlust is up and often hunters shoot other hunters—one of my teachers shot a sheep. Nothing's safe. There's a lot of excitement, hundreds of thousands of deer are slaughtered and they call it a sport.

Now, here I was, a guy who wouldn't kill an ant or fly—though I did sometimes make exceptions for mosquitoes and if you'd ever lived in Minnesota you'd understand—but I could be shooting at other men pretty soon. I like to be good at the things I do ergo if I was going to hunt I'd probably be a lot better at shooting a human than a deer. They aren't as fast. Only two legs you know; might as well start slow.

I could just see the headlines in the Whiskey Creek Journal: WHISKEY CREEK BOY KILLED IN SHOOTOUT WITH *FEDERALES*; or maybe: WHISKEY CREEK BOY NABBED IN SHOOTOUT. "AND HE WAS SUCH A GOOD BOY," TOWNSPEOPLE LAMENTED. "IT'S ALWAYS THE QUIET ONES," FORMER TEACHER SAYS. "HOW DID HE GO BAD?" Who knows? Either way it wouldn't sit too well with my mom.

As we ran, I could see the cliffs and rocks were receding, and ahead, the beach was once more abutting jungle and this was good. There were trees and palms and brush and it was getting thicker as we ran and there were various types of detritus on the sand. It looked like the same kind of lagoon we had traversed the night before. Maybe we could escape without fighting it out to the death, but one thing for sure: they'd never take me alive.

I felt sorry for Marat. Here he was so close to that enormous pipe and he didn't even get his toes wet, not to mention trading tales with *Fidel*.

"Grab some of those palm fronds," Marat said. Quickly, we each picked one up. "We're going to wipe out our tracks. Then we will run back up the beach about fifty yards, walk into the jungle, then walk backward, keeping our feet in the tracks so it looks like we left the beach at that point. Then we rub out our tracks for another fifty yards up the beach and go into the lagoon."

"Why don't we just run at the water's edge?" I said. "The incoming waves will rub out the tracks."

"No," Marat said. "This is the way the army taught us."

"French Army," I said innocently.

As we disappeared into the muck, the first thing I did was listen for mating calls.

"Sorry about the surfing, Marat," I said as we crawled across a huge log. "And *Fidel*."

"*No problemo*," he said. "*Ce la vie*. I will come back another time."

It was much hotter in here and more humid. Both of us were sweating profusely. Marat took in everything.

"Watch where you step," he said, looking up. "And what is above you. Believe it or not, many people are killed by coconuts falling on their heads."

I knew that.

We tore through the jungle. It seemed like we covered a mile in less than a minute. It wasn't long before we came to a fast-rushing stream, and totally out of place, right in the middle and on stilts, was a wooden shack with a thatched roof. Even more strange, to my eyes anyway, was a bridge over the river made up of a long single log running straight up to the door of the shack. I could see another log ran out the back to the other side.

"This is too inviting," Marat said. "Like some kind of trap."

Well that surprised me. Maybe Marat was losing his nerve a little bit and I liked that. I guess when you travel with somebody for awhile, you kind of blend. He was becoming a little more like me, and vice versa—hopefully the qualities we were transferring weren't each other's worst qualities.

"What d'ya say?" I asked.

"We cross on the log," Marat answered. It came down to wrestling with crocs, fer-de-lances and *piranas* or chancing the trap.

I went first, balancing my way over the log as incense emanating from the shack filled my nostrils. I quickly made it across and saw a sign hanging above the door, a shingle you might call it, with what I took to be a name, Masala Dosa. I started to feel hungry. Polite as ever, I knocked on the warped wooden door, wondering if Marat's fear was justified. I also wondered what new personage we could offend enough to want to chase us.

The door creaked open. I heard a high-pitched voice bid me to enter. When my eyes adjusted, I saw a smoke-filled room, piled from floor to ceiling with a dust-covered mishmash of books, vials, cups, plates, potions, candles and golf clubs—the messiest room I'd ever seen, even worse than my college apartment.

In the middle was a little, shriveled-up *Zapotec* Indian lady sitting at a table with bones, Tarot cards and stacks of loose tea leaves. A few goats, lizards and cats meandered around to complete the ambience.

Great! I thought. She had to be one of the sisters. And right when I needed her. Glancing around, I could see she knew her stuff.

She stared at me, motionless and silent. Then I heard footsteps.

"Are you here for a reading?" she asked as Marat entered.

"How do we get out of here alive?" I blurted out. "Are we headed in a good direction?"

"Calm down, Mr. Tomas," she said. "Have a seat. Take a load off."

We sat and she looked us over. She knew my name. Yup. She was talented.

"Unfortunately," she said, "the future. It gives me a head-ache. So I only tell the past."

I should've seen that one coming. Too bad I had so little time, being chased and all. Still, there were things I wanted to know about the past. Did my Nordic girlfriend really hate me? Or was it just her way of showing love? More recently, what if we'd stuck to the plan and gone to Mexico City? You know, "the road not taken." So, I wanted to know. Was there fate, deter-minism? Would they have found us anyway? I sat across from her and as my dad would've said, got down to cases.

"Don't you have something to say to me?" she asked.

"We are really short on time," Marat cautioned.

"Take it easy," I said, thinking hard. "Oh yeah. Hello from your sister, Granola."

"Thank you," she said. "It's actually Granola Chip."

"Oh. Sorry. What's this gonna set me back?" I asked.

She looked us up and down again and answered, "Ten pesos." She looked at her watch. "Up front."

Hmm. Either we looked pretty down and out or we were in big trouble. I handed over the money.

She put the bones into a hat, shook it and then dumped them out on the ground, shaking her head in a none-too-good way as she examined them.

Then she put tea leaves into a pot and hung it over a fire. Next she sharpened a long knife and started running after one of the goats. It was a small room and cluttered. During the chase, almost everything was knocked to the ground at least once.

"Darn *chatchkahs*," she cried (for those not in the know, *tzatzkees* can be spelled eleven different ways, all of them incorrect).

"Do you need help?" I asked.

She only grunted while continuing to run after the wily goat. I think he'd been chased before.

"Could you be quick about it?" I asked politely, looking at my watch. I could tell Marat was getting antsy. "We are in a bit of a hurry."

"Oh my God!" she said as she did a triple lutz over one of her tables, thus spilling horned toads, feathers, beetles of all shapes and sizes, bric-a-bracs and other knickknacks onto the thatched floor. Regaining her feet, she looked at me and yelled, "The damn tea leaves have to boil and I have to kill the *verstunken* goat and pull out the goddamned entrails. And I just had the place cleaned." Then, more calmly, she added, "Rome was not built in a day, you know."

"Maybe we should come back later," Marat suggested.

"I could give you a partial reading," she countered as she jumped through my legs and snagged the goat, which then started bleating loudly.

"Perhaps you could just do the tea leaves and bones," I helpfully suggested.

"Now you tell me."

Then she glared sternly at Marat who was staring at the teapot.

"And if you're in such a hurry," she scolded him, "don't watch the water boil."

So here we were sitting leisurely in front of this old lady, while mother-hating, peasant-killing, peon-whipping, father-raping, surfer dudes from the underworld tracked us down, hot on our tail, breathing down our necks, and all three of us trying hard to not look at the water in the pot, lest it wouldn't boil.

Soon, the Indian lady poured three piping hot cups of tea (a strong, black Darjeeling), closed her eyes and went into a trance. "Do you take milk or sugar?" she asked, opening one eye.

"Milk," I said.

"Milk and sugar for me," Marat answered.

Tossing Marat a sugar cube, she put one in her cup, then poured milk in all three, then reclosed her eye.

"Could I have another cube?" Marat asked. "I like mine sweet."

She flipped him a second, dumped the tea leaves onto a sheet of white paper alongside the bones, and went back to her trance for a minute, got up, pulled all the shades, then sat back down and went into her trance again.

I started to get suspicious.

It was dark in the cramped room, the only light coming from candles and tiny embers on the incense sticks.

Then she started to sing and I recognized the tune.

"Give me the beat, boys, to soothe my soul; I wanna get lost in your rock and roll and drift away."

Then I guess she drifted into her trance. Never underestimate the power of Rock and Roll.

After a few seconds, in a strange and much lower voice, she said, "So, what d'ya want to know?"

"You're the medium," I said. "Why don't you tell me?" I'd always wanted to say that in the right circumstance.

"You want to know about the road not taken," she said in a kind of Nya Nya Nya tone.

I told you she was talented. A chill ran down my spine. I nudged Marat to see if he'd told her anything about my bio. He shook his head in a no, and a bigger chill ran down.

"If you had gone to the *Yucatan,* you would have eaten something bad. By night, it would have been coming out of this end and coming out of that end." She pointed to her mouth and her rear as she talked for a visual aide. "Then it would have come out of both ends at the same time and you would have been up all night and lost five pounds. But then your friend here, Marat, would have given you *Entermo Viaform,* and it would take your intestines, and done this and stopped the fun." Here she brought her hands together and made a motion like she was wringing out a wet towel.

Ok. Ok. Ok! I've heard enough," I said. "How about on to the less recent past."

"Ok," she said, "but this *Entermo Viaform,* it has been known to kill people."

"Thanks a lot, Marat," I said under my breath.

"A word of caution," she said. "Don't drink the water here."

"So I've heard."

"When you were fourteen," she said, "you made a wrong turn on Horseshoe Island in the Boundary Waters National Park. Is this correct?"

"Ah, yeah," I stammered.

"And you got lost, correct?"

"Ah, yeah," I stammered.

"Well, see," she said. "If you'd taken the other road, you would not have become lost. The road not taken led back to camp...Need anything else?"

"No," I said. "I meant what would've happened if we'd gone to Mexico City?"

"You should be more specific."

"Sorry."

"If you went to Mexico City," she said. "The man you call Assad would not have found you."

"See," I said, turning to Marat. "Our fate was already determined. We were bound to come here. Because he was coming here."

"But if you went to Mexico City," she went on, "you would have run into the albino. He has business in Mexico City and he would have called Assad."

"Determinism," I shouted, slamming my fist down onto the table. "We would've run into Assad no matter where we would've gone."

Unfortunately, one leg of the table was shorter than the other three, and the book that had rested under that leg to prop it up had been kicked out during the goat chase. The table tipped over, dumping everything onto the floor.

"Thanks a lot," the Indian woman said as Marat and I picked up the table, the tea leaves, the bones and various other unknown objects off the floor.

She looked the mess over. "Perhaps I should re-boil the leaves.

"Just give us what you have," Marat said. "Time's money."

"But had you given the albino his five bucks," she said, "he would have gone back to the States and not called Assad."

"Ah," I said. "So I would've had free will in Mexico City."

"But we came here," Marat said.

"And the storm turned you away from the *Yucatan*," she said.

"Bringing us here," I lamented. "Tolstoy was right! It doesn't look good for free will. Everything is predetermined. I'm really bummed."

"And Monsieur Marat had to come here because here is the heaviest sand bottom tube in the world." She looked me directly in the eye and intoned, "Just like the butterfly flapping its tiny wings in South America causes someone to put *chorizo* in their *torta* in *Veracruz*, Mexico, which causes someone to be towed in Waco, Texas, which eventually results in someone buying deer hide gloves in Whiskey Creek, Minnesota, so does every previous action or thought you took in your life, or even your past lives to who knows how many generations back, effect every new action or thought you have in your present life."

Boy. She was good.

"But he chose not to surf," I said hopefully, still trying to worm my way back to believing in free will.

"He is too smart for that," she said. "He has two PhDs. you know."

"Aio!" I said.

"Don't worry, my son," she said. "All will work out for you in the end...although whether it will be good for you or not, I can't tell."

"Huh?" I sputtered.

"I calls 'em as I sees 'em," she said.

Now a different thought hit me. "Was it foreordained that I would be hit by a car and not be able to play tennis?" I asked.

"You couldn't play tennis before," she said, adding, "Ba dump bump." But then she adopted a serious expression.

"You are sad because you don't believe there is free will. But it was your choice to stop here, even though you have *Federales*, *banditos* and rebels on your tail, and have your fortune told, though everything would argue against you stopping."

My head was spinning. The *banditos* and rebels followed us here as well?

"Are there any police or army chasing us?" I asked.

"I don't see any," she said.

"Who's the albino?" Marat asked. "I have a thing about albinos."

"You and me both," I said.

"So you think there is free will?" I asked the lady. "Doesn't that contradict the whole butterfly spiel?"

"I am getting really bored," Marat said.

She gave him a dirty look. After all, this was her life's work.

"I like to cover all bets," she said. "And now you will have another chance to have it your way."

"I will?" Somehow, it seemed that asking a medium about free will and determinism either was an oxymoron, begged the question, or was a contradiction in terms—I'm not sure which one, but I'm sure it was covered by at least one of them.

"Because you can stay, and try once more to ask me about the future which is what you want to do, or you can hightail it out of here because any second now, Assad is going to be knocking on my door."

"Wait a moment," she said, looking at her sundial. There was a knock. "Ah," she said. "Right on time."

"Is there a rear exit?" Marat asked.

She pointed to a neon "Exit" sign above the rear door. We ran to the door.

"Thanks for the heads-up," I said as I flung open the door. Then I hesitated. "Do you have any good stock tips?" I asked.

"Ten pesos," she said.

I threw a ten spot at her.

"Microsoft. Your deliverance shall come through sport," she said. "And don't let the door hit you on your way out."

"By the way. That girl really hates your guts," she yelled.

So much for looking the girlfriend up if I ever got back home alive.

As I ran onto the log, I heard her exclaim, "Man! Ever since the *verstunken* Conquest."

We no sooner had stepped out on the second log, when Assad's men, seeing us from the other side, opened fire and bounded unto the log on their side.

"What I wouldn't give for some C-4," Marat said as we sprinted across.

Visions of the bridge blowing up under the bounty hunters in *The Wild Bunch* filled my mind as we jumped to the riverbank and disappeared into the jungle, bullets whizzing by our ears.

CHAPTER 18

Cubans Are Nice and Smoke Good Too

"A traveller has a right to relate and embellish his adventures as he pleases, and it is very impolite to refuse that deference and applause they deserve." –Baron von Munchausen.

We ran through mud and tall grass, hurtled logs and swung on vines in our bid to escape. I wondered why I hadn't asked if it was our fate to be caught, then figured that was against her mission statement and she wouldn't have told me anyway. Then a worse thought came to mind. She saw that *banditos and* rebels were chasing us. Well, where were they? Was she right? Had they come to surf too? Man! Too much knowledge can ruin your day.

The shooting from our rear had dissipated down to nothing, probably because they couldn't see us. And then, we entered a marshy area where there was not a lot of cover. Still, we sped on. But all of a sudden we heard gunfire from our front and left.

"What the hell!?" Marat exclaimed.

"I believe that would be the *banditos* and rebels," I explained.

Quickly, we made a right turn and sprinted toward a small clump of coconut trees and fallen logs. We dove down between two of the larger tree trunks.

"Wow," I said, as I looked up. "Look at the size of that coconut. It's at least a three pounder."

"*Sacre merde*, Tomas. Stop worrying so much."

"But it's right over you, Marat. It could squash your head just like a grape."

"Stop it!" Marat cried. "By the way, it's over your head too."

"Well, I don't like to think about my mortality too much, you know, after my close call."

"Aye yi yi. That's all you think about."

"And free will versus determinism."

"Aye yi yi."

Soon, bullets were hitting everywhere around us from three different sides. The *Federales* had caught up.

We were on the fourth corner of a square. The *Federales* were behind us, the rebels were on a corner to one side and the *banditos* on the other, all pouring rifle, pistol and AK-47 fire into our trees. That bastard albino was with the *Federales*. I had an idea to cut the odds a bit. Searching around for something with heft, I found a rock. I took a piece of paper and a rubber band out of my pack, then found the five-dollar bill. Wrapping the bill in the paper and securing it with the rubber band, I hurled it at the albino. He tried to catch it but fumbled and it hit one of Assad's henchmen on the forehead, knocking him down. I waited for the albino to unwrap the package.

"What about interest, man?" the albino yelled, in the meantime putting an icepack on the henchmen's head.

"Jesus!" I said. "You're killing me!"

I found another rock and wrapped up a one spot, tying some grass around it because I was out of rubber bands. I threw it and he flubbed it again—it caught the same henchman on the nose.

Tossing him another icepack, the albino stood and yelled, "No hard feelings," waved goodbye to Assad and split.

"What's with the albino?" Marat asked.

"He's a butterfingers."

Intermittently, the *Federales*, *banditos* and rebels would turn their guns on each other for awhile, I guess when they got bored or from force of habit. Then we'd have peace for a few moments, but soon, they all remembered us, and once more we were in Hell.

Marat took the Uzi out of his bag, pulled back the slide and cautiously edged up over the log.

At about this time, I decided to change my quest to just getting out of here alive. I wasn't even concerned if it was in more than one piece—just alive. Still, I had to admit, it was pretty cool.

"This is pretty cool," I said.

"Huh?!" Marat said, slipping back down for cover.

"Just like Butch and Sundance."

"They didn't make it," Marat deadpanned.

"Well, we don't actually know that," I rejoined.

"Yes, I guess that is true." Then he peeked over the log once more. Marat was quite surprised by what he saw.

"You won't believe this. Assad's waving a white flag."

I quickly edged my head over the top of the log.

"*Senors.* I want to talk. A truce," Assad yelled. He bravely stood up, showing the flag in all directions.

There was a moment of doubt and lots of silence.

"*No problemo,*" soon rang out from all sides, and "Ok, you bet," and "whatever."

"What d'ya think?" I asked Marat.

"It's his funeral," Marat said. "Hide your gun and I'll tell him to come over."

"No. You stay put. He hates your guts. I better take care of this," I said. "*Buenos noches!*" I shouted, peering over the log and I slipping my Uzi into the belt at the small of my back. "*Pero no las gatos.*"

Assad made a big show of taking a large gray cat from under his shirt, held it over his head for all to see and then handed it to one of his henchmen.

Marat tugged at my shirt, shaking his head and whispering in my ear.

"*Pero no los pestolas!*" I amended.

Assad made a big show of taking his pistol out of his holster and handing it to one of his men, then he slowly walked over the swampland in a straight line towards us.

We declined to stand, not knowing how many trigger-happy people were in attendance, but we knew one thing they didn't: we had Uzis.

It wasn't long before he stood towering over us. Damn! For the first time I could see he had a unibrow. And it was furled.

A contemptuous smirk came to his lips, like he thought we were cowardly for not standing, but we were very content to sit and let the logs shield us, only our heads visible to him.

Assad was over six feet tall, sallow complexioned and with a heavy five o'clock shadow even though it was only about one. It was obvious he thought he held all the cards.

You don't want to mess with the luck of Marat, I thought, but I guess Assad did, because he then spit contemptuously on one of the fallen tree trunks, barely missing Marat's face.

"*Senor*," he said to me. "I don't want you." Then he shouted, "I only want that pig-sucking canaille, bastard, *puta, chingando*, that, that, that..."

Wow! He still couldn't even bring himself to say it. I've heard of long standing grudges—the best being Darius' servant having to say, "Remember the Athenians" to him every dinner for ten years; maybe Darius had A.D.D. or smoked grass and had short term memory problems—but Assad's was also a pretty good one.

Assad let out an anguished, teeth-gnashing scream.

"He is right, Tomas," Marat said. "I brought this on us. It is all my fault. I'll go with him."

"We're in this together," I said, addressing Assad, my hand slowly edging toward the Uzi. I had to remind myself who this man was, and what we'd almost seen him do. I needed to buy time, throw him off his game. "But I have a question for you."

"*Que?*" Assad asked in a dumbfounded manner.

I had been wrestling with many philosophical problems for the last few weeks, ever since I was hit by the car and survived.

A traumatic situation like that always wakes one up to one's own mortality. Some people might use that impetus to try to find God, or turn there life on a completely different path, do something they've always wanted to do but never had the time or guts to. Others might try to get laid, thus reaffirming life. Me, I had questions. Now here was a smart man, though rather Ahab-like in his pursuit, but who ever said megalomaniacs couldn't be intelligent? He found us all the way down here, didn't he? It probably wasn't the right time, maybe not the right place, but I wanted another opinion. Besides, I couldn't help myself so what better way to stall? I asked him, "Sir, do think this confrontation was predetermined, and for that matter, all life?"

Assad looked at me and sneered. "Ah, *comprende*. You mean can you escape your destiny." There now appeared a twinkle in his eye. "But *senor*. Your destiny is to die."

"Sheesh!" I muttered. "Thanks for enlightening me. We're all gonna die."

Right then, Marat stood up and shouted, "Just shoot me!"

"*Si*," Assad said as he reached behind his back.

"Die Yankee scum!" Assad cried as he produced a pistol and aimed it at Marat's head.

I knew I'd never get my Uzi out in time, but just then, we heard the sound of chopper blades. I could tell it was closing fast. But who cared, we'd be dead by the time it got here.

I looked up. Marat looked up. No doubt the rebels and *banditos* looked up out of force of habit, but I didn't really notice because I was looking up. Then I remembered Assad.

Assad looked up. And just as I saw him look up, I heard this gigantic "Whoosh sound." Then I saw this streak come down and I heard a big "Whomp!" as it squashed Assad's head like a grape and splattering it over a five-yard area. It was the coconut.

"Wow!" I said. "The coconut. That *was* a big one."

"*Mucho grande*," Marat added.

Assad's men saw him go down. Now one of them yelled out, "Hey *gringo-putos*. We don't care so much about you. We are open to bribery if you want to leave."

"We're open to bribery too," I yelled back.

"It doesn't work that way, Tomas," Marat whispered to me. "You are so inexperienced, no? We have to bribe *them*."

I figured I only had enough money to get home. "Would you take a check?" I yelled.

We could hear some murmuring.

"Is it from a good American bank?" the *Federale* shouted.

"Chase Manhattan," I yelled.

More murmuring. I guess they had second thoughts.

The *banditos* yelled, "We don't trust banks. They're too big to fail."

"Ditto," yelled the rebels.

"They screw you coming and going," yelled the *Federales* and they all began shooting at us again. Once more, my blood was up and I brought out the Uzi, but Marat stopped me.

"Save the ammo," he cautioned. "Wait till you see the whites of their eyes."

By now, the helicopter was right over us and coming down.

All the shooting stopped as the copter came to within ten yards of the ground and hovered smack dab in the middle of our square and very near our log fort. A rope arced to the ground and three men in olive green fatigues slid down into our midst; two were heavily armed.

Marat's eyes almost bugged out as we recognized one of them as *Fidel Castro*.

Soon as he hit the ground, *Fidel*, a take charge guy, asked, "*Que pasa*?" But he did not wait for an answer.

"Come in," he commanded. "All of you." And such was his prestige in all of Mexico, Central America, South America and the Caribbean islands that the *banditos*, rebels and *Federales* all came forward, each alternately aiming their weapons at one enemy, then another, switching on and off between groups, but ultimately at us. We were surrounded.

Our Uzis tucked into our pants in the small of our backs, we stood up defiantly.

"I see the whites of their eyes," I whispered to Marat.

"Chill," Marat said.

"What's the beef?" *Fidel* asked.

Everyone told their stories, and surprisingly, they were all quite truthful, and were mostly comprised of complaints against Marat. The sole complaint against me was that there was a dim, miniscule possibility that I'd sent a signal to the army concerning the whereabouts of the rebel camp. And of this, I assured them I had no such intention because I was really fond of the *commandante*—and this, of course, led to renewed snickering amongst the rebels.

"Where is the *commandante*? Did she, I mean he, get away?" I now asked.

"He went to Chicago...to look for you," one of the rebels said.

"Geez!" I exclaimed. "I told her, him, I mean him, Minneapolis."

"He is always getting lost," the rebel said.

"He can't even pronounce Chicago," another chimed in and all the rebels snickered again.

My heart skipped a beat.

Fidel listened with great patience to all of the stories, while Marat stayed speechless, knowing he'd done all he was accused of.

Then *Fidel* yelled up at the helicopter and they tossed down a folding director's chair, which he caught with one hand. He stamped on the marshy ground to find a secure spot, unfolded the chair, set it down and sat on it, his hands supporting his chin. He began to contemplate.

I knew our fate was in the balance. I tried to remember what the Indian lady had said. Something about sport. That's it. I'd brown nose.

"Sir," I said to *Fidel*. "When you're done, could you tell me more about your tryout in the majors? I'm a huge fan."

He looked up at me for a second, then went back to his deliberation. His chair legs began to sink in the mud until only the seat was above ground and his legs were stretched out straight. But other than that, he didn't budge—his powers of concentration were legendary.

Having laid on the ground while under fire, I knew that the seat of his pants was probably getting wet.

Still, he remained calm, much like a modern day Solomon.

Chunks of time passed. Would my baseball ploy turn the tide I wondered hopefully?

Fidel jumped up, pulling his chair out of the ground and throwing it to one of his men, who began to wipe it off.

There was a dark splotch in the rear of his pants.

"I think you are wasting your time," *Fidel* finally said. "The American does not betray the rebels because he loves the *commandante*."

More snickering from that quarter.

"The cuckold has a squashed head and *Dulcinea* wanted to see the big city," *Fidel* continued. "These are matters of *amor* and not much else."

"She wasn't *your* sister," *Dulcinea*'s brother said angrily.

Fidel looked at him with shining dark eyes. "In your country, don't you usually go up to foreigners and say, '*Senor*, you want my sister?'"

The bandit stared at him for a second as though he was thinking. "*Si, si*," he said. "I guess you are right."

"What did I tell you?" *Fidel* said. "I like this Frenchman. Even the *Norte Americano* ain't so bad..." He looked at me. "Even if he was trying to suck up." Then he grinned, but the grin only lasted for a second.

I rolled my eyes, gazed skyward and whistled softly.

"Here is my decision," he said to the *banditos*, rebels and *Federales*. "I will give you three choices: one, you can come to Cuba and become part of the socialist experiment and revolution."

"I thought you were a Communist?" one of the rebels interrupted.

"I am not a Communist," *Fidel* said. "That is a running dog imperialist lie! Don't call me a Communist. I have enough troubles."

"Two. You can leave here but without the *gringos*, and go back to whatever it is you do, or three, my men kill all of you."

He pointed up to the hovering copter where at least a dozen machine guns were aimed into our midst. "Now. What do you choose?"

They all chose number two and without much adieu, faded back into the jungle toward the beach.

Fidel grabbed the rope to the helicopter. "Now, *senors*," he asked. "Can I drop you somewhere?"

"Where are you headed?" Marat asked. Obviously, neither of us trusted the *banditos*, rebels or *Federales* to stick to the bargain if they saw us back at the beach.

"We're on our way to *Cancun*," *Fidel* answered. "There are some good breakers there."

"So we can tag along?" Marat asked.

"Ah, s*enors*," *Fidel* said, beaming. "You will be my guests."

With that, he shinnied up the rope into the chopper. He was fit—you kind of get that way after leading a rebel army in the mountains.

Thankfully, they sent down a rope ladder for us and before you knew it, we were on our way, our troubles long past us.

We'd only flown for fifteen minutes, barely enough time for me to suck up again and ask him about his baseball, when we landed on the tarmac in *Puerto Angel*—it was too noisy in the copter anyway. Following *Fidel's* lead, we got down, quickly walked over to an olive green ten-seater Cessna with an assortment of red stars painted on the wings and fuselage; we were airborne again in minutes and I could see the Pacific.

It was loud in there, but nowhere near as loud as the helicopter, and *Fidel* began to tell me about his baseball career, how disappointed he'd been at the time to not make the "Show," but how all in all, he was happier being a dictator. "You know, I don't have to worry about being cut or traded."

"I remember you had a pretty good lefty slider," I said.

"*Si*," *Fidel* said. "But my split-fingered fastball was the best. Nobody could touch it...I invented it you know."

So we talked and talked. Somewhere along the line my tennis playing came up, and Marat asked questions about the

Revolution, the Bay of Pigs, the October Missile Crisis and the sanctions.

I don't know where the idea came from, but suddenly, I just blurted out, "You know, Mr. *Castro*, I have an idea for you. Now don't get angry…"

Quickly Marat drew his finger across his throat like I was going to get us killed or something. Maybe he thought *Fidel* would toss us from the airplane.

But I couldn't help it, I had started and the words came pouring out. "First, I have a question," I said, tugging his shirt sleeve. "Is it true you wanted to nuke us during the missile crisis?"

Fidel looked at me sheepishly as though I had caught him red-handed. He hung his head and said, "*Mi malo.*"

In the meantime, Marat crossed himself.

I cleared my throat and went on. "You know there's no way you could ever defeat the United States even if you still had nukes," I said as Marat covered his eyes in despair. "I mean, look at the size differential."

Fidel was quietly staring at me. I couldn't tell what he was thinking. But I was sure I had muffed the start.

"Even if every person in your country could bear arms and invade us, you still wouldn't have a chance. Forget about the military, just in my neck of the woods, Minnesota and Wisconsin—everyone has a gun. No, five or six guns. Think about it. They'd turn to hunting Cubans instead of deer. Owning guns is a right in America, you know."

Marat had moved as far away as he could, trying to disassociate himself from the loony.

I now had a full head of steam. "Anyway," I said. "The point is, and don't get me wrong, I don't dislike my country. The fact is I love my country. Sometimes though, I don't care too much for the leaders. But the point is, with our leaders, we probably have contingency plans to poison your cigars, contaminate your cane fields, maybe even assassinate you, take over your country. You know what those guys are like."

"*Si,*" *Fidel* said. Surprisingly, he was listening with keen interest. Even Marat had moved a few seats closer.

"Think," I said slowly. "What would be the best way for you to, let's say, get back at the U.S., really put it to 'em?" And I thrust out my hand like a spear or a knife and kind of turned it from side to side like I was twisting it in someone's belly. "What could you do to really dig at them, sort of spit in their eye? Something that would really piss them off, but that they couldn't do anything about."

"I don't know," *Fidel* said.

"And something, that at the same time you're really putting it to 'em," I continued, really getting into it, "that the rest of the world will praise, and think this is just the greatest thing they've ever heard of...and will make you even doubly a hero to your own people. You're already a hero of course, but this will make you even a bigger hero, and world-wide."

By now, *Castro* was listening intently, and so was Marat.

"Not only that," I said. "You would go down in history as a man akin to Gandhi or Einstein or Churchill."

Both *Fidel* and Marat had puzzled looks on their faces.

"What do I do?" *Fidel* asked.

"It's very simple," I said. "And it's almost like a practical joke on the Americans, if you're into that sort of thing...But it involves sacrifice."

"Yes, yes," *Fidel* said. "What do I do?"

"You're going to have to think about it for awhile," I cautioned.

"*Si, si,*" *Fidel* said.

I paused. I wanted to wait till his interest peaked.

"Ok," I said. "Here's what you do...You unilaterally declare a democracy."

"A democracy?!!" *Castro* asked in wonder.

"A democracy?!!" Marat said in amazement.

"Think about it," I said. "You declare a democracy, federation, republic, whatever you want to call it. You become a ceremonial President, an elder statesman who does ceremonial duties, entertaining heads of state and the like, *but*, you relinquish all power and influence. You call for free elections for a Prime Minister to run Cuba. *But*, neither you nor your relatives, nor high-ranking persons in your military, nor anybody in your cabinet or secret service can run for office. There can be no sign of your influence in any election, and the election has to be run by the UN, which will also work to set up political parties, free speech, and an open press, as well as dismantling any repressive remnants of the present government. Not only do you go down in history as the greatest of men, but there would be nothing like it ever before in the history of mankind."

Fidel nodded his head.

"I don't think any ruler has relinquished absolute power and turned it over to the people," Marat said.

"And isn't that what Communism is actually supposed to evolve to?" I asked.

"I am not a Communist," *Fidel* said forcefully.

"Whatever," Marat said.

I guess they had a lot in common.

"This is a plan that would be unequivocally supported by the French, Germans, English and most of the peace-loving people of the world. That includes the people of the United States by the way."

Marat came on board now that I'd mentioned the French.

"You would be the first man to bring freedom to the people of Cuba," Marat said.

"And it's about time you started thinking about your legacy," I said. "Your choice of how you leave the stage, not the U.S.'s. This is a unique chance. You could go down in history as a modern day Ghandi, plus, the U.S. would be obliged to lift sanctions. If they didn't, they would look like total assholes, while you come off as the greatest benefactor in history."

"Not to mention," I said, "that other countries would probably be snickering at the U.S."

"But does this not simply give the *Estadios Unitas* what it wants?" *Fidel* asked.

"Good question," Marat said as both of them stared at me for an answer.

"That's the point," I said. "It gives the States what it wants, but not on its own terms...It's on your terms. You determine your own fate."

Marat rolled his eyes, slapped his forehead with his hand and yelled, "Free will. Could you stop it with the free will already?"

"What do I do with my time?" *Fidel* asked.

"You could turn your time to building more libraries, schools, freeways, bridges and hospitals," Marat said. "You could lecture other countries on how to do the same. You might just set a precedent."

"You squirreled away a lot of money didn't you?" I asked.

"No no no," *Castro* said, looking around at his fellows. "Don't say that."

"Come on," I pressed. "Every tinhorn dictator squirrels away money. It's in the job description."

"The money of Cuba is for the people!" he protested.

Marat edged away from us again.

"Well," I said, not to be deterred. "Just suppose you had...what you might be able to do, is buy into a baseball club. Like the Yankees. God knows they need better management. I know this is a love of yours."

"If you're not interested in that, I'm sure we could find a way to get you season tickets to the team of your choice."

"The Yankees and the Dodgers," *Fidel* said.

"You like them both?" I said, surprised.

"*Si*," *Fidel* answered. "I like them both."

"What about the Twins?" I had to ask.

"No," he said. "I just wish I could have taught Whitey Ford or Sandy Koufax that split-fingered fastball. They could have really been good."

Fidel then shouted to one of his men, who brought over the mud-stained director's chair and unfolded it, setting it down in the aisle in front of the Cuban.

Handing out cigars to Marat and I, *Fidel* sat in the chair and lit a new cigar for himself, put his chin in his hands, and began to think.

He didn't say another word till we landed in Cancun. As we got off the plane, *Fidel* looked at me very seriously.

"Could you show me how to hit a one-handed backhand?" he asked. "I always have the trouble with this shot."

Right there on the tarmac, I gave him a few tips, using my Uzi to show him the motion and the grip.

"*Gracias*," he said. "*¿Cuánto?*"

"It's on the house," I said.

"You know," he said in a very positive tone. "I think your idea about democracy is perfect for Cuba. I'll *do* it."

Both Marat and I were flabbergasted.

"You mean you'll really do it?" I asked excitedly. "That's fantastic!" And I had immediate visions of becoming an international diplomat and winning the Nobel Peace prize.

"Naw," *Fidel* said, with perfect timing. "I'm just fucking with you." Then he and all his men laughed so hard, Marat and I had to help them up off the runway. See what happens as soon as you think you have it in the bag?

As he recovered from the hysterics, he put one arm around Marat's shoulder, and the other around mine, squeezed and said, "Keep in touch. Come visit me when the sanctions are lifted." Then he said to his men, "Surf's up!" and off they went.

Marat was beaming after his encounter with *Fidel*.

"See," he said. "This is why this is the best of all possible worlds."

"Oh yeah," I said. "Well, I think I'm going home to just tend to my forehand."

Marat and I split up soon after—Marat left for Columbia to make his fortune and I wanted to get back to the States and my tennis. I hadn't realized how much I missed it. I suppose I could have flown back, but I didn't want to spend the money—a habit I guess I picked up from Marat. Besides, if I was going to travel to play tournament tennis, I couldn't be extravagant. My brothers would be in India soon and I decided I might as well play there. I missed them too.

So, I walked to the outskirts of town and started hitching as though it was the most natural of things to do. It didn't even hit me for a couple of hours. I was hitchhiking back to the States by myself.

I pulled out a dog-eared map. Hmm. A little over 2000 Ks to Nogales. No big deal.

I had to admit it was exhilarating to be on the road again. What a difference from a month ago.

THE END

45896111R00153

Made in the USA
Charleston, SC
05 September 2015